A SEASON OF MIRACLES

HEATHER GRAHAM

A SEASON OF MIRACLES

ISBN 1-55166-873-4

A SEASON OF MIRACLES

Printed in U.S.A.

With best wishes for every season
and many thanks for many things to
Sandy Hyacinthe at American Airlines,
Renee Smilek, the Dolphin Hotel,
Joy Wawrzyniak, Starwood
and
Jennifer Goodman, the Plaza.

PROLOGUE

The Burning

He had never ridden harder in his life. Desperate as he was, he became aware of each slight sound and scent, every sensation. The day was cold, crisp. The sky was blue. His horse's hooves made thunder, striking again and again upon the ground. Distant thunder, muffled by the thickness of the snow. The cold seeped into him, though he was sweating as he rode.

His horse's hooves seem to beat out words. We will not make it. We will not make it.

But they had to try. He had sworn that he would allow no evil to happen. He had sworn to love, to honor, to protect. He had done so in secret. What had seemed logic had been cowardice. And now...

Now they would pay.

"Hey-yah!" he shouted, heels digging into the sides of a

fine animal already doing its best to travel the slick, snow-covered roads.

"Sweet Jesu, Michael, you'll be the death of us all," Justin called, riding hard behind him with the others.

"There is no time!" he roared. "No time!"

"We'll be no good to the lass with broken necks," Justin said.

"Worry about your own, then, because I will trust my neck to God."

"Aye, God be with us."

The snow flew. The ground trembled.

They rode. Harder, harder.

God was with them.

How had he underestimated the evil of his enemies? Michael wondered bleakly. It was incredible, chilling beyond death, the lengths to which men would go out of jealousy, bitterness and greed.

"Faster," he insisted, fear bringing out the sharp command in his voice.

Again he felt the sweat that trickled down his chest despite the whipping wind and the harsh chill. The air was fresh, as fresh as the scent of *her,* clean, enticing, invigorating. How her scent seemed to haunt him now, despite the mad rush of their reckless ride, the whistle and groan of the wind whipping in a tempest around them. Snow flew, great chunks of it, filthy with dirt and grass, as their horses tore up clods of it under their racing hooves. His heart hammered in time, thudded, thundered, and still the words rang in his head. *We will not make it, we will not make it, we must make it, at all costs, for if we don't...*

If we don't...

The fear that seized him was unbearable.

"We're nearly upon the valley," Raynor, another of his men, riding at Justin's side, called out. "It's over that hill. We've nearly made it."

Nearly. They were so close.

* * *

The sun.

How glorious, she thought, feeling it on her cheeks.

The day was cold and she so barely clad that she shivered, yet still she felt the kiss of the sun on her cheeks. What a wondrous feeling. Something that heated, warmed, giving her the illusion, if only for precious moments, of a deep, encompassing warmth of bliss and well-being; the illusion of being cherished, secure...

As she had felt with him.

But it *was* but an illusion, for the day was cold, bitterly cold. And she would feel real warmth soon enough.

Her arms ached from the ties. She had not felt them so much at first. Now, they ached with a vengeance.

"You have not as yet begun to know pain."

Her enemy stood before her again, watching her eyes, seeking her panic, her pleading. How he longed for it. And God knew, if it would bring her release, she would promise him anything, swear to anything. God help her, indeed, she would *do* anything.

But she knew, meeting his eyes, that no plea, no "confession," nothing whatsoever on her part, would change things.

"You know I won't beg," she said simply.

"Aye, you're too stupid."

"You'd accuse me now of stupidity? I thought you considered me far too clever for my own good."

"Not so clever. You are about to die hideously. Or do you believe in miracles?"

Her eyes fell from his. *God, how she wanted to believe in miracles!*

"I would never beg you, because I know that it would change nothing, that you've no intention of sparing me, that any plea on my part would be nothing but sheer entertainment to you."

"So you stand calmly, thinking aye, there might be a miracle. Salvation might come."

"It's the Christmas season, is it not?"

"For some, dear lass. For you...I think not."

He wanted her to break. To burst into tears. To confess, to plead, to throw herself in abject humility at his feet. Well, she couldn't quite do that. Not bound as she was.

But she would not cry or break or give a confession.

Her tormentor leaned against the stake. "He will not come, you know."

"If he can, he will."

"There are no miracles. Ask me, and God, for forgiveness."

"God knows my soul. And *you* should be asking *my* forgiveness."

"I do what I must to preserve what is right."

"What is right? You betrayed me."

"You betrayed us all. As he betrays you now. You turned your back on your heritage. Now...ah, well, you had your chances. Wait until you smell the fire," he said, and he came close to her, fingers entwining in her hair as he forced her to look down at the dry tinder and faggots at her feet. "The scent. Oh, God, you cannot begin to imagine the scent of burning human flesh. It's a sickening smell. Enough to make the staunchest man vomit."

"Then, you must move on quickly from here. I wouldn't have the scent of my burning flesh ruin your Christmas Eve repast, good sir."

She saw his face change, saw the fury, but there was nothing she could have done to prevent the blow he leveled against her face. Her head rocked against the stake that held her. Pain shot behind her eyes.

And still, she knew, she had not as yet begun to know pain....

He stiffened then, knowing he should not have allowed the

others to witness his show of emotion, his lack of control. He was a man of right; God knew, he followed the law. To execute her was his duty.

He came very close to her face. His breath touched her cheeks, replacing the warmth of the sun. "You do not begin to understand. I will smell you roast, and I will savor the scent. Indeed, I will take pleasure. And tonight I will enjoy my meal with a gusto you cannot begin to imagine. The taste will remain on my tongue forever."

"Forever may not be long," she noted, amazed that she could offer him a smile.

He shook his head. "Poor, naive beauty that you be. But are you so beautiful now? Hair tangled, cheeks windburned, clothes in tatters, your body but bones for the flames to ravage. Would he be so enamored now? What fools you were. What fools."

He had said that he would come for her. He had sworn. Sworn...

Had he, like God, forsaken her? Had her sins been so great? No, he would come...might still come...

"I cannot help but believe you will one day find yourself the fool," she whispered.

"That day will not be today," he said grimly, his features, once striking, marred with cruelty and taut with fury. "I could have had you strangled. I might have saved you the agony. But you are a little fool, with your dreams of love and the pleasures of the flesh. Even now, you dream of his touch. But what you will feel is the kiss of the flame, the lick of the blaze, the warmth of hell's damnation."

He watched her eyes.

"Not even my death, my agony, will free you, will it? You are the one who will suffer. You will spend your life in bitterness. Eaten by flames from the inside out, burning in the hell of your own hatred."

He looked as if he would strike at her again, but he managed to turn away.

He stepped toward the crowd, raised a hand. The murmuring grew silent.

"I have tried, pleaded, begged...but she has no words of remorse, she offers no prayer for redemption. God help her, forgive her her transgressions against her country. Pray for her, though it seems her tormented soul must return to the Devil, her maker. Let the fires cleanse her, and ourselves, and let us then pray from our hearts in the joy of the season we now enter, a time of God."

The faggots were lit.

Flame quickly blazed before her. Around her.

She longed to cry out, to curse him. To tell the world that the real monster was there before them, clad in a cloak of law and respectability. She wanted to say that no one was safe, no one who stood in his way, no one who coveted anything he wanted...

Instead she found voice and strength to say, "God forgive you, sir. God grant you ease from the torture and agony you will suffer again and again—"

She broke off, choking. How quickly the flames had risen. Gone was the warmth of the sun, in its place the growing heat of the fire. She could speak no more. Her skirt was aflame. She tried to twist away, but it was no use. She burned! Dear God, she burned, the agony entering her lungs, her flesh.

She began to scream....

They rode over the rise and looked down into the valley. And saw.

He closed his eyes, damning himself, raging within, without.

He had imagined her scent.

He could smell it now.

On the air.

Oh, God.

"Jesus! Our Lord Father, Jesus, Mary and Joseph," Justin intoned.

"Help her, for the love of God, help her!" Raynor demanded. "You know what you must do."

"God help me, I cannot."

"You must!" Raynor said.

"For the love of God!" Justin cried, tears in his eyes. "Will you look? It is too late. It has gone too far. You know what you must do!"

Tears streamed down Michael's face. He prayed, he begged forgiveness, God's forgiveness—and hers. Split seconds passed.

He knew what he must do.

"By God, by heaven, by hell, I swore..."

He had sworn that he would come for her.

"By the angels, by God, by Christ, I swear, the time will come—"

He broke off. Each second meant great agony.

He did indeed know what he had to do.

CHAPTER 1

Present day Manhattan

It all started with the tarot cards.

And then the dreams of burning.

And of course the cat.

But at two o'clock on that Halloween afternoon, those things were still in the future.

Jillian sat at her desk at Llewellyn Enterprises, tapping a pencil on the wood as she stared at her new design. She'd set out to create a contemporary cross, with clean, sleek lines, to be available in yellow and white gold, and platinum. Every year since she'd finished college and joined the company full-time, she'd done a special Christmas design, available in a very limited quantity. By tradition, the invitation to purchase went out November fifth, all orders had to be received by the twentieth, and the pieces were delivered by special courier one month later. She loved designing jewelry. There was something so permanent about it. Pieces could be handed down through generations. A beautiful piece could be timeless—or speak volumes about the decade of its creation.

This piece, however, wasn't saying what she had intended at all. It wasn't that she disliked the design—on the contrary, it was coming along beautifully. She simply hadn't envisioned it quite this way.

"Wow, that *is* pretty. I guess you're worth your paycheck." The voice, masculine and amused and coming from over her shoulder, was so startling that she nearly bolted out of her chair. The speaker was her cousin, Griff, handsome and too charming at thirty. Tall and well built, with sandy hair and hazel eyes, he wore Armani with runway perfection.

She hadn't seen him enter her office. She had been so intent on the drawing that she'd been oblivious to everything else.

"Thanks."

Griff stretched out playfully on her teak desk—à la 1930s Hollywood movie. "Excellent, sweetie. Excellent. It speaks 'new millennium' loudly. Unfortunately, it appears that the new millennium you're planning on promoting is man's movement into the 1000s—Celtic-looking thing, isn't it?"

"Hmm," she murmured.

He traced the pattern she had drawn, grinning away. "Oooh, the old boy is going to go ballistic over this one," he said flippantly, referring to Douglas Alexander Llewellyn, her grandfather, his great-uncle, and CEO of Llewellyn Enterprises. "Could his angel have failed this time? He does think you're an angel, you know. He's unaware that you're half angel, half fire-breathing dragon."

"He realizes it completely. He's just very fond of dragons. And, Griff, get your body off my desk. I have work to do, and I don't need your scrawny self getting in my way."

"How dare you?" he asked, in a tone of genuine indignation. "My body isn't scrawny. It's practically perfect—in every way.

In fact, it's too bad we're cousins and that we'd have horrible, two-headed-monster offspring, or I'd let you see just how perfect."

Jillian wrinkled her nose and sat back, looking at him. "Thank God that the possibility of two-headed children is going to spare me. I shudder to think of it. You're just going to have to share all that perfection with someone else."

"Actually, we're only second cousins. Maybe the kids would only be pathetically cross-eyed. Come to think of it..." he mused, "did you know that William of Orange married his first cousin, Mary Stuart, and they ruled together as William and Mary?"

"And they left no heirs," she reminded him pleasantly.

"Half the royalty of Europe was closely related. Everyone out there was a descendant of Queen Victoria."

"And half the royalty of Europe was—and is—very strange," she said. "Griff—"

"C'mon, the old boy is kind of like a king, and he'd be so happy to think he was leaving his little kingdom to those of his own blood, don't you think?"

"No, I don't think, and I'm thanking God at this moment that surely you're not serious," she said, shaking her head.

"You're just refusing to see the possibilities."

"Griff, was there a point to this visit?" she asked pointedly, glancing at her watch. Griff liked to torture her—good-naturedly, of course, or so he claimed, as did the rest of her family members who were part of Llewellyn Enterprises—Daniel, Theo and Eileen. Jillian knew that she tended to be her grandfather's fair-haired child, despite the fact that she hadn't risen to the head of the family class on purpose, nor was she calling the shots at the company now. But she had grown up with her grandfather, she knew him best—and loved him best. Jewelry design was her favorite part of the work, while Theo was a crack marketer, and Eileen's expertise was public relations.

Daniel was the one with his hands on the reins, though—right behind her grandfather's. He knew the business, every aspect of it, and with the scope of their various concerns, she was glad. Perhaps her grandfather could control everything, but he was the only man who could. People tended to think of the company as one giant prize. It wasn't. It was a giant jumble of various enterprises, and it took a variety of talents to keep it in its current excellent shape.

Griff always told her that his expertise was looking good and pretending to be busy, whether he was or wasn't. And, of course, being charming. He had a point. She couldn't help but like Griff herself.

Eileen was her first cousin, an only child like herself. The boys were the grandsons of her grandfather's brother, who had perished in the ever precious "Old Country." Douglas had outlived not only his brother, but also his two sons and his nephew, the boys' father, Steven. Jillian often thought of how it must have pained him to lose so many people he had loved so much. But he never faltered; he went on, giving his devotion to the remaining Llewellyns. No one had been forced into the business; they had come because of the same fierce sense of family pride and loyalty.

"You know," Griff said, wagging a finger at her, "you could do a lot worse. I am handsome, witty, urbane and charming."

"Of course I could do worse. But you're my cousin. So, Griff—"

"Don't you remember playing naked together on those fur rugs when we were babies?"

"Griff, we never played naked together on any fur rugs."

"I guess not. If we had, you would have remembered."

She groaned and laid her head on the desk. "Griff, what's your problem? You're cute, you're—"

"Cute? I want to be sexy and devastating."

"Okay, you're sexy and devastating."

"That's better."

"And I'm really trying to finish up and get out of here today."

"I'm really here on an errand of mercy."

"Oh?" she queried carefully.

"It's Halloween. I didn't want you going home alone. You know, poor little rich girl, all alone in the family mansion. That big old place where none of the rest of us are invited to live."

She leaned back, grinning. "You are such a pathetic liar."

"Well, in a way, but not really. I don't want to live in the family mansion. I like my privacy. And believe it or not, the family fortune isn't my bag, though I do like to live with a certain style."

"Griff, I have no fear of you ever changing."

He grinned. "I'm worthless, totally. And happy. And smart enough to be grateful."

"You pretend to be worthless, but you know you're not. Anyway, I need to get out of here."

"So you can sit by the fire like a little old lady and hand out candy to the kiddies? No. Ever since Milo died, you don't do anything or go anywhere. It's time for you to start doing things again. You're not a mole. Not to mention, you're far too young and...yes, good-looking. Why, Jillian, some people might even call you beautiful. Thanks to good family genes, of course. And right now all that beauty is just being wasted. You need to get out again."

She felt a rush of air escape her. It was odd how life went on, but that, at strange moments, grief would come sailing back and, like a blanket, wrap itself around her. She had known what she was doing when she got married. She had always known she would lose Milo.

And she knew that Griff really was here to help her.

So she smiled. "For your information, I *am* going out."

"A date?" he queried.

"Maybe."

"With Robert Marston?" he asked carefully.

"Robert Marston?" she repeated impatiently.

Robert Marston had just started working for the company. He wore Armani just as well as Griff did, but he came with sharp, very dark eyes and, in Jillian's opinion, a sharper—possibly darker—mind. He was handsome, intelligent, deep-voiced and very articulate. He had gone to school with Theo, and spent the past five years with one of the fastest-growing computer companies in the world. He was the type of man who walked into a room and drew attention. By his physical nature he seemed to exude authority.

She had felt wary of him from the moment she had first seen him—and that had actually been from quite a distance. She didn't even know the color of those dark eyes of his. There had been far too many rumors flying about for her to willingly meet the man her grandfather had brought into the business.

Was he stepping on her cousins' toes? Or were her cousins in agreement with the situation, content for Marston to be the one with the power? Somehow, she doubted it.

"Why on earth would you assume I'm going out with *him?*" she asked too sharply. She had wanted to convey courteous impatience. She was afraid that her tone had given away concern.

His grin told her that he had, indeed, heard far more than impatience in her voice. "Well, are you going out with him?"

"No, I haven't even met him yet. I saw him across a room. And I don't believe in going out with business associates."

"So?"

"I'm going out with Connie."

"With Connie?" he repeated. Was that relief she heard in his voice? Connie had been one of her best friends forever, way back to grade school. Connie was also her administrative assistant. And since it was such a family enterprise, Connie's husband, Joe, also worked for the company. He was on Daniel's staff.

"Yes, Connie and I are going out. As we do every Halloween," she reminded him.

He dropped his teasing manner for a moment and looked at her seriously. "You're really going to go—"

"Christmas shopping, yes."

"As everyone does on Halloween," he responded with a fine line of sarcasm.

"It's a personal tradition," she said with feigned indignation. It was a strange tradition, she knew, and it had started when they were little kids who went trick-or-treating together. Now Connie had two daughters, a dog, a cat, a bird and in-laws coming out the kazoo, so she traditionally started her Christmas shopping on October thirty-first, convinced that the best Christmas sales came on Halloween, when everyone was doing last-minute scrambling for a costume. They had a great time shopping, then going trick-or-treating with the girls, and then, usually, just spending the evening together checking out the acquired candy.

"All right," Griff said. "Just so long as you're really going out."

"I really am."

"Not to baby-sit or hand out candy."

"No." Her voice was steady. She wasn't baby-sitting, and she wasn't handing out candy.

"And you're really going to have a good time."

"Really."

"Because if you came with me, I'd show you a good time, you know."

"I'm sure you would."

He slid off her desk at last, brushing her cheek with his fingertips. "I'd show you off to all my friends. You are gorgeous, you know."

She caught his hand and squeezed it. "Thanks, Griff."

"Oh, by the way, Daniel asked to see you. His office."

"When?"

Griff looked at his watch. "Hmm...a while ago, I guess."

"Griff, why didn't you tell me?"

"I'm sure it's nothing." He placed his hands on her desk and leaned toward her again. "Why don't you defy him? Just go home!"

"Because it might be important," she said impatiently. She stood and walked past him.

"Hey, Jillian?"

She turned back.

"Happy Halloween. And merry Christmas shopping."

Eileen Llewellyn paced in front of the storyboards set up in her office, looking at the newest sketches for the catalog campaign. Of medium height, with coal-dark hair that was expertly styled to flatter her heart-shaped face, she was elegant, efficient and a picture of total sophistication. She liked business suits with tailored jackets, short skirts and high heels. She walked with an aura of confidence and authority. One look from her cool blue eyes could silence a room. She had been born to soar in the business world.

But at the moment she was agitated. She groped for the pack of cigarettes on her desk, slipped one out without looking and lit it, grateful in the back of her mind that the company owned the building and she could smoke in her own office whenever she damn well pleased. Exhaling a cloud of smoke eased her aggravation slightly, but still, she continued to stare at one storyboard, in particular. It showed a woman in an off-the-shoulder, long-sleeved, dramatic gown with a flowing skirt; it somehow had the look of something from another time, another world. The woman was draped across an iron chair near a fireplace, and a man was bending down before her, his fingers brushing the bare flesh of her throat while he set a locket around her neck. It was a wonderful sketch. Striking. Seldom could one piece of art speak so clearly, especially in the commercial world. The artist was to be highly commended. It conveyed everything it should. The timelessness of a gift of fine jewelry. The pure romance of such a gift. The class, refinement...more. It was wonderful. What she could do with this one sketch alone...

But, damn, it was irritating.

There was a tapping on her door.

"I'm busy," she called out sharply.

The door opened, anyway.

Theo walked in. He was a tall man, imposing in stature. Though barely thirty, he had already acquired a few gray strands in his dark hair. They gave an impression of wisdom and authority. He knew how to use his physical presence well, but he didn't intimidate her. She glanced at him over her shoulder, irritation evident in her eyes.

"Theo, I said—"

"Yeah, I can see you're busy, puffing away."

"What do you want?"

"It's great, isn't it? I want to use it for more than just the catalog. I want to pull some of the ads we've already got for December and rush this in, instead."

She flashed him a frown. "Theo, it's way too late to go changing the Christmas ads! December magazines are already on their way out."

"I was thinking newspapers. And maybe a television campaign, after Christmas."

"Television? It's a sketch!"

Theo was silent for a moment, arms folded over his chest, eyes on hers. He smiled slowly. "We both know the real thing isn't a sketch."

No, the real thing wasn't a sketch. It was Jillian. A perfect likeness. The woman was tall, elegantly slim, but shapely, as well. The hair was long and a beautiful reddish blond. The eyes were deep green, like expensive emeralds. It was Jillian.

And she had been drawn with love. Or at least with pure infatuation.

"Eileen?" Theo said.

She let out a sigh of impatience, stubbing out her cigarette. "Jillian is a designer. Yes, she's good-looking, Theo, really good-looking, but she isn't an actress."

"She could carry this off, and we both know it."

"Brad Casey in art must have a hell of a crush on her. Besides, who knows if she'd even be willing."

"Brad Casey saw something and used it in this drawing. As to Jillian being willing? Our Jillian? She *is* Llewellyn Enterprises. She lives and breathes the company."

"Careful. She gets angry when you say that," Eileen warned.

He arched a brow. "Hmm. I'm just a hard-working second cousin—you're a direct descendant of the old boy, just like our Jillian."

"Well," she said sweetly, leaning back against her desk to light another cigarette and survey him with cool blue eyes, "Grandfather doesn't seem to care about that, does he. No one compares with Jillian, but you're right up there, aren't you, Theo?"

"Eileen, it sounds as if we need to supply your office with a scratching post."

"Would you stop, Theo? I didn't start this. Look—"

"Eileen, you know I'm right, you know this is brilliant. Pure accident, and yes, that poor sod Brad Casey probably does have a crush on Jillian. But it's perfect."

A hard rap on the door interrupted them. Griff swept in, bearing a silver tray with a tea serving and Halloween cookies. He slid the tray onto Eileen's desk and looked at the sketches.

"Wow! Our golden girl is a beauty, isn't she? I mean, for real. No wonder the old boy dotes on her."

"Griff, some of us want to get out of here today," Eileen said, walking around behind her desk.

"Television spots would be perfect," Griff told Theo. "I heard you through the door," he said in response to Theo's quizzical look.

"Thanks for the input," Theo said briefly. "What's with the cookies?"

"The old boy sent them out to all of us—his idea of trick-or-treat, I guess," Griff said. "I gallantly swept them from the hands of the young office assistant about to hear you two airing the family laundry."

"We weren't airing the family laundry," Eileen said impatiently.

"Think Jillian will be willing?" Theo asked Griff.

"We can persuade her."

"I want to move on this before Marston gets any more involved."

"Endear Jillian to us before Marston gets his hands on her, huh?" Griff teased.

"What are you talking about?" Theo asked impatiently.

"He's brilliant, right? And the old boy has pulled him in above all of us."

Theo turned away, studying the sketches again. "Don't be ridiculous. I suggested Marston. I went to school with him."

"He'll be just like Big Brother—watching," Griff said.

"This is a company, not a kingdom," Theo said impatiently.

But Eileen was studying Griff thoughtfully. "Douglas Llewellyn is all about family. Marston is nothing, really, not without—" Eileen said.

"Jillian," Griff said. "Ah, but then..."

"What?" Eileen asked.

"There's you, of course. Another direct descendant. You could slip in and cut her out of the running, keep an eye on him."

"Griff, you're ridiculous. I've been engaged for—"

"Oh, yeah. You and Gary Brennan have been engaged for

what—five years? You won't give the poor fellow a wedding date. He might want you to go by Mrs. Brennan. Horrors," Griff said with a shudder. "Would you give up the family name, Eileen? Even for love?"

"Many businesswomen keep their maiden names, Griff," Eileen said icily. "I adore Gary—we just haven't had time to plan a wedding."

"No time in five years. Imagine that," Griff said with mock solemnity.

"I told you—I adore him," Eileen said sharply.

"I'm sure you do. But you'd throw the poor boy to the sharks in two seconds if he were any threat to your position at Llewellyn Enterprises," Griff teased.

"There is no threat to me—I actually work," Eileen snapped back, eyes narrowed.

"Touché," Griff told her.

Theo let out an impatient sound. "I hope to God we're not being overheard. We sound exactly like a pack of squabbling children, and we're supposed to be running a major company. We all work here, and we work hard." His eyes fell on his brother, and he shrugged. "All right, most of us work hard. But to suggest that there was an underlying reason for bringing in Marston, to even think that anything should go on is..."

"Is what?" Griff demanded

"Sick," Theo announced. "And the old boy is in perfect health. To begin to imagine that anything is going on is—"

"Theo," Griff interrupted, "your lack of curiosity is positively boring. Don't you think it's just a little bit strange? I mean, we've been dividing the executive duties here since we got out of college."

"You've had executive duties, Griff?" Eileen asked.

"You're not being very nice," Griff said.

"I *am* nice," she snapped back, a trace of hurt in her tone. Griff heard it, she knew. He always saw the smallest sign of weakness in those around him. "I am nice. I'm simply efficient. When people are 'artistic,' they don't have to be quite so efficient."

Theo came around behind her, speaking softy. "Artistic? Like cousin Jillian?"

"Theo, I love Jillian dearly. We have a bond. Just like you boys have the bond of brotherhood."

"We're all Llewellyns," Theo said flatly.

"And you're just as nice as can be," Griff told Eileen, grinning.

"God himself is going to come down and slap you right across your silly face one day," Eileen told him.

"Did I just say she's nice?" Griff asked Theo.

"Griff, some of us do have work to do."

"I know. That's the point. I'm getting scared. I may have to actually start working around here, now that Marston has suddenly been called in. The old man has been watching Jillian grieve all this time. She's been widowed a year now," Griff said. He looked at the other two. "Almost a year. The traditional mourning time is coming to an end."

"The old man has figured out that there's more work than all of us can handle, and he's brought in a crack management and numbers man who happens to be an old school friend of mine. That's all there is to it. And I've got things to do," Theo said impatiently. "Eileen, this image here is the one I want to go with. When I meet with our major accounts, I'll be letting them know that a Llewellyn will actually be displaying our jewelry in our next ad campaign. Get busy with it. See what kind of guest shots we can get on the talk circuit. You can use the family name when you're trying to land guest spots on radio or television. It may be a bit crass to try to cash in on our good works, but God knows, we give enough to charity at Christmas."

"We like to get our tax breaks in before New Year's," Griff muttered.

"If we didn't make a fortune, we wouldn't be able to give away big bucks," Theo snapped. "Get on with it, both of you."

He walked out of the room.

Griff grinned at Eileen. "Get on with it, huh?"

"Get out of here, Griff."

He left, and Eileen sat down, drumming her beautifully manicured nails on her desk. How dare they accuse her of jealousy? She loved Jillian, who was the closest thing to a sister she had. She made a face and mimicked Theo's tone. "Get on with it. I'm not a servant, Theo. *Get on with it?*"

She was silent for a minute, then she said softly, "Oh, I'll be getting on with it, all right."

She picked up a cookie with pumpkin-orange icing and little black chocolate-drop eyes. She took a bite—a savage bite—glad she made the cute little cookie snap.

Then she set the cookie down, stared at the tea service.

"Oh, yeah. I'll get on with it, all right."

Jillian swept past Daniel's secretary with a quick smile and knocked on his door.

"Yes?" he said sharply from behind the wood.

"It's Jillian."

"Get in here."

She froze for a moment, disturbed by his tone. Then she gritted her teeth and walked in, closing the door behind her. He was behind his desk, writing, and he didn't look up. She stood before his desk, feeling like an errant school child. Then she grew angry and impatient.

"Daniel, you asked to see me," she reminded him.

He looked up at last, staring at her as he recapped his pen. "Yes, quite some time ago," he told her.

Like his brothers, Daniel was an attractive man. He liked clothing and appearances, and dressed well. His eyes were a deep brown, a true deep brown that could appear black. His gaze was always fathomless. Many times, when she'd been young, Daniel had been her protector. Ten years her senior, he had often taken her to and from school. In those days, he had been like a big wolf between her and any danger—be it real or imagined. She had loved him deeply; he had been her favorite relative.

But that had been a long time ago.

In the past several years, with her grandfather handing out more and more responsibility, things had changed.

Daniel had held the reins of power for a long time.

The fact that she was a direct descendant seemed to be raising a barrier between them—though he didn't seem to show the same reserve to Eileen. Maybe it was all in Jillian's mind. And maybe she had been so involved with the details of her work—and the death of her husband—that she had built her own walls between them.

"Sorry," she said briefly. She decided not to mention the fact that Griff had forgotten to tell her that she was supposed to come here. "Really."

"I thought you were trying to get out of here today?"

"I am. But I gave Connie the day off—" She broke off at his frown. "Daniel, she never misses work. She had some things to finish for the kids."

"And the two of you are off together this afternoon. I'm not so sure it's a good thing to have your best friend as your assistant," he told her.

"Daniel, we don't miss a beat as far as work is concerned. You know that. Joe works for you, and he's a great employee."

"Sit down," he told her, indicating one of the chairs in front of his desk.

She sighed and did so. He heard her sigh, and looked at her

sharply. "Daniel, no one puts more time into this company than I do," she reminded him.

"Oh, I agree," he murmured. "It's as if you're married to it." There was a note of bitterness in his tone. Did he think she was trying to make herself the indispensable one?

"Daniel—"

"Never mind," he said curtly. He thrust his copy of her design for the new cross toward her. "What is this?"

She inhaled, staring at him. "A cross."

"Yes. It's supposed to be a contemporary design, Jillian. Sharp, hot, contemporary. A look to the future."

"Yes," she said, and faltered. "I know."

"So?"

"I don't know what happened. But—"

"It's a great design. Beautiful. But not contemporary."

He was right. Definitely right. They'd all been in the meeting, and it had been Douglas Llewellyn himself who had stressed the need to look to the new millennium.

She seldom failed, but she had failed this time. Her voice wavered as she told him, "Well, we can use this in the general line, and I'll just start over."

"No."

"No?"

"We don't have time, and this...it's not what we planned, but we can go in another direction. You know. Something like, 'As we enter the first decade of a new millennium, we welcome the new—and cherish the beauty of our past.' I'm not sure if that's quite right, but something like it. I haven't talked with the old boy yet, but I'm sure he'll go with it." He was quiet for a minute. "Especially since it's you who designed the cross."

"Daniel—"

"I just wanted to let you know that we would go with it," he said, interrupting her. "I'm sure you were aware yourself that it doesn't fit the original concept."

"Of course."

He lifted his hands in dismissal. She met his eyes, feeling that she needed to apologize for something. She hadn't done anything, she reminded herself. The design was different from what they had planned, but...

It was also very good.

"Daniel—" She broke off.

His secretary had tapped on the door and now hesitantly stuck her head in. She was a capable young woman, but to Jillian, Gracie Janner had always given the impression of being a doe caught in the headlights of an eighteen-wheeler. She had frizzy dirty-blond hair that seemed like a puffy halo around her head, and huge hazel eyes. Jillian was as nice and soft-spoken as she could be to the woman, but Gracie always seemed to be on edge. Nervous.

Afraid.

"Cookies and tea, Mr. Llewellyn," Gracie said. "Jillian, I believe your tray has been sent to your office, but I can run down and get it—oh, my God, I called you Jillian. I should have called you Miss Llewellyn. Or are you still going by your married name? Oh, I'm so sorry."

"Jillian is just fine, Gracie. I've told you, please, my first name is just fine."

"Cookies and tea?" Daniel said impatiently. "You brought me cookies and tea?"

"From the Great Pumpkin above," Gracie said, trying to joke. She was as slim as a saluki, and appeared frazzled. Joking wasn't her forte. Maybe she was perfect for Daniel. He didn't seem to know how to joke anymore, either.

"Thanks, Gracie, but we're finished here. I'll just run back to my own office," Jillian said. "Happy Halloween to you both," she murmured as she got up and moved toward the door.

"Um, happy Halloween," Daniel said. Then, to her surprise, he called her back.

She paused in his doorway.

His voice was slightly gruff when he spoke again. "Go out and have a great night. And remember, it's only Halloween. You and Connie leave some Christmas stuff out there for the rest of humanity, hmm?"

"Will do," she promised. Her voice was light. But tight, as well.

She was sorry about whatever it was that lay so strongly wedged between the two of them, but for the moment, there was nothing she could do about it.

She had been dismissed.

She hurried back into her own office.

Her tray of cookies and tea had been left on her desk. With a few things to clear up, she poured herself tea. She usually liked milk in her tea, but it had gotten cold, so she just shrugged and sipped it black as she started clearing her desk. She picked up one of the cookies, then put it back down, drawn again to her design for this year's Christmas cross.

What had possessed her?

The design was beautiful. Intricate, delicate. One of the best things she had ever done. But contemporary? Definitely not.

She picked up the cookie again, studying the cross. She leaned low, looking at her own work. It really was so Celtic.

She set the cookie down again. "Am I unintentionally...stealing?" she murmured aloud. "Did I take that off a gravestone in Ireland or a picture somewhere or—?"

She heard the tinkling of a small bell. Jeeves, a big black alley cat who had one day made his way inside and become a company pet, suddenly leapt up on her desk.

She absently stroked his back. "Am I a cheater, Jeeves?" she murmured. "Can't be." She shook her head and threw the design into her upper right-hand drawer. Once again she stroked the cat, then poured him a saucer of the milk intended for her tea.

"Drink up, buddy. Have some cookies, too."

The cat let out a mournful cry, looking at her with huge golden eyes.

She smiled. "Excuse me, you're a cat, not a dog. Lap up that milk."

The cat did so, needing no more invitation. Jillian stroked the animal one last time, making a mental note to leave her office door open.

The litter box was down the hall in Griff's office. Her cousin did, after all, have his responsibilities. Cat food, water—and the litter box.

It had been his idea to keep the cat and feed it. Studies had shown that pets were good for people, lowering blood pressure, making them calmer, more friendly. Eileen had pointed out that cat hair also made many people sneeze.

The cat had stayed. Luckily, no one in the office had been allergic.

"It's all yours, Jeeves," she said cheerfully.

She was leaving. She glanced at her watch one more time. Taxi or subway? She was due to meet Connie in fifteen minutes.

Feet. She wasn't that far from the coffee shop where they had planned to get together. She would just walk fast. That would be her best bet.

"'Night, Jeeves," she told the cat. *Happy Halloween. Trick or treat.*

She grabbed her coat and her handbag, and exited her office.

The cat, heedless of the comings and goings of mortals, gave no note. It greedily drank up the milk.

Suddenly the animal's body went rigid, then convulsed.

It collapsed by the tea tray.

The body twitched once. Twice.

And then it was still.

Dead still.

CHAPTER 2

"I didn't think I was ever going to get away this afternoon," Jillian told Connie when she met her at the little coffee bar off Fifth. She'd been in such a hurry to leave. She had actually gotten here first. But now, out of the office at last, she was beginning to relax. Not even the caffeine in her café mocha could start her blood rushing again.

"You shouldn't have given me the day off," Connie said sadly, stirring her tea.

Jillian looked at her friend. Connie Adair Murphy was petite, dark haired and blue eyed. Her face was round and always pleasant; she had a dimpled smile, and could be a powerhouse despite her small and cheerful appearance.

"You always take Halloween off. And I don't think anyone could have helped. It was just one of those family kind of days," she said, rolling her eyes, then grinning.

"They were feisty today, huh?"

"Moody, I think."

"Over the cross?"

"Only Daniel."

"What did your grandfather have to say?"

"He didn't come in today. He likes to take Halloween off, too."

"Are you going to start over? It would be a shame. It's such an outstanding design."

"No, Daniel says we're going with it. We'll just put a different spin on it." She looked at her watch. "My God, it's getting late."

"No, it's not so bad, only three-thirty."

"It gets dark so early."

"Doesn't matter," Connie assured her cheerfully. "I told the girls we'd head out at five-thirty or six. We've got a little time. It won't take long to get home on the subway. We'll just shove anyone in front of us away from the platform. We're fine."

"If we hustle."

"So we'll hustle."

"Let's do it."

They hustled. And to good avail.

Connie found darling dresses for her daughters. And though Llewellyn Enterprises offered an elegant line of evening wear, they took pleasure in finding the bargains that could be had in haute couture by other designers. They went on to find some fantastic gowns for the season's parties, and there were going to be a lot of them. They would be celebrating the fiftieth anniversary of Llewellyn Enterprises, and the rounds of activities and events planned for the estate in Connecticut were endless. Naturally Connie, as Jillian's assistant, was included, as was her husband. There were benefits to having both members of the family working for the same business. Connie had met Joe right out of college, during her first year working for Jillian; Joe had already been a rising star in the management division.

At the end of their whirlwind shopping spree, they happened upon a costume shop, with a last-minute sale. Connie was to-

tally incapable of passing a sign that stated—in large black letters—50% Off, Today Only!

"Wow! Will you look at this?" Connie said.

Inside, Connie pulled a costume off a rack and brandished it before Jillian. It was a witch's costume in silk and velvet, decorated
with rhinestones. It had a high collar, draping sleeves and a suggestive bodice. It was fitted at the waist, and flowed from there.

"Exquisite," Connie breathed.

"Buy it. Fifty-percent off," Jillian suggested.

Connie shook her head sadly. "Too long and too tight for me.
But..." She paused and looked at Jillian. "It's you."

"Me? I'm not wearing a costume. And there's no time. We
have to take the girls out. In fact, we need to take them soon."

"Yes, and I'm going to find a costume. I've decided I'm
going to be one of those fun moms, all dressed up like the kids.
Oh, look, there—"

Jillian looked where Connie was pointing and saw a large
horse's head. "That one? Oh, no, Connie, even if I decide to
come with you, I am not playing the rear end of a horse so you
can be a fun mom."

Connie started to laugh. "No, not the horse. I'm going to be
a princess, and you can be the witch. The gorgeous witch, I
might add. And when we finish the trick-or-treating bit, we'll
meet Joe at Hennessey's." She made a face and shrugged. "It
will be fun. You know Joe. He'll take a few pictures of the kids,
tell them they're adorable, then leave me to do the candy bit.
But he's going to the annual Halloween party at the pub, and
he's always telling me to get my mom to watch the kids and join
him. We'll do it. We'll get dressed up and go together."

"An Irish pub for Halloween?" Jillian asked skeptically.

"Why not? It's sure to be filled with pixies and leprechauns
and maybe a banshee or two." Connie cocked her head, looking at Jillian hopefully. "All right, so there are sure to be a few

big bad wolves around, as well. Actually, you could use a big
bad wolf or two in your life."

"My life is fine."

"You can't mourn Milo forever," Connie said, studying her
friend.

Jillian felt another twinge of loss. People still tiptoed around
mentioning Milo's name most of the time. Today, though, he
seemed in the forefront of her mind, and she reminded herself
again that she had married Milo Anderson with her eyes wide
open. She had known about his cancer. He had tried to talk her
out of marriage on the basis that she pitied him but didn't love
him. She had insisted, though. Because he had been wrong. She
had loved him very much.

Even more than Connie, he had been the best friend she'd
ever had. Maybe she hadn't been *in* love the way it was in
movies and romance novels, but she wasn't so sure she wanted
to be in love that way. Loving Milo had hurt enough.

Neither all the king's horses and all the king's men—nor all the
Llewellyn money—had been able to stop the growth of the dis-
ease. Milo had died almost a year to the day after their wedding.
Almost a year ago now. No one in her family ever told her, "Well,
you knew it was bound to happen," and for that she was grateful.

"I'm not going to mourn Milo forever. I'm glad for the time
we had together, glad for what he did for my life, glad for what
I was able to do for his. But it's not as if I've been wasting away
for years. He hasn't even been gone a year. I don't go out a lot
because I'm busy. I—"

"You need a life. And I happen to know that you refused a
get-to-know-you with Robert Marston for this evening, when
your grandfather suggested it."

"And how do you know that? It wasn't even a real suggestion."

"You poor innocent! Word is all over the company. You know
we love to talk about the bosses."

"I'm not the boss."

"Your grandfather wants you to be."

"No, he doesn't. He doesn't want to let go of the reins while he's living, and I don't think he should."

"He knows he's not going to live forever."

"It's a huge operation. I'm in design, not business. I don't want the headaches of everything my grandfather has his fingers into."

"A few of your cousins would be happy with the reins."

"I'm sure they would be."

"And they all despise the fact that Douglas has hired Robert Marston. They hate him."

"They don't hate him. He's an intelligent man, a top-notch businessman, and he'll be great for the company."

"I bet they think your grandfather brought Marston in to marry you and create a new dynasty."

"Connie! How ridiculous. This is the twenty-first century. That's archaic."

"Archaic, schmaic. I think it's what's up. And I think a few Llewellyn noses are going to be out of joint."

"Connie, I'm not marrying Robert Marston. I'm not dating him. I haven't had a business lunch with him. I haven't even been close enough to him to really see his face."

"There hasn't been time yet."

"Connie, come on. We're not a dynasty—and we're not going to rule New York fashion design and marketing together. You know I would never marry anyone for business reasons. I can't believe anyone would think such a thing."

"Jillian, look at the facts. Suddenly, when you're...when you're getting accustomed to the fact that Milo is gone, your grandfather brings in a handsome, powerful, *unattached* businessman. Out of the clear blue."

"The company has gotten huge."

"Marston isn't working under Daniel, is he?"

"No, he's—"

"Aha!"

"Connie, I'm not in a position of power. You know that. So an alliance with me wouldn't get him anywhere."

"You have your vote. And most people do see you as the natural heir to the company."

"Eileen is a grandchild, too."

"Yes, but Douglas dotes on you."

"It just appears that way because I was orphaned very young and I grew up with him. But I don't want to run the company. Why would I? It's huge, and I'm happy to share the legacy with the family. Please, are we buying costumes or not?"

Connie sighed. "I'm dying to dress up. But only if you will, too. Will you buy that outfit? It would look gorgeous on you."

"I...yes. I guess."

"We'll have fun. I promise. Let me call my mom and tell her she's definitely staying on, that we're going to go and meet Joe. Don't look at me like that. I won't talk shop anymore, I promise. We'll have fun, fun, fun."

It did turn out to be fun. They dressed up at Connie's apartment in Chelsea, went with the kids to the Safe-Haunt party arranged by one of the churches, then took the candy-laden kiddies back home, where they excitedly told their baby-sitting grandmother everything that had gone on. Kelly Adair, Connie's mother, oohed and aahed over the two women's costumes, and got into the fun by helping with glitter makeup. Jillian admitted that she was having a terrific time; she so seldom had a chance just to play this way. She worked constantly, went to charity dinners, plays, the opera and political fund-raisers. She almost never got a good night out at a pub or spent time with friends for no reason other than to have fun.

Connie called her the oldest twenty-six-year-old she knew

and teased her that she needed to have a good time before moving to a retirement home, where she would get her kicks out of watching reruns and waiting for grade-school children to come and sing Christmas carols. But Jillian knew—instinctively, and due to the fact that it had been pounded into her all her life—that she was a Llewellyn of Llewellyn Enterprises; she had a responsibility to uphold, as did all the family. Once her grandfather had entertained dreams about her father going into the White House. He'd become one of the most popular senators ever to be elected to public office, but then he had dropped dead. An aneurysm had felled him at the age of forty-one. That was when she had really come to love her grandfather. She had watched him swallow his own grief and anguish to console her.

She understood that she had been born with a silver spoon in her mouth, but when people called her lucky all the time, she wasn't sure why. Luck wasn't money. She would have traded every dime in the family coffers to have her father back. Connie told her that it was worse to be in agony *and* broke, and she guessed that must be true, but she felt it was more than enough that she'd lost her mother and baby brother in childbirth, and then her father. She had been raised in a huge, cold house and a huge, cold apartment—though not by a cold man. She adored Douglas Alexander Llewellyn. At the age of eighty-five, he remained the iron-fisted, tough-as-nails ruler of all he surveyed.

But it had never been fear of him that had made her work so hard, take such care in school, or behave with complete responsibility at all times. She loved him. She wanted to please him. And though she loathed politics, she did want to do her part to change the world. Douglas had taught her about giving back; Connie had shown her why she must do so.

"Jillian," Kelly said, bright blue eyes sparkling, "I have never seen you look lovelier. Not even in all those chic gowns you own."

"She's a vamp," Connie said with a laugh. "We look okay, Mom? I mean, how about me? Your daughter, remember?"

"Cute as a button," her mother said.

"Cute? I want to be sultry. Stunning."

Kelly laughed. "Your husband adores you, and you're devastating. You're both devastating—in fact, I'm afraid to let you go out to that pub."

"Just Hennessey's, Mom. And Joe will be there." She looked Jillian up and down and angled her head in thought. "Though, come to think of it, we may pick up every sodden Irish-American—hell, every sodden man of any nationality—but what the hey, you only go around once, right?"

"Well, off you go, then."

They kissed the girls good-night. Tricia was five, and Mary Elizabeth, or Liza, was the baby at four. The excited little girls raved over Jillian's costume, and as she kissed and hugged them, she found herself loving the clean, baby-powder scent of them in their jammies. They were such a wonderful part of real life, and one day she wanted something as wonderful as what Connie had: a cozy little apartment and people all around her who loved her, really loved her. Family. True, she had a family, but it wasn't the same as having a husband who'd chosen to love her and children born of that love.

"We're off," Connie said, kissing her mother's cheek.

"Behave, now," Kelly admonished.

"Behave? Good heavens, Mother. I want this witch to go wild, have a little fun."

"She can't go too wild, and you know it."

"Why not? I'm buying her the biggest Guinness in the place the moment we get there. But don't worry, because I'll be there, protecting her."

Jillian grinned. Connie was the closest thing to a sister she had. In school, Connie had been a class ahead of her, and from the start, she hadn't been in the least intimidated by the Llewellyn power, money or prestige. She had allowed Jillian to see the streets of New York, the real streets. They had gotten into a few scrapes, but they had also gotten out of them. Thanks to Connie, she had seen harsh things firsthand: prostitutes on the street turning tricks so they could afford another line of cocaine, AIDS victims dying with no hope, kind priests, rabbis, laymen and women determined to help them.

"You are going to let loose, right?" Connie asked her, angling her dark head in question as she studied Jillian.

"You bet I am!" Jillian teased back.

"You can drink like an Irish potato digger, cuss like my pa, and trust in me to see that you're okay."

"Aye, and that I will," Jillian agreed, putting on the appropriate accent. She was good with accents and loved the theater. She still played with the idea of heading out to audition for Broadway one day.

"All righty, then. Jillian and I are on our way out, Mother."

"Toast me, ladies."

"We will," Jillian promised, as Connie dragged her out the door. They flagged down a cabdriver, who, despite the absurdities rife on the street that night, kept staring at them in the rearview mirror.

"See?" Connie teased. "He's watching you."

"Hey, you're the princess tonight."

"Sad but true, everyone loves an evil woman best," Connie advised.

In a few minutes they reached Hennessey's Pub, down in the Village. Though the place was rocking, it was doing so in the nicest way. The music was loud, but not too loud. The band was Irish-American, playing mostly rock, some folk, all with a wee bit of the Old Country thrown in. Drinks had been flowing, but not to the extent that too many drunks were weaving around.

For the most part, the clientele was in a good mood. Many people were in costume, from the group dressed as the different colors of M&M's to the brawny exercise guru in the Carmen Miranda skirt, bra, sandals and fruit headdress. He greeted Connie by name right away. Connie introduced him to Jillian—no last name—as Sergeant Tip Guyer of New York's finest. Connie did the introductions, and the cop instantly offered to treat them to a couple of beers while telling Connie that she could find her "old man" just inside by the bar, watching ESPN.

"Can you imagine? A party—and they're watching sports," she said with disgust. "Tip, if you think you can reach the bar, we'll take you up on those beers."

Tip nodded, flashing an appreciative smile at Jillian.

"He can't believe his good luck," Connie said, when the man had gone.

"His good luck?"

"Getting to hang with you."

"Oh, Connie, please."

"Not because of who you are—just because he wants to bask in your gorgeous nearness."

"Connie..."

"And there's good old Joe, not even noticing us, just watching the game."

"I'm sure he can't hear too much, with all the music, so he has to study the TV closely," Jillian teased. There was a tap on her shoulder. A giant leprechaun was asking her to dance, but she wasn't ready for that quite yet, so she declined politely and asked him to come back in a while.

"Dancing is fun, and you're out to have fun," Connie reminded her.

"I intend to dance. But you've asked Carmen Miranda to bring us drinks, remember?"

And then she saw the tarot card reader.

"Hey, look, there's a fortune-teller."

"A fortune-teller? What fun!" Connie said.

"She's great." Tip had rejoined them, bearing glasses of ale. He passed them over as he went on. "She's interesting. She has you lay out the cards, then she tells you what they mean and how the future might affect you. I have a confrontation coming in my future."

"How unusual—for a cop," Jillian teased.

He shrugged. "A nonbeliever. So many are. But she's really good. It's not just hocus-pocus. Maybe she's a psychologist by day, desperate for more interesting characters by night. She told me to watch my temper. Can you imagine?"

"Yes, Tip," Connie said thoughtfully, "I'm afraid I can."

As Tip and Connie started discussing the idiocies he saw on the streets of New York every day, Jillian had the strangest feeling. It was as if she knew him. Of *course* she knew him she told herself; Connie had just introduced her. But she felt as if she had known him before. A long time ago. Was it true, she wondered, that you recognized people in life who you might like, who would be your friends, given half a chance?

Suddenly she noticed that the conversation had stopped and he was staring at her, seemingly unable to tear his eyes away from her. "Look at you, looking so solemn. Lighten up. It's Halloween. Ghosts and goblins and ghouls. Okay, maybe that's a bad example. Think Christmas. Santa Claus. Ho, ho, ho. Pine trees, packages, Christmas carolers—"

"Really bad traffic, people shoving each other in stores over the newest toy craze, badly wired lights sizzling families to a crisp."

They all spun around. Connie's husband, Joe, had joined them. Despite his words of doom and gloom, he spoke cheerfully.

"Back to Christmas," Connie said sternly. "Pine trees, packages, the girls giggling, Santa Claus—and miracles."

"You don't really believe in miracles, do you?" Tip asked.

"And why not?" Connie demanded. "There are plenty of strange things in this world."

"And the next, too," Joe said with a depth of sincerity that caused his wife to stare at him again.

"What is this? We're not here to ponder the next life," she protested. "We're partying. Think good times only."

"All right," Joe said. "Let the good times roll. But let's test out the world of the occult. We won't say a word to the tarot card reader. I'll go to her with Jillian on my arm. Connie, you go with Tip. We'll test her powers."

"She doesn't claim to have powers," Tip reminded him.

"Tip, did I ever tell you how good you look in that color bra?" Joe teased him.

"Ah, honey, you're going to make me blush. But go ahead—test her out. I've already seen her. I'll escort Connie, then you come along with Jillian. You'll see."

Carrying their drinks, they joined the line for the tarot card reader. She was a beautiful woman. Her skin was a tawny copper color, her eyes a hazel that gleamed golden in the candlelight. She was dressed for the part in gypsy attire—a sweeping, multicolored skirt, a gold-colored peasant blouse, and a scarf in various shades of gold and copper tied around her head. She was, according to the glittery name plaque in front of her, Madame Zena.

From her place in line, Jillian sipped her Guinness and watched as the woman laid down the cards. The customer, a pretty young woman in a harem costume, tapped one of the cards in dismay. "Oh no, that means death, right?"

Madame Zena shook her head patiently. "It's not just the cards themselves that speak to you, it is their arrangement. These cards warn you..." She looked up, staring at the girl sternly. "Were you planning on taking the subway back out to Brooklyn alone?"

"Brooklyn—yes, it's where I live. I'm a Fine Arts student."

"From Omaha," the guy behind her teased.

"Don't go home on the subway alone," the reader warned.

The young man put his hands on her shoulders. "She won't," he said protectively.

"But you'll be ridiculously late if you come back to the dorm with me."

"I'll sleep on the floor. Janice won't mind."

"All right, all right, Madame Zena—can you tell me about my midterms?" the girl asked.

Madame Zena leaned forward, then tapped on a card. "You passed. But barely. If you want to stay in New York and avoid Omaha for the next few years, you'd better get cracking."

"Yes, ma'am."

The girl slid from her seat, her eyes wide. She was a believer. Jillian had to admit to being pretty impressed herself.

"She goes for the obvious," Joe whispered.

"How so?" Connie demanded in a soft hiss.

"The kid is obviously a student."

"Maybe, but there are colleges in Manhattan, too, you know."

"She made a good guess."

The young man had sat down in front of Madame Zena. He grinned. "Am I going to get lucky tonight?"

"Lucky?" Madame Zena queried. "Are you going to survive the drunks driving around the city tonight? Yes, you're very lucky. Will you be smart enough to avoid the big pothole on Willoughby Avenue and avoid a broken ankle. Yes, again, if you pay attention. That will be lucky. Are you having sex? Not a chance. Janice is going to be there, and she's going to throw you a pillow on the floor."

Those standing around Madame Zena's table all laughed. Madame Zena smiled, tolerant of the laughter. Jillian decided that the woman was very good at what she did, that she wasn't psychic, she just used some good solid sense on her clients.

There were a few more people before them in line. Jillian watched, enjoying what she heard, along with the Guinness. Tip refilled their beers while they waited in line and the band kept playing.

Finally their turn came. Tip led Connie forward. Madame Zena studied her briefly, her amber eyes intent. She looked up to the line and motioned to Joe. "Come sit with your wife," she said.

"You told her," Joe accused Tip.

"I did not," Tip protested.

Madame Zena noticed Jillian. Her lashes flickered, as if something disturbed her.

"Well?" Joe murmured.

"Shuffle the cards," Madame Zena said. "Let your wife go first. I'm using the three-card spread. They reveal past, present and future. There is a meaning to all cards, and a reverse meaning, as well."

She laid out three cards, side by side. For a moment she studied them, then studied Connie. "Temperance. You are a good human being. You've made those around you happy, and you have chosen your friends wisely."

"That's me," Connie said happily.

Her husband sniffed.

"Joe!"

He caught her hand and kissed it. "You're the best human being."

Madame Zena looked at the cards, then past Joe and Connie to Jillian.

"Madame Zena?" Joe queried, tapping the table.

Madame Zena pointed to the second card. "The Nine of Swords. There is discord in your life."

"But there isn't!" Connie protested.

"Maybe it's in the future," Joe suggested gravely.

Madame Zena shook her head. "The future is here... The World. It symbolizes...completion, rewards."

"So everything comes out okay?" Connie said hopefully.

Madame Zena looked at her. "You must *make* things come out okay, because the reverse meaning here suggests that success is yet to be won, that you may be lacking in vision. You must take care to see, to see everything, beyond the physical eye, do you understand?"

"Yes," Connie said. But the tone of her voice said "no."

"So the cards don't like me?" she asked in distress.

"The cards are to be used for good. They warn you. Nothing in life is free, nothing comes without a price. Except for the occasional miracle. The cards warn you that you must be firm, steadfast, loyal. You must always control your own future."

Madame Zena wasn't going to say more.

"Okay, me now," Joe said.

Madame Zena looked over his head at Jillian once again. She looked troubled. "Shuffle the cards," she told Joe.

He did, and the reader laid them out. Three cards. Past. Present. Future.

The exact same lineup as his wife.

"Hey, that's not possible," Joe protested.

"Shuffle them again."

He did. They fell the same way. Madame Zena shrugged. "You know what they mean."

"They mean you do card tricks as well as readings?" Joe suggested.

"No, young man, I do not do card tricks. You're a good man, you've made good choices."

"The best of men," Connie said loyally, slipping her arm through her husband's.

"You're passing through a rough time. Only your own courage and determination will show you the way to go. They will bring you through to triumph or success." She stared at Jillian again. "I don't want to read your cards."

"What!" Jillian said, astonished, and dismayed by the little chill that swept through her.

"I'm sorry, I'm tired."

"Madame Zena, she's been in line for nearly an hour," Tip protested.

Joe and Connie had risen already, and Tip was ushering Jillian forward. She sat, and Madame Zena stared at her, then handed her the cards. Jillian felt as if a rush of electricity jumped into her flesh.

"We are all part of our own destinies, you know," Madame Zena said. "The soul can be very old, and the soul can learn. A good soul remains so. Sometimes there are second chances." Madame Zena's strange hazel eyes were hard on Jillian. "In life and in death. Energy does not die. God is great. Hand me the cards."

Instead of the three cards, Madame Zena laid out more, creating a cross on the table before her. She had Jillian turn them over, then was silent for a long time.

"You've had tremendous upheaval, tragedy."

"Of course," Joe said. "Her husband died."

Madame Zena asked, "Violently?"

"Cancer," Connie supplied softly.

Madame Zena shook her head. "No, something worse, far worse. There was a lack of faith, a terrible betrayal...there was a fire."

"Nope, no fire," Jillian said positively.

"Yes, there was a fire," Madame Zena insisted. "Betrayal. And the night. There was one who came and enticed and laughed and...betrayed. And there you see the Moon. Rising in Pisces... You are in danger. You have enemies."

"Well, she's a big shot, rich executive. Of course she has enemies," Joe said.

"Really?" Tip asked, looking Jillian up and down all over again. "Cool," he said. "And I just thought you were one sexy redhead."

"Thanks," Jillian murmured.

"Now you've gone and told half the world who she is," Connie murmured.

"Enemies," Madame Zena murmured. "Enemies."

"I still don't know who she is," Tip told Joe. He gave Jillian a charming smile, and she tried to respond, but by then Madame Zena was beginning to get to her.

"Beware..."

Madame Zena's voice was suddenly so low and husky that it seemed to reach out and touch her with fingers of ice, running along her spine, her nape.

"Beware..."

Jillian leaned forward, forcing her lips to move. "Of what?"

"Christmas...Christmastide..."

"Oh my God, this is going too far," Joe said impatiently. "Beware of Christmas? Of what? A psychopathic Santa? Come on, Jillian..."

"Beware, take warning."

"Jillian, come on, get up," Joe urged, but she couldn't seem to move.

"Witch, witch, witch, witch..." Madame Zena said.

"Which? Which what?" Jillian murmured.

"W-i-t-c-h," Madame Zena whispered.

Dear God, but she sounded so weird and looked so spooky. Scary. Maybe it was a holiday act.

Madame Zena leaned back, gripping the table. They all stared at her blankly as she fell silent, her eyes closed. When she opened them, they had rolled up into her head until only the whites showed. "Witch," she murmured. "Witch." The cry grew louder. *"Witch."* Louder still, and different, as if several voices were speaking through the woman. Her voice rose so high that Jillian, staring at her, horrified, was afraid that the cries would echo above the sound of the band.

"Madame Zena, stop it!" she protested.

"Witch!"

"It's a costume, just a costume," Jillian said.

"Come on, enough is enough," Joe told her. He drew back the chair, gripped her elbow and pulled her to her feet.

"Too much," Tip agreed.

"We need some air," Connie said.

"I'm all right," Jillian said, but they were already headed for the door.

As they neared it, it opened and a man entered. He was tall, broad-shouldered. He wasn't wearing a costume, just a long leather coat against the autumn chill. Jillian barely noted him at first, except as someone who was blocking the door.

Then the light touched him.

He had dark hair, almost pitch in color, cropped at the collar, swept back in the front. His face was strongly chiseled, with clean features and a square, well-defined jaw, a generous mouth, large, dark eyes—maybe dark blue, she thought, rather than brown. He was good-looking and moved with confidence.

"Built like a brick shit-house," Connie whispered in her ear.

Still, Jillian would have walked right by him. The city was home to lots of good-looking people, models, actors, even businessmen.

Then this man looked at them. And when she looked back, she realized that she knew him.

"My God," Connie breathed. "I didn't recognize him at first."

Of course, she knew him. Or *almost* knew him.

She'd just never seen him so close.

Nor seen him...*look* at her.

She felt his eyes on her. Then, suddenly, pain seared her. Rocked her. Hit her in the chest as if she had been struck by lightning. Pain so vibrant that fire seemed to flash before her eyes.

She staggered, doubling over in sudden agony.

"Jillian?"

She heard Connie's concerned whisper.

Then the pain radiated through her. *Fire!* It was as if she were on fire.

And then she blacked out.

CHAPTER 3

He was bending over her, his head slightly turned as he calmly ordered everyone to move back, give her some room.

Then his eyes fell on her again.

They were blue. Navy. The closest thing to black she'd ever seen that still carried the touch of a hue. And she wasn't in pain anymore. Not in physical pain.

But she was in mental agony. Total humiliation.

What in God's name had seized her?

She had been kept from falling by someone and transported to the Victorian sofa that sat just inside the main entry to the pub. Connie was on one side of her, Joe on the other. Her new friend Tip, the cop, was hovering somewhere nearby; she could hear him talking. But it was Robert Marston who was right in front of her, barking out orders, touching her forehead and her throat—checking for a pulse, she assumed.

She wished she could crawl under the couch.

She sat up, an act easier planned than managed. Marston was

so close that she crashed right into him, forehead to forehead. He smiled as their heads cracked, while she paled all over again.

"I knew I wasn't exactly welcomed by everyone in the company, but I never thought I could cause fainting spells," he joked.

She shook her head quickly. "You had nothing to do with it. I didn't even know who you were. I—"

"Are you all right?" he enquired more seriously.

"I—I—of course," she stammered.

Then she was aware of Connie's gaze. "Jillian, are you sure? My God, you were white as a ghost. We were so worried."

"I'm...I'm fine," she protested. "Thanks, really. I'm just embarrassed and—"

"Maybe we should get you to the hospital, get you checked out," Marston suggested, interrupting her with a note of authority.

She stared at him, wishing she could crawl away.

What in the world had caused this?

She hadn't felt threatened by his hiring, had she? Wary, but not threatened. She hadn't really talked to him yet, because there hadn't really been the opportunity. A simple, *normal* opportunity. But she hadn't been worried about it. She was in design, he wasn't. In all honesty, she wasn't sure why Douglas had suddenly brought him in, but she had neither felt threatened nor overly impressed.

But at this particular moment, he seemed extremely imposing. The man was very tall, even down on one knee the way he was now. His shoulders were broad, though he seemed as sleek and agile as a man more slimly built.

"A hospital couldn't hurt, other than the hours you're likely to spend in the emergency room," he told her.

She realized that she hadn't responded to his earlier comment; she had just been staring at him. "No, I don't want to go to the hospital. Really, I'm fine," she protested. "Please, I just—" She broke off, aware that a sea of faces seemed to be looking on.

In the distance, she even saw the face of the tarot reader. The

woman was watching her gravely, as if she weren't at all surprised by this turn of events.

For some reason the sight of the woman was disturbing. Jillian felt uneasy again, as if something was wrong but she just
couldn't put her finger on it. It was as if the tarot card reader
knew something she didn't.

Something that she *should* know.

The woman turned away, and Jillian's uneasiness dissipated.
She felt simply and completely like an idiot.

"What?" Marston asked quietly, seeming to sense her unease.

"I just need to get out of here," she said. Her voice was soft.
Raspy. "I could really go for some air."

A second later, she regretted her words, as Marston lifted her
into his arms, striding from the pub. "Excuse us, the lady needs
air."

She wasn't white anymore. Her cheeks were flushed with
mortification.

Outside, she found herself seated on the hood of a silver
sports car. She heard Connie's heels hitting the pavement as she
and Joe hurried out to join them, followed by Tip, still in his
Carmen Miranda getup.

"Is that better?" Those uncannily dark blue eyes were on hers.

And her hands were on his arms, she realized; she had
gripped him to steady herself. She snatched her hands back and
grasped for some dignity. "Look, Mr. Marston, I appreciate
your concern, but I'm fine now. I just—"

"Had too much to drink?" he suggested.

She straightened in indignation. "I never have too much to
drink."

"No?" A spark of humor touched his eyes.

"I don't believe your job description includes anything about
picking me up from barroom floors, though I do appreciate the
concern. However, I really am fine."

"She does seem to be okay," Tip said.

Marston turned around, his eyes widening at the sight of the big cop in drag. "Sorry, I didn't realize you two were together," he said briefly.

"No, no, they're not together," Joe said quickly, explaining. "Tip is a friend of mine."

Jillian could have knocked him silly. She offered him a scathing glance, but he didn't notice.

"I think I should get off this car before the owner sues for damages," she said, starting to move.

"Give yourself another second."

His hands were on her shoulders. Long fingered, clean, neat, powerful. She glanced down at his touch and felt a strange, warm tremor. Barely remembered. Not welcomed now.

"I'm on someone's Mercedes."

"It's mine," he said.

Naturally. The Mercedes said everything there was to say about him. Smooth, cool. Sporty but mature. Handsome, powerful, sleek.

"Maybe you should take Jillian home, Mr. Marston," Connie said, concerned. She looked from one to the other. "We haven't actually met," she said to him. "I'm Connie Murphy."

"Joe's wife. I know," Marston said. He smiled and took her hand, and his eyes met Joe's. "Your husband and I have already worked together."

"Yes, of course." Connie looked flushed. It had been one thing for her to tease Jillian about company gossip, but now that she was actually meeting Robert Marston, she seemed a little awed herself. He did make an impression.

Was that why Douglas had brought him in? Connie wondered. She answered her own silent question quickly and defensively. *No. Daniel, full of confidence, ability, authority and composure made quite an impression himself. Theo was equally presentable. Eileen was pure elegance and assurance. And Griff...*

Griff excelled at being Griff.

"Office meeting over," Jillian murmured with false cheer. She tried to slide off the car, but Marston stopped her. She looked at his hand, then met his eyes. "I told you I'm all right."

"If you won't go to the hospital, at least let me take you home."

"I'm fine. Tip can see me home. He may look like Carmen Miranda, but in real life, he's one of New York's finest."

"So you're a cop. Nice to meet you."

"Ditto," Tip told him, as the two men shook hands.

"Did you drive, Tip?" Marston enquired, those dark eyes settling on the cop.

"No, 'fraid not," Tip told Jillian apologetically.

"I don't need a ride," Jillian protested.

"Jillian, you passed out cold," Connie said.

"Thanks, Connie," she murmured.

"You might have hurt yourself."

"But I didn't!"

"You were leaving, anyway," Marston reminded her. "So let me take you home."

"You just got here, so I'm sure you don't want to leave. Go on in and have a good time."

"And what would I tell Douglas in the morning?" he asked, a half smile curving his lips.

"That his granddaughter is pigheaded?" Joe supplied.

"Joe..." his wife said warningly.

"I really don't think that watching me is part of the job," Jillian began.

"I wouldn't want to bet on that," Joe said.

"Okay, okay. I'll go home with Marston," she said, aggravated.

"You can call me Robert, Bob, Rob, or even Bobby. Most of the time, when people call me Marston, they put a 'mister' in front of it," he said, his tone conversational but with a slight edge, his dark eyes on her.

She eased off the car, meeting that gaze. "I'm so sorry, Mr. Marston."

He smiled. An honest smile. She looked away, biting her lip.

" 'Night, then," Connie said.

"Good night." Jillian hugged Connie, kissed Joe and then Tip on a cheek, and walked around to the passenger side of the car. He was already there, opening the door for her.

Call me, Connie mouthed.

She would call her, all right.

A moment later, they were in traffic.

He drove competently, assertively, but not recklessly. He was playing a Celtic CD; a woman was singing about a highwayman. Partiers filled the sidewalks, all laughing, some loaded, some simply happy. Taxis veered in and out; horns blared.

"I live at—" she began.

"I know where you live," he told her.

Fine.

A few minutes later, they pulled up to the house on Manhattan's upper east side. It was one of the few old mansions that remained. Among a sea of skyscrapers, it stood three stories tall. A brick wall with wrought-iron gates separated it from its neighbors.

Here, away from the throngs, the streets were quiet. Marston didn't opt to enter the driveway but slid into an impossible spot on the street.

Before the engine had died, Jillian was reaching for the door handle.

"Are you afraid of me?" he asked her. She could hear his amusement.

"No, of course not." Her fingers fell from the handle.

"Do you resent my being hired?"

He was blunt. "No. Why should I?"

"Want to hear all the rumors?" he queried.

She shook her head. "No. Do you want to hear the truth?"

"Sure."

"I like design. I enjoy what I do. I especially like jewelry, but make occasional forays into fashion, as well. I don't want my grandfather's kingdom. I don't even think my grandfather wants all his kingdom anymore. So why should I resent you being hired?"

He smiled, looking not at her, but straight ahead at the road, at the night. "Because in a kingdom, you always have to have a king. Or a queen."

"Well, if we have a king, it's Daniel. Are you planning to push him from the throne?"

"I've been given shares in the company and a very satis-factory title. Part of the package when I came over. Daniel has his own role."

"Then, we all ought to be just peachy-keen," she murmured. She looked at him. "Thanks for the ride. I'm sorry to have trou-bled you." She fumbled with the door. He reached over her and opened the door easily.

"Thanks," she muttered.

"I would feel better if I walked you in."

"I wouldn't."

"But you don't resent me?" he queried lightly. He stepped out of the car as she did.

"Okay, walk me in."

"You did have quite a reaction to seeing me walk through the door tonight."

"I wasn't reacting to you," she said, her heart pounding. What *had* she reacted to?

The pain. The pain had been unbearable, and the world had gone black.

"Then?" he pressed.

"The tarot card reader," she said.

"What?"

"There was a woman reading tarot cards. She started screaming, rolling her eyes—and calling me a witch. She wouldn't stop. She was pretending to be in a trance or something, and we decided to get out. I just needed air," she said, finishing rather lamely. "I had nothing to do with it?"

She met his gaze again, black in the shadows. She still felt...wary of him. But curiously drawn, as well. She had to admit he was being polite, and he seemed to have a sense of humor.

She shook her head. "No," she lied, then smiled. "Honestly, I don't resent you. I think you've got great credentials, and I really don't want to run the company."

"If that's a welcome, thanks, I'll take it."

"Sure. It's a welcome. In fact, please come in, if you'd like. Have a drink here, since you never got your chance at Hennessey's."

"Despite the much-appreciated-but-debatable sincerity of that offer, I'm afraid I have to refuse."

"Ah, a date," she murmured, lashes flicking downward. She was definitely losing her mind. She hadn't wanted him to take her home, and had tried very hard to shake him. And now...

She was disappointed. And curious.

Jealous? She wondered who he was meeting.

"An appointment," he said lightly. "You're sure you're all right?"

"I've never felt better. Honestly."

"All right, then."

But he stood there, watching her.

"Well?"

"I need to see you in."

"Oh." She slid her computer key into the lock. The gate swung open; she stepped through, closing it behind her.

He nodded, then turned away, starting back toward his car.

"Mars—uh, Mr. Marston?"

He turned back.

"It was nice to meet you. And thanks for your concern."

"Of course."

He walked to his car, and she watched him drive away. Though it was cold, the bars of the gate suddenly seemed to burn against her hands.

She released them quickly.

Strange, strange night.

Robert returned to Hennessey's.

Parking the car in the street—easy enough, with most of the evening's revelers Halloween-ed out and headed home—he left the driver's seat and checked his watch.

Too late for his original appointment, but he'd wanted to come back here, anyway.

He'd never seen anything like the way Jillian Llewellyn had looked at him. He hadn't expected to be welcomed into the company with pure joy and enthusiasm, but he'd never imagined anything like what he'd encountered.

She had looked at him with...hatred? Horror?

Maybe pure blind terror. Or something else. He didn't know quite what. A combination of all those emotions.

He had felt shaken. For a moment a chill had settled over him, like something cold and horrible beyond words, and then...

Then she had started to fall, and the feeling had slipped away, and now he couldn't even recall exactly what it had been. Maybe he'd imagined it. And yet...

At the bar, he ordered a beer. They'd dyed the beer with food coloring. Black beer. Interesting.

As he sipped, he eased back and surveyed the room. Nearly midnight. The band was playing ballads. The bar was still full, but the customers at the tables were beginning to head out. When people moved, he saw the fortune-teller.

Tarot card reader. Whatever. It was all just fun and bull.

As he looked at her, she suddenly stared up at him. Her eyes were golden. Amber, glimmering. She was an arresting woman, metallic in color. Even her skin was copper. She was both stunning and disturbing.

As she looked at him, she suddenly leaned back in her chair, gripping the table. She didn't seem to be doing anything else, certainly nothing threatening, but the couple who had been having their cards read suddenly pushed their chairs away.

He wasn't sure why, but he rose, walking over to her. She straightened, pointing at him.

But she didn't see him. He knew that, her eyes had rolled back into her head.

"Betrayer," she whispered. She began to croon and moan, weaving in her chair.

He felt the cold again. Like ice. Fear unlike anything he could remember. Yet he wasn't afraid for himself. He just knew that...

His head hurt. Pounded. He leaned forward, putting his hands on the table. "Stop it," he snapped. "Stop it."

She jerked forward; her eyes rolled into place. "You shouldn't have come," she told him, visibly shaken.

"I shouldn't have come to the bar?" he asked.

"To Llewellyn," she answered.

He eased down into the chair, staring at her. "Who put you up to this?" he demanded. After all, this was Hennessey's. A favorite hangout of Daniel's, Theo's, and probably Griff's, as well.

The name Llewellyn was Welsh. But Robert knew from his long conversations with Douglas that the family had been in Ireland for hundreds of years before he had picked up and made his way to the States.

"Madame Zena," he said firmly, looking around the pub again for some sight of any one of the Llewellyns, "who put you up to this?"

"No one," she told him.

"Well, then, listen to me," he said, leaning forward. "I didn't come to Llewellyn to hurt anyone. As a matter of fact, I intend to protect certain people, even though they may not trust me. Protect them, and their interests. So you can call off the mind games. I—"

"You know nothing," she said softly. "You are dangerous. More dangerous than you can ever imagine. You're so powerful and arrogant." She leaned toward him, suddenly angry, but very still and quiet as she spoke. "You know nothing. And you do not care to learn."

"Excuse me, Madame Zena," he interrupted, puzzled and angry, and not knowing why he felt he needed to defend himself to a fortune-teller. "Look, I'm a decent human being, responsible, concerned, intelligent—"

She didn't seem to hear him. "You may be all that, but it's not enough. Fear is a good thing, young man. Fear can create a quest for knowledge, because no man is so strong he can defy God, Heaven and Hell, and all the Fates. Get out of here. And don't come to me again unless your mind is open."

She stood and, with a flourish, spun away from him, then rushed from the bar.

Startled, he sat back in the chair.

"Wow, that was...scary!"

He turned around and saw that the girl who had been in his chair just moments earlier had spoken. A pretty young brunette, she was clinging to her lanky escort, eyes wide, cheeks pale.

"Well," he said with a shrug, "it's Halloween, after all."

One of the bartenders—a freckled redhead wearing bobbing bug antennae—came walking over, wiping a glass as he looked out the door. "She didn't even get her money," he said, then shrugged fatalistically. "Oh well, I imagine she'll be back."

He returned to his position behind the bar.

"Look at the card that's turned over now," the brunette said.

She grabbed her boyfriend's lapel. "That wasn't my card." She stared at Robert, scared again, shaking her head. "It's your card. It has to be your card."

"So? I don't believe in prophecy. Fate is what we make it," he said firmly.

"It's...it's still your card," she whispered, then turned, heading out.

"Women," the man said. "You know the old saying. Can't live with 'em, can't shoot 'em, either."

He hurried after the brunette.

Robert looked at the card on the table. He didn't know much about tarot cards, and he certainly didn't believe in their ability to foretell the future.

But even he recognized the Grim Reaper.

The dream came suddenly.

She smelled smoke. And then there was the rustling sound of dry kindling as it caught fire. The acrid smell of something burning...

Flesh.

Pain, a searing pain...

She awoke with a violent start and jumped out of bed, screaming, "Fire! Henry, get Grandfather!"

With her eyes open, she saw that there was no fire. She stood dead still. No smoke, no fire, no scent of burning flesh.

Her door suddenly burst open.

There was Henry, Grandfather's assistant.

Henry was seventy, a spring chicken compared to Douglas Llewellyn. He stood in her doorway in his proper pajamas and robe, snow-white hair beneath a bed cap, as if he were a character right out of a Dickens novel.

"Jillian?" he cried, looking frantically around.

Embarrassment filled her. She'd been dreaming.

"Oh, Henry, I'm so sorry. I had a nightmare, I...I guess."

He exhaled a vastly relieved sigh. "Oh, my dear girl," he said.

She walked to the doorway, setting a hand on his shoulder. "Henry, are you all right? My God, I can't believe I was screaming like that. I wouldn't have worried you for the world. How ridiculous. I guess it happened because it's Halloween."

He smiled. "Why, Miss Jillian, you've never been afraid of Halloween, or the dark, or things that go bump in the night."

She lifted a hand. "I'm at a loss myself. But I'm sorry." She set her palm on his chest. His heart rate was slowing.

"I'm fine, Miss Jillian. Just fine. The old ticker is pumping just as it should. Shall I fix you a drink? A hot toddy?"

"No, no more alcohol," she said.

He arched a brow.

"I had a few Guinness Stouts," she told him.

"Well, then, what say we share some hot chocolate?"

She smiled. "Sounds good."

As she had since she'd been a little girl, after her mother died, she slipped her hand into his. They walked out to the second floor landing and down to the kitchen together.

As they chatted, memories of the awful vividness of the nightmare faded.

She didn't tell him much about her Halloween evening at Hennessey's, though. And she didn't say a word about the tarot card reader, or the arrival of Robert Marston.

Eventually, warm and relaxed, she yawned, thanked Henry and headed up to bed.

She tried to sleep, but she couldn't. Suddenly, after all these years, she hated the dark.

She rose. The main light would be too bright. Even the reading light by her bed would be too much. She turned on the bathroom light, then left the door open a crack and lay back down in bed.

Better, but still...

She'd never been afraid before. Of the darkness, of the night. If there were ghosts in her life, they were good ghosts. People who had loved her. Her mother. Her father.

Milo.

Her eyes fell on the snow globe that sat on her nightstand between the lamp and the silver-framed picture of Milo and herself. Always smiling. No matter what pain had plagued him. He had loved art and music, dance, theater, the world. An eternal optimist. The pain was okay, because he was living, still with her, still seeing the world. Death would be okay, too, because then the pain would be gone, and there was a better world.

He had given her the snow globe. It played a beautiful, if somewhat sad, tune, though the title was a mystery. It held a wilderness scene, with horses and riders racing through a winter landscape. She shook it and watched the snow fall.

"I wish you were with me, old friend," she said softly.

A few minutes later, she felt an odd sense of peace settling over her.

Finally she slept. And the dream didn't come again.

Connie was the first to enter Jillian's office in the morning. She stepped in humming, then came to a dead halt. A scream escaped her, and she clamped her hand over her mouth to stop it.

Someone rushed in behind her, and she spun around. Daniel Llewellyn.

Like her, he stood dead still. Staring. At the cat.

"Jeeves is...dead," she said.

"Sure looks like it," Daniel said.

"Hey, what's all the commotion?" Griff demanded, walking in behind them.

They both looked at Griff with almost as much surprise as they had stared at the cat.

"You're early," Connie said.

"Keeping on my toes," Griff said lightly, then saw the cat.

"Whoa, what happened to him?"

"Connie?" Joe rushed in, looking anxiously at his wife. "I heard you screaming. What—"

"It's the cat," she explained.

"The cat?" Joe queried, puzzled.

"Jeeves apparently climbed up on Jillian's desk to die last night," Daniel explained. "We shouldn't have kept a cat in the office in the first place," he muttered.

"I looked after him," Griff said, walking over to the dead cat, picking it up. "He's cold. Dead a long time. What could have happened to him? There are no dogs in here, no cars to run him over—"

"Maybe he was just old," Joe suggested tactfully. "I mean, no one knew much about him."

"Should we have...an autopsy?" Connie asked. "An investigation?"

"Cut him up?" Griff demanded indignantly. He stroked the dead cat, looking hurt and troubled.

"I don't think we can call the police in over a dead cat," Daniel said dryly.

"But..." Connie began, and shivered suddenly. "A black cat...just dead. On Halloween."

"In Jillian's office," Joe said.

"And after last night," Connie moaned.

"Last night?" Daniel queried.

"She passed out at the bar," Joe explained.

"The golden girl got drunk and passed out?" Griff said skeptically.

Connie offered him a withering glare. "Of course not, she just—"

"It was the fortune-teller," Joe said.

"Tarot card reader," Connie corrected.

"What?" Daniel demanded, incredulously.

"She started screaming that Jillian was a witch."

"Well, I'm sure we've all called her a name or two along the way," Griff drawled.

"It was spooky," Connie informed them firmly.

"Yeah, it was kind of uncanny," Joe agreed, setting his hands on his wife's shoulders. "Then Marston appeared—"

"Robert Marston showed up at the bar?" Daniel asked sharply.

"And Jillian passed out?" Griff said, brow furrowed as he tried to understand the chronology of events. "Because of *Marston?*"

"No...no..." Connie murmured uncertainly.

"It was the bar, I guess," Joe said.

"The bar or the beer?" Daniel asked.

"She wasn't drunk," Connie told him.

"The fortune-teller made her think she was a witch?" Griff asked, as confused as his brother.

"No...but I..." Connie began.

"I don't think we should let her find Jeeves like this," Joe said flatly. "She loved that cat."

"She loves anything with fur," Daniel commented.

"Is that true of her men, too?" Griff asked Connie, teasing.

"Griff..." Daniel began warningly.

"Hey, she's coming!" Joe alerted them, stepping in and closing the door. "She's on her way down the hall."

Griff quickly slid the dead cat behind his back. Connie rushed over to him, standing behind him so the dead cat was fully hidden.

"The tray of cookies is still there," Daniel muttered.

"I'll just grab it," Joe volunteered.

When Jillian stepped into her office, it was more than weird. Connie and Griff were standing to one side, were very close to one another, looking like Tweedle Dee and Tweedle Dum. A very guilty Tweedle Dee and Tweedle Dum.

Daniel was standing by her desk, Joe beside him, looking like a butler, last night's tray of cookies and tea in his hands.

"Good morning, Jillian," Joe said brightly.

She frowned. "Good morning, Joe." She looked around her office again. "Daniel, Connie, Griff," she said, greeting each of them in turn.

"Morning," Connie said.

"Good morning, Jill," Daniel murmured.

"Ditto," Griff told her.

They were all staring at her.

"Okay," she said. "What are you all doing in my office?"

"Meeting," Daniel said.

"I stubbed my toe," Connie said.

"She stubbed her toe," Joe repeated. "And screamed."

"Yeah. She screamed. We all came running," Griff told her.

They were still staring at her.

"Are you all right now?" she asked Connie.

"Of course I'm all right. Why wouldn't I be all right?" Connie said.

"Your toe," Jillian reminded her.

"Oh...I...yes. It's fine now."

"So what about this meeting?" Jillian said.

"What?" Connie said, frowning.

"Meeting. Didn't you say you were here for a meeting, Daniel?" Jillian asked.

"Yeah."

"About what?"

"A quick meeting. Just to say that, uh, we're definitely going with the Celtic cross."

"You told me that yesterday."

"Yeah, but...there's also an ad campaign we need to discuss." He looked at his watch. "Can't now. Have to be in a marketing meeting in two minutes."

"But—" Jillian began.

"Marketing. That's me," Griff said.

"Since when have you actually bothered to attend a meeting?" Jillian asked.

"Today. It's an important one." He was walking toward her door. Backward.

And Connie was going with him.

"I'll get some coffee," she said, smiling in response to Jillian's confused frown.

"And I'll get rid of the tea," Joe said cheerfully, rushing out, the tea service rattling.

"Marketing," Daniel said, sounding ridiculously awkward, not at all like his usual assertive self. He followed Joe, passing by Connie and Griff—old Tweedle Dee and Tweedle Dum—who nearly crashed into one another in their haste to exit her office.

She watched them go, then walked around to her desk and sat, still staring at the door. She groaned aloud and dropped her head into her hands.

The tarot card reader.

The nightmare. The feeling of burning...

And now her family and friends being entirely bizarre.

Like Alice, she might as well have fallen down a hole.

Her world was going mad.

CHAPTER 4

There *was* a meeting that morning. At eleven a.m., Jillian found herself in the conference room with her grandfather and all her cousins.

It was a family affair, except that Robert Marston and the artist who'd created the sketch Eileen and Theo had discussed, Brad Casey, had also been invited.

Jillian had heard—via Connie, who had heard it from Daniel's secretary, Gracie Janner—that Douglas, Theo and Daniel had already met earlier. Now the whole family had been brought together.

She didn't think her grandfather had been planning on this meeting earlier. She'd seen him briefly at the breakfast table that morning, since he'd been finishing up when she'd come down. He looked good—even at his age, he was tall and straight as an arrow—but there had been concern on his features when he'd poured milk over his cornflakes and said, "I heard you had a bad dream last night."

"Halloween. I guess I'm still impressionable," she had tossed back lightly.

He hadn't pressed the point, which had worried her a bit.

Now, he was staring at her down the length of the beautiful hardwood conference table. "I guess everyone knows what's going on here," he said, watching her. "Except for you. And Robert."

She looked around uneasily, feeling a strange sense that maybe everyone really had gone mad and she had been brought here to be told she was to marry Marston or else be thrown to the wolves—whatever form of wolves still lurked in Manhattan, that is.

She didn't doubt that there were many.

"Douglas, I—"

"It's about our next ad campaign."

"What?" she breathed, feeling instantly at sea. Whatever he was getting at, it was nothing she'd been expecting.

"I have to hand it to Eileen and Theo. They saw the possibilities first."

"I'm sorry. I haven't the faintest idea what you're talking about."

"Neither do I, Douglas. What's up?" Marston asked.

He was seated to her left. Cool, smooth, impeccable. A powerful, neatly manicured hand wrapped around his coffee cup.

"Brad, show the sketches, please."

Brad Casey was a nice guy. Tall, slim, with thinning, long blond hair, he had a gift for taking a spoken concept and translating it onto paper. He flushed uncomfortably as he rose from his position at the far end of the table and lifted the cover from an easel. Jillian gasped.

He had drawn her. In an incredibly flattering way. She was sure she was far more electric in his sketch than she had ever been in life. She was looking at a man, her eyes alive, conveying a warmth that seemed to come from the soul, as he fastened a locket around her throat. The entire image was stunning. It captured something more than the giving of a special gift to a special person. It seemed to evoke the very essence of two people together, living for one another, understanding the gift not so much of a locket, but of love. The very best, and most tender, of human emotions.

"Wow. That's—that's outstanding, Brad," she said softly. "And extremely flattering, by the way. Thank you."

She made sure to add the last. He was a brilliant artist, but never really convinced of his talent. A capable man, but often very shy.

His flush deepened.

"Well, of course, it is idealized—" Eileen began.

"Jillian glows," Daniel said.

"Just like Rudolph's nose," Griff said cheerfully.

The others stared at him.

"Show the next sketch, Brad," Douglas advised, breaking the silence.

Brad flipped the page. This time, it was a beach setting. She stood by a palm tree. Branches and fronds dipped over her head; the ocean rolled ahead of her. It was dusk, hues of incredible beauty captured on the page. One hand was on the tree, the other reaching for the man coming toward her.

She almost choked.

It was Robert Marston.

She couldn't look at him. She felt deeply humiliated, as if he had been paid to come here—for her.

"Grandfather, did you—"

"No. Brad admits to using you as his model, but he didn't know Robert, so that likeness is purely coincidental," Douglas informed her.

Marston was studying Brad with his fathomless dark eyes. "Quite a coincidence," he commented.

"Yes, sir," Brad said. His eyes touched Jillian's. "I'm sorry. I didn't mean to upset you. We usually hire models, though we've been doing more and more on computer lately, but when

I heard what type of feeling they wanted...really, it was me. Just me. And I'm truly sorry."

It was an incredible speech for Brad Casey, who looked even more desperately miserable than she felt.

"No, no, Brad, what you did is...incredibly flattering, as I said. I'm certainly not angry with you."

Douglas leaned forward, hands folded on the meeting table, powder-blue eyes steady on hers. "We think it's incredible. An accidental piece of genius. What better way to promote Llewellyn Enterprises than with a real Llewellyn? We want to make this the centerpiece of a major campaign. Naturally, though, it has to be all right with you. And Robert."

"They're wonderful sketches. And if you think that they'll increase sales, by all means, use them," she said, though she still felt shaken by the power of the art.

"It's more than that, Jillian," Eileen said, sitting forward. "You'd have to be really out there."

"Really out there...how?" she enquired.

"A campaign, Jill. We want to do a campaign. We want to do some stills, maybe some TV ads. Theo was the first to see it. The sketches are just the beginning."

Jillian must have been looking at Theo blankly, because he added, "We're hoping to get you on some of the talk shows."

"What do I have to talk about?" she asked.

"The company. We can increase our Christmas sales, and by doing so, we'll be able to increase our charitable donations. We'll even do a special campaign, something for the children's hospital you support."

Theo, she thought, was really trying to talk her into it. She wasn't sure she shared his enthusiasm, though. She wasn't convinced that her image would sell more jewelry or improve sales at all.

"We can focus on your piece this year. We haven't worked it

all out yet," Douglas said. "But the campaign will have something to do with the timelessness of beauty, relationships, the human need for love and permanence. And a full ten percent of each sale will go to charity."

Marston leaned forward before she could speak. "Don't you think we might be putting Jillian in danger by making her so well known?" he enquired, not quite sure why the fear loomed so large in his mind.

"Danger?" Eileen exclaimed.

"All our images have already been out there," Daniel said. "For Douglas's last birthday, family shots ran in a number of national publications."

"And the press was all over Jillian last year when Mi—" Eileen began, then broke off.

"When Milo died," Griff ended quietly.

"There was a tremendous amount of press then. Especially in the city. You must remember," Theo told him.

"Anyone with money and influence stands in danger," Douglas said, breaking in at last. "I see your point, Robert. But I also believe that what the others are saying is true—we've all been out there many times. Our faces are certainly recognizable. I've always had the best and most up-to-date security on the house, and the company that handles this building is top-rated. From the richest man to the poorest, no one is safe from random acts of violence. We need to be smart. But I have always refused to live like an ostrich. I came from nothing, and I was blessed to create this empire—a small empire, but an empire all the same. I like this campaign. It gives back, and it shares the spirit of the season."

"That's another point. Most Christmas ads are already ready to run, and ours are no exception. Marketing strategies have been carefully put into place—"

"Yes, but we all know ads can be pulled, changed. And TV time is always available. We've got power, and they get cancellations." Douglas turned to Jillian once again. "Jillian, the decision is yours. Though, I would like us all to be in accord." He looked at Marston as he spoke.

Marston shrugged, deep blue eyes on Douglas, his jaw set. "Just for the record, I still think it's dangerous." He turned to Jillian, his gaze suddenly hard. "It's you. You should object."

She couldn't bring herself to agree with him, though she wasn't sure why. It wasn't that he had done anything to her, or been rude to her in any way.

On top of that, she wasn't fond of the idea herself. In truth, for some reason, it made her nervous.

But she wasn't about to agree with him.

"If you all think it's good, then we'll go with it," she said.

She didn't realize that they had all been leaning forward, looking at her, until they all leaned back, relaxing.

"I told you that she was Miss Llewellyn Enterprises," Eileen said. She was smiling as she said it. No sting intended.

"We'll take a vote," Douglas said.

All hands went up. Except Marston's.

"We were hoping you'd agree to do the campaign, too," Daniel told him. He pointed at the second sketch. "That is you to a tee. And the man in the first one could be you, as well."

"You would be perfect," Eileen said with a sigh. "I'm so sorry you don't feel the same."

"Oh, I'll do it," Marston said, leaning back with a shrug. "I disagree with the entire thing, but I've been outvoted. So I'm your man."

"I'll call for coffee, and we'll bring in the staff," Douglas said. "Let's get started now."

His longtime assistant, Amelia Yancy—silver haired, sharp-tongued and nearly as old as he was—was the first to arrive. Coffee and pastries were arranged, the room filled, and the planning began.

And through the entire meeting, Jillian felt Marston at her side. It wasn't an easy feeling.

Robert Marston gave his last instructions to the young temp who was doing his clerical work until he had the time to find a permanent assistant, then sat at his handsome desk in his handsome office. He looked out the floor-to-ceiling windows that offered an excellent view of the Manhattan skyline and idly tapped his pencil on the desk. *Why the hell had Douglas Llewellyn brought him into the company?* He had no lack of confidence; he'd worked his butt off through school and done very well at Hydro-Tech, his previous employer, but the point was, Llewellyn Enterprises wasn't lacking for leaders. Why had old Douglas been after fresh blood?

The campaign they had decided on was good. Excellent even. But he still didn't agree with it. Douglas was going to parade his granddaughter in front of the public for the benefit of the company, whether it would be personally beneficial to her or not. That didn't alter the fact that the campaign was good, ingenious, and it would also benefit charity. It was important to Douglas to give back to the country that had truly been the land of opportunity for him. Robert had learned that Douglas never walked by a bum in the street, he always gave a down-and-outer at least a buck. He had caught Robert studying him once when they were walking along Fifth Avenue, and he had shrugged and said, "You know the old saying, 'There but for the grace of God go I.'"

Robert had felt a little jaded. His own parents had brought him up with a sense of responsibility for his fellow man, but he donated checks to known institutions and he used them as tax deductions.

After that walk with Douglas, he'd found himself handing out cash. New York gave a man plenty of opportunity. Just the other day, he'd given money to a woman down in the Village, who then had leapt up and kissed him. He'd thought she was about sixty. At closer glance, she was about thirty. "I really do have a little kid to feed, mister," she had told him. He'd believed her, then given her another twenty.

So had he come here just because he admired Douglas Llewellyn? Or because Llewellyn had intrigued him with his offer—and his strange honesty at the end of their final interview? Granted, the salary and shares had been hard to refuse. But the job he'd left had been darn good, too. And despite having a vote on the board here, he was still an outsider. There were few other businesses like Llewellyn Enterprises, so big—and still family owned and operated. There had been a few insinuations, of course....

And more than insinuations. There had been that last interview before he'd accepted the position.

"I worry. I worry sometimes because we are all family," Douglas had told him. He had shaken his head. "Family. In all the world, there's nothing so important. I've felt that way all my life. I sometimes feel even now as if we're still in the last century, and I'm just a dreamer sitting on a stone wall in Dublin, swearing I'll change the world. Family is everything, but you know, back there, back in the old country, I saw a father tar and feather his own daughter, and a mother turn from her own son. Over religion, politics...money. That's what it boils down to, eh, money. Family can be damn scary, son. I fear..."

"You fear...what?"

"Ambition. You've got to have it. But too much of it..."

"Douglas, there are all kinds of rumors that you want to bring in fresh blood to mingle with your own."

Douglas let out a wheezy laugh. "I'm an Irishman, boy, not a matchmaking old woman." He'd laughed again, but then he'd grown serious. "You were with the special services in the navy." It was a statement; not a question. Douglas Llewellyn had read Robert's dossier a dozen times over, he was certain.

"Yes," he responded, anyway.

"You saw some action."

"A little. Middle East."

"Well, it's good to have a smart man on board—and a wary man. One who can watch out for himself—and others."

Robert had leaned back, grinning. "Okay, Douglas. I get it. I'm a crack businessman—but I'm really here because you think I have the skills to investigate what goes on at your office, as well."

"You're here because you're a crack businessman—it doesn't hurt that you can protect yourself—and others."

"Which others?"

"My granddaughter."

"You have two granddaughters, sir."

"Jillian."

"Why Jillian?"

The old man was quiet for a minute.

"Because I had a dream," he finally said.

"A dream...?"

"Do you want the job? You'll instantly become a rich man."

"I'm not doing badly on my own."

"I'm aware of that."

"Why me?"

Again, Douglas hesitated. Then he told him, "You were in the dream."

"But if you think that your granddaughter is in real danger..."

"That's just it. I don't. There's nothing. Nothing concrete. Nothing I can see, just something strange and hazy...an old man's dotterings, perhaps."

"I'm not a cop."

"I'm aware of that. Are you going to take the job?"

"Yes. Yes, I am."

Strange. But stranger things had happened in life, he was certain. He was being offered a king's ransom—because of a dream.

And then, of course, the first time he'd actually met Jillian Llewellyn up close, she'd screamed as if he were a psycho killer or a six-foot tarantula, then passed out cold. Great protector he was. Well, he was here. Though the place seemed to move as smoothly on its own as a Swiss clock. Still...

Would he always be outvoted? Always be an outsider? He wasn't a fool. He had heard all the rumors, and though rumors didn't mean squat, it was true that he hadn't been called in just on account of his business acumen. He was there to watch out. For Jillian.

And he'd tried today. He sure as hell had.

The old man hadn't given him a bit of help. But then, Douglas didn't think the danger to Jillian would come from the outside. He was afraid of his own flesh and blood.

Robert suddenly stood and walked down the hall to Daniel's office. Daniel's secretary, Gracie—Whippet Girl, as he silently termed her—started to rise, but he waved her down. "Don't worry. I'll be just a minute."

He tapped on Daniel's door and entered. Daniel had risen and was closing his desktop drawer. "Hey, Robert. I was just heading out. Want to stop somewhere for a drink? Since we missed last night?"

"I did show up," Robert told him, thinking of their missed appointment at Hennessey's. He wondered what Daniel had planned to talk to him about.

Daniel's eyes were dark and grave. "I heard. My cousin passed out, so I was told. You gave her a ride home."

"They told you at the bar?"

"Yeah."

"I came back."

"Sorry, I'd left."

"I see..."

"What's that supposed to mean?"

"You didn't put the tarot card reader up to giving me a hard time, did you?"

He'd been certain of it. But now, the way that Daniel looked at him, he wasn't sure at all.

"I didn't talk to the tarot card reader. I don't believe in any of that nonsense. Why? You mean, you went to the woman for a reading? You, of all people."

"Not exactly. But she knew a lot about me."

"Practical jokes. More Griff's line of work. Talk to him. I did hear what happened, and before I left, I gave old Henry a call to make sure Jillian was all right. He said she seemed to be fine. Joe Murphy told me this morning that you'd taken her home. I should have hung around a while longer last night. I'm sorry. Anyway, I'd meant to tell you about this ad campaign then, so you wouldn't be taken by surprise."

"Hey, it's a good campaign."

"But you don't like it."

He shrugged. "It still sounds dangerous to me."

Daniel watched him for a moment. "Jillian isn't a potato-head, Robert. She's strong, smart and resilient."

"I'm sure she is."

"There's a 'but' in there."

"She's rich. And beautiful."

"And that makes her...?" Daniel asked carefully.

"A target," Robert said. "Want to get that drink?"

They started out. Gracie—old Whippet Girl—came nervously up to Daniel as they were leaving. "I was getting ready to lock up, but I haven't seen that cat all day. I always make sure he's out of your office, Daniel."

"The cat was Griff's idea and he's Griff's responsibility," Daniel said, impatient. "Just leave my door open."

"But I haven't seen him all day," Gracie protested. "I set tuna out for him at lunch—"

"Gracie. He's a cat. Don't worry. Go on home. Leave the office door open."

"All right," Gracie said with a sigh. "All right, sir."

They left the building. "Anywhere special you want to go?" Daniel asked.

Robert hesitated a minute. "Yeah. It's entirely out of the way, though."

"Shoot."

"Hennessey's. I want to go back to Hennessey's."

At five, Jillian went around to Connie's office, a cubicle outside her own. "Connie, I was about to leave, but I just realized, I haven't seen Jeeves all day."

Connie looked up, startled. "Jeeves?"

"Jeeves, Connie. The cat."

"Oh," Connie said vaguely. "Jeeves."

Her friend was acting very peculiarly. "Connie, have you seen him?"

Connie hesitated, then shook her head vehemently. "Uh...not lately."

"I guess I'll look around for him."

Easier said than done. The corporate offices were large, taking up the entire floor. She slipped in and out of meeting rooms and those offices that were open, to no avail. Most of the time people worked late, well past five, but today, it seemed, everyone had left early. She found Gracie still outside Daniel's office, preparing her last batch of letters for the mail room.

"Hey, Gracie. I'm looking for Jeeves. Have you seen him?"

"No, Miss Llewellyn, I haven't. But I've been concerned, as well. I opened a can of tuna for him at lunch, then called and called, but he didn't show up."

"Strange," Jillian said.

"Daniel—Mr. Llewellyn—didn't seem concerned. He told me that he's a cat and he'll show up."

"Well, I suppose that's true."

"I'm still worried."

"I'll try Griff's office. You go on home, Gracie. Don't worry." Griff had already gone. And his office was locked. She frowned. "Well, I hope you're in there, Jeeves, or we'll have little kitty presents all over the place tomorrow."

She turned back, heading for her own office. Connie was there but reaching for her coat, ready to leave. "I was heading off. Unless you need me?"

"No, I'm on my way out, too." She hesitated. "I think I'll head downtown with you."

"You will?"

"Yeah, I've got an urge to stop in at Hennessey's."

"Do you think that's a good idea?" Connie asked, concerned.

"Don't you want me coming with you?"

"No, no, it's not that. It's Hennessey's. I mean, after last night..."

"After last night, it's important. I don't want to be afraid of going back to a pub."

"I guess it's okay. I mean, the tarot reader won't be there tonight."

"I don't intend to be afraid of tarot readers, either."

"But really, in your day-to-day life, just how many tarot readers do you run into?" Connie asked with sheer practicality.

"That's not the point. I just have an urge to go to Hennessey's."

"I'll go with you."

"You have to pick up the kids. I'll just head down to the Village with you. I'm a big girl, and I can go into a friendly Irish pub alone."

"You're a big girl, and the world is full of wolves. We've discussed that before. I'll stop for a quick drink. Mom is still at my place. She won't mind."

"All right. I guess I'll appreciate the company." She studied Connie for a minute. "By the way, I didn't find the cat."

"No?" Connie wasn't looking at her.

"Connie, do you know something about that cat that I don't?"

"Jillian, what am I, the cat-watcher now? If we're going for a drink, we've got to get moving."

"Connie, you don't have to come with—"

"I want the drink. I *need* the drink. Can we go?"

It was 5:45 when they reached the street. Traffic was at its worst. They opted for the subway, though it was every bit as busy.

People milled about the platform, the whole crowd lurching toward the train that was just pulling into the station. The mob was pushing Jillian closer, until she was afraid she was going to fall into the path of the train.

She felt a sudden pressure against her chest, heard a whisper. "Get back."

The crowd behind her grumbled as she stopped dead, holding up their progress. Who...?

"Jillian!" Connie was calling to her across a sea of heads. The train stopped, the door opening almost directly in front of her. She pushed the whisper out of her head and rushed on, one with the crowd.

Eileen was into her second martini when the doorbell rang. Barefoot, she walked across the impeccable white tile of the foyer of her penthouse apartment to swing the door open. She knew who was coming. Gary Brennan, an up-and-coming name in the stock market, the man to whom she had been engaged for a rather long time, had reached the summit of the building.

He was blond, with the perfect business haircut, the perfect business suit, a clean-shaven, scrubbed, impeccable face, and—not the least of his many fine virtues—the world's most perfect teeth.

"Hi, sweetheart, you—"

He didn't get to finish. She had opened the door, then swung around and headed back into the living room, with its huge, panoramic windows. She had a fake fire burning in the fake fireplace—a real one might create soot, which she loathed. The mantel was white; the furnishings were white. In fact, the entire room was almost as white as Gary's perfect teeth.

"As I was saying, hi. Hard day?" he enquired, shedding his coat. He almost dropped it over a chair, then he remembered where he was and walked back to the foyer closet.

"It was a fairly usual day," Eileen said.

"Oh?"

"I poured you a drink."

"Thanks," he said lightly. She seemed so somber. Eileen had always had her eccentricities. Most of the time she admitted to them, even laughed about them. She wasn't mean about them, either—she was fastidious, but she understood that others didn't always share her hankering for a bleached clean that bordered on hospital sanitation.

"Shaken not stirred, of course," he teased.

"Two twists, not one," she returned, but she sounded tense.

He helped himself to his martini and slid onto the comfortable sofa before the pseudo fire. Snow was falling. It was beautiful from here. Of course, by tonight it would be sooty gray slush, but right now, as it flew, white as angels' wings, it was beautiful.

"All right, Eileen. What did your wicked family do today?" he asked. She had once told him he was more than welcome to take a job at Llewellyn Enterprises. If he hadn't been engaged to her, it would have been an attractive proposition. But he would never have a relationship with Eileen *and* work for her. Because he would, of course, wind up working *for* her.

"Nothing. It was a good day."

"Um. So what did Jillian do?"

"Oh, nothing, you know Jillian. What's good for the company..."

"I thought you told me that you agreed the ad campaign would be a good thing?"

"Yeah, it will be great."

"Then...?"

"I'm sick of her agreeing, I'm sick of her being so irritatingly decent, I'm just sick of her being...being..."

"Disgustingly beautiful, charming, hardworking—"

She creamed him with a pillow. He had to make a desperate save in order to balance the martini glass.

"Sorry." He laughed.

"Why do I feel this way?" she asked, curling up next to him.

"Because you're afraid Douglas will leave her all his shares in the company?"

"Is that it?" she mused. "I don't think so. She's my closest relative, my only first cousin. And we're friends, really friends. We talk, she listens. God knows, she did go through hell with Milo, and I didn't mind her so much then."

"She's in the limelight. She's going to be representing Llewellyn Enterprises," Gary suggested, still trying to speak lightly. "She's just too damn...perfect," he suggested.

"She's making me crazy," Eileen said, getting up to walk around the room.

"Well, then, I have an idea," Gary said.

"What?"

"We just do away with her."

"What?"

"We do away with her." He pretended to form a shotgun with his arm and forefinger. "We shoot her. Up in Connecticut, out in the snow."

"Gary! I'm not—"

"Oh, I know, I know. Nowhere near clean enough for you."

"Gary, get serious."

"I *am* serious."

"Gary..."

"Okay, shooting her might be a bit drastic. Can we shove her out a window? Nope, not from the Llewellyn Building. The windows are all permanently sealed. Well, surely there's a garden on top of the building somewhere that we can get her to—"

"Gary!"

"Then there are the streets of New York. God knows, the taxis can be deadly. We can write about it afterward. We'll call it 'Death on Brooklyn Bridge.'"

"Gary, stop."

"Why?" he asked innocently.

"You're being far too obvious," she told him. She pounced on the sofa next to him, and he had to make another wild save for the martini. But she was smiling again at last. Eyes bright. Devious. She snuggled up beside him and laughed. "If I ever were to plan a murder..."

"Yes? Oh, I know, my dear, darling, sumptuous little schemer. It would have to be far more ingenious. And subtle."

"Subtle. Of course, darling. Subtle," she agreed.

CHAPTER 5

"I still dislike it," Robert said, easing back in the leather-lined booth at Hennessey's. Oddly enough, he'd opted for a Guinness today. Something Irish. Dark.

Moody.

He was referring to the ad campaign.

"I don't really understand why," Daniel said, frowning. "Look, you know Jackie Kennedy was an editor before she died. Now who could be more high profile than Jackie Kennedy? But she went up the elevator every morning with dozens of other people. This is New York City. We're pretty impressed with ourselves at Llewellyn Enterprises, but in the end, what are we? Just a business. Look, Jillian is my cousin."

"Second cousin," Robert reminded him. He wasn't sure why he was going for that detail.

"Second cousin. My point is, she's family. She's the little kid I looked after the whole time I was growing up. I love Jillian. If I thought this campaign would harm her in any way, I'd be the first to veto it." He drained his beer and set down the glass. "Excuse me, will you? I'll be right back. Nature calls."

After Daniel left him, Robert drummed his fingers on the table. Their waitress came by. "Mr. Marston, can I get you another?"

He looked up. The young woman looked vaguely familiar. She was slim, with a face that appeared a bit worn and prematurely lined, but she had nice eyes, warm eyes.

"Do I know you?" he asked politely.

"Not really, not as I am now."

"Well, that's an interesting answer. How do you know my name?"

"I asked if anyone knew who you were the minute you came in."

"Oh?"

She nodded. "You gave me money when I was about as low as I could get." She bit her lip. "Cocaine. I had a baby, hit the streets, worked the streets, picked up a drug habit, then got too ugly even to support it. The night you gave me the money, you said you'd like to have a kid one day, too, and you gave me another twenty and...I realized I was lucky, incredibly lucky, to have such a wonderful, healthy little girl. So I went home. And my folks took us both in. My dad is an old customer here, so he got me the job."

"Wow," he murmured, studying her. "Good for you. *Damn* good for you."

"I'd never have done it without you."

"I think that's a bit too—"

"I'm not trying to embarrass you or anything. I'm just trying to thank you. Accept my thanks graciously, okay?"

He laughed. "Okay. You're welcome. And in return, may I tell you, if I've improved your life, you might well be my greatest accomplishment."

She flushed. "Well, I don't know about that. I hear you're a pretty important man. But if I can ever do anything for you..."

"I'll let you know. Thanks."

"The next beer is on me."

"Thank you."

"Here comes your friend. Excuse me."

She left the table as Daniel returned, but before he slid into the booth, he hesitated, glancing out the window.

"Well, look who's here," he murmured.

Robert half rose, twisting around. Jillian was coming into the pub, followed by Connie Murphy.

"Hey, cuz!" Daniel said, summoning them.

The two women had been talking as they entered, and Robert noticed that Daniel had startled Jillian. For a moment, as she glanced their way, her expression was unmasked.

She was disturbed that they were there. Had she come here with a purpose in mind, and were they about to destroy it?

She quickly masked her surprise and walked over to them, Connie in tow.

"Sit, ladies, I'll buy you a beer," Daniel said.

Connie slid in next to Daniel, leaving Jillian no choice but to sit next to Robert. She still seemed uncomfortable around him, he noticed, though pleasant. Courteous but cool—was that how she'd decided to behave around him?

"I'll have a Guinness," Connie said. "Though I think dark beer makes you fatter."

"Fatter than what?" Daniel queried.

"Well, fatter than whatever you were," Connie told him.

The waitress came up behind them with a full tray. She had seen the two women enter, and there were four glasses of Guinness on her tray.

"All on the house," she said sweetly, setting the glasses down.

"Thanks," Jillian said. "And to what do we owe—"

"Just a thank-you for your patronage," the waitress interrupted cheerfully. "We're always happy to serve the Llewellyn family here."

"Well, thank you," Jillian murmured. "Thank you very much." Her words were genuine. Robert noticed her eyes when she spoke, and the beautiful flecks of pure emerald in them. Her features were all but flawless. She really was a striking woman.

She didn't notice his perusal, just sipped her beer, seeming to eye it suspiciously.

The waitress had walked away. Daniel was telling Connie to remind her husband about the meeting they were having with some buyers the next morning.

"I don't think it's really that evil," Robert told Jillian.

She almost jumped, apparently startled that he was watching her. "Evil?"

"You're staring at your beer as if you think it might bite."

She flushed and smiled. "No, but I had two...maybe three last night. Then a fortune-teller spooked me, and I passed out and later had nightmares. I'd actually been thinking of something a bit lighter for this evening."

"Then, we'll get you something lighter."

"Oh, no, it's all right. I don't think the beer..."

"That the beer caused the situation?"

"I wish it had," she murmured.

"Do you think *I'm* evil, then?"

"No, of course not," she protested, flushing more furiously.

He glanced across the table. Daniel and Connie were still deep in conversation.

"Good, I'm glad. Because I'm not. In fact, I intend to be there for you," he said. He had meant it lightly, not intending to betray Douglas Llewellyn's trust in any way. He was disturbed himself by the sudden intensity of his voice, but he spoke again, anyway. "I swear, when you need me, I'll be there for you."

The words had an echo.

As if he'd spoken them before, he thought.

And she was staring at him. Completely perplexed.

As if she'd heard him speak those exact same words before.

"Wow, sorry," he murmured, easing back against the wall. "I didn't mean to get so scary there. I just meant that..."

"That you'd be there. On my side," she murmured.

"Yeah."

"I should probably leave—"

"No, don't, please."

"Hey, you're the one who wanted to come here," Connie protested, picking up on their conversation.

Jillian didn't move.

The waitress came back to the table. "You all said that you'd just come for a drink, so I didn't mention that the special tonight is shepherd's pie. Really excellent, if you'd like to stay for dinner."

"Shepherd's pie," Daniel said, looking across the table at Jillian. "You know who used to make the best shepherd's pie in the world?"

She smiled back. "My mother, so I've heard."

Daniel nodded. "I wasn't all that old myself when she died, but I'll never forget how good a cook she was. She could whip up a masterpiece with a whole kitchen full of little terrors. And her shepherd's pie was the best. Let's stay."

"Gee, I can't," Connie said.

"Jilly?" Daniel said.

"Well..." Jillian murmured.

"Hey, isn't someone going to say, 'Sure, Connie, you can stay. Call your mom. We'll all be so disappointed if you don't have dinner with us. Maybe Joe can come, too.'"

Daniel grinned at Jillian, then turned toward Connie. "Sure, Connie, you can stay. Call your mom. We'll all be so disappointed if you don't have dinner with us. Maybe Joe can come, too."

"Mr. Llewellyn, you're a quick study," she told him. "Excuse me, I'll make a call." She slid from the booth.

"Connie, I have a phone right here," Daniel said.

"I don't want to sound as if I'm having too much fun. And I may have to beg and plead a bit. Embarrassing in front of friends—and the boss."

"Robert, can you stay?" Daniel enquired.

"Wouldn't miss it," he agreed.

"Is this in his job description, Daniel?" Jillian murmured, sipping her beer, speaking to Daniel, but studying Robert's eyes.

"Dinner with fellow employees, especially at friendly Irish pubs. Bitch of a job, but hey..." Robert murmured back.

She smiled, the slightest stain of a blush touching her cheeks. Something inside him churned. She was stunning. He felt an almost overwhelming urge to wrap his arms around her and protect her. More than that. The feelings inside him had little to do with protection. She suddenly seemed as hot as the sun. He reached out and touched her cheek. *She would fly like a doe at the scent of a hunter!* he thought, instantly ruing his action. But she didn't. She was studying him, as if she barely realized he was touching her—

"So is it shepherd's pie?"

The waitress had returned. They both jumped away from each other. No one else seemed to notice.

But they knew. They both knew.

Connie came back to the table announcing that Joe would be joining them. He arrived within a few minutes. They talked about work, the city, the weather, politics, inane things.

Robert felt her presence all the while. Heard her laughter. Her perfume was intoxicating. Her laughter was more so. Her warmth seeped into him. Her every smile, her every move, seduced him.

Get a grip, buddy. Get a life, he warned himself.

She was a fire he longed to touch, burning beside him.

When dinner was done, coffee served and they were all ready
to leave, he turned to Jillian. "I'll see you home?"

He was holding his breath. Like an adolescent, afraid she
would refuse him.

"Hey, you came with me by cab, remember? Left your car
home this morning," Daniel reminded him.

"I'll come along and make sure your cabdriver knows the
way," Robert said to her, smiling ruefully at his own lapse.

She hesitated. He felt the constriction of his heart. She needed
to hesitate, needed to stay away, he thought briefly.

"Sure," she said softly.

He almost forgot why he had wanted to come back to Hennessey's, but just before they left, the women went off to the
ladies' room.

He walked over to the bar. The man on duty was big and dark-
haired, with hazel eyes; from his accent, he appeared to be right
over from County Cork.

"Excuse me, I was interested in the woman who was in here
the other night. Madame Zena."

"Yeah?" The bartender studied him curiously. "Now, you
don't look like the kind of fellow who'd be into all that."

"She said some interesting things. I'd like to know more
about her."

"Ah, well, curious thing. She came back for her money just this
mornin'. But we'd checked out the address she'd given us and..."

"And?"

"Well, that address would put her in the middle of the
Hudson River."

"Do you have a phone number?"

"I don't, but the owner, he just may. I'll find out for you,
Mr. Marston."

"Thanks."

When he turned away from the bar, he saw that Jillian had

returned. She was standing with her coat and purse in hand, waiting, watching him. She was alone.

"The others have left," she said, then asked him, "You want to find the fortune-teller?"

He shrugged. "I'd like to ask her a few questions."

"Why?"

He took her coat, placed it around her shoulders. "I came back here when I dropped you off last night. She said some strange things to me."

"Maybe it *is* something in the beer," Jillian suggested solemnly.

"I don't think so."

"Someone put her up to telling specific fortunes?"

"I thought that might be the case. I'd been supposed to meet Daniel here. I thought maybe he'd told her to say a few things."

"But he denied it?"

"Yes. He suggested Griff."

Jillian grimaced. "Yes, he may be your culprit. He's the eternal joker."

"He certainly wants people to think so," Robert said. She arched a brow. "I didn't come to Llewellyn blind, or without doing a great deal of research. Griff has suggested some of the best marketing policies the company has going. He knows about incentives, and keeping goods out on the market. Shall we?"

They headed out the door. He hailed a cab, then paused after opening the car door. "Want to see where I live?"

"Now?" she asked. She sounded a little breathless.

"It's not that late, only nine."

"Well, I, but—"

"Take a chance," he said softly. "Do something strictly on instinct."

"If I were going to go on pure instinct, I'd run as fast as I could right now."

"In what direction?"

"Any direction—away from you." Her words were wry, but she was smiling.

"Then, you really should come see where I live."

She was going to say no to him; he was certain. She didn't.

"I guess it is early," she said, and slid into the cab.

He took that as her agreement and slid in behind her, giving the cabbie his own address.

When they entered his apartment, he was suddenly anxious for her approval. And for the first time in a very long time, he studied his own surroundings. The floors were hardwood, but covered with thick, rich Persian area rugs. He especially liked the one in front of the hearth. Rich cobalt and crimson, it depicted medieval horsemen racing through dense forests. Tapestry pillows still lay at one end; he had come home and read last night before going to bed, trying to forget the strange things the tarot reader had said to him.

He liked leather—brown leather, well upholstered, comfortable—and books. The room was lined with bookcases. He loved collecting first printings and rare editions, and his two prize pieces were a very old almanac with notations in it by Thomas Jefferson, and an even older New England prayer book with notations by the fire-and-brimstone Puritan minister Cotton Mather. The art on the walls tended to be old or historic, as well; he had a lithograph of the first subway system in the city near the floor-to-ceiling windows that opened to the terrace, prints of works by Raphael, Titian and Michelangelo, and oils he had purchased at shows from contemporary or lesser known artists.

He had opted for a view of the river and the Brooklyn skyline beyond, and a very contemporary entertainment system. He liked music, old and new, and very much appreciated being surrounded by it. The fireplace was real, and after he had taken Jillian's coat in the foyer, he went straight to the fireplace, surprised to find that he wasn't his customary competent self.

His hands trembled as he set the blaze. She followed him into the room, staring into the rising flames.

"I had the strangest dream about a fire last night," she told him. He held very still. Was she telling him not to get any stereotypical romantic notions? He turned, still hunkered down as he stoked the fire, and looked at her. "Should I put it out?"

She flushed, shaking her head. "No, no, I love a fire on a cold night. I was watching you and just thinking...it was such a strange night."

"Yes, it *was* a strange night. Well, except for the fact that I don't really believe in 'strange.'"

"What does that mean?"

"It means I still think someone set us both up with the tarot card reader. Eventually I'll find out what went on."

"You're not worried about me, are you?"

"Worried about you? In what way?"

She walked over and bent down by him. "You know," she told him softly, "I'm not at all delicate. I don't have the blinding desire to seize the company in my own two hands, but I'm not a doormat, either. I'm opinionated, and very strong and determined."

A slow smile curled his mouth. "I don't doubt it."

"Good."

She straightened and walked to the windows, looking at the view beyond the glass. "The lights twinkle like a million stars."

He walked over to her. She smelled of soft and subtle perfume, an evocative scent that seemed to reach out and infiltrate his senses.

"Do you like the view?"

"It's incredible."

He stood just behind her. "I like to go out on the terrace, preferably when it's a bit warmer, lie back and look up. All you see are the stars, and sometimes it's quiet enough that you can imagine all Manhattan gone, and that there's nothing but the earth, the air and the stars."

"Nice. I get that out at the estate in Connecticut. Well, you'll see. So much goes on out there as we get closer to Christmas." She stopped staring out the window, turned and smiled at him. "I love Christmas at the estate. Everything seems possible. Everyone is relaxed. And there's something so special about the lights and the music and..."

"And?" he prompted.

"I don't know. There's something about Christmastime. All things seem possible."

"Like it's a time for miracles?" he murmured.

"Ah, so skeptical," she said.

"Not skeptical. Just realistic."

"A doubter," she judged teasingly, her eyes still alight. "Well, that's the whole point. You have to believe in miracles for them to be able to happen. Let's go out."

"It's cold."

"I've been cold before."

"Out there, it's very, very cold."

"Ah, but you'll be there. To warm me."

The length of his body tightened and his heartbeat quickened. "It's not just cold. On a night like tonight, it's freezing."

Her eyes remained on his. An enigmatic smile still curled her lips. "I'm willing to take a chance. And besides, you have a fire burning in here."

"All right. We'll go out. If you wish."

He opened the locks and slid open the glass. They stepped out.

The wind blew fiercely, enhancing the coldness of the evening, as he had known it would. The location of the building along the river allowed for a strange tunnel of air. Snow had begun to fall. Light, dusting flakes, but wet and bone-chilling.

The flakes whirled around them, as if they were standing inside a snow globe. The heavens really were alive with stars that night. A beautiful full moon burst out from behind the snow clouds, then was swallowed again by the dark mist and the snow. The wind began to moan.

He slipped an arm around her. "Okay, we came out. Now we should go in. You must be freezing."

She turned in his arms, looking up, about to speak. Her eyes were a brilliant green, her lips curved in a smile. He felt suddenly humbled, but as if he had known her forever, as if she had listened to his hurts and his dreams, as if they had planned a lifetime together. As if he were sworn to buffer her from the winds and the snow.

As if she knew all his strengths, all his weaknesses.

He lowered his head slowly, giving her every chance to move. But she didn't. And when his lips touched hers, the heat of a thousand fires seemed to burn through him.

He burned....

Against the wind, the snow, the cloud-misted darkness, they seemed to spin. Their kiss deepened; the fire surged. She was stunning, soft, evocative, and more. In some strange way, older than the fierce wind sweeping around them, she was his.

He lifted her.

Her eyes met his again.

And she knew it.

Confidence returned. A touch of arrogance, as well. He felt as if he had conquered the world. He lifted her in his arms, then turned from the wind, from the blinding snow, and entered the apartment, slid the glass closed with his foot and walked with her to the fire, where he lowered them both to the ground.

The heat of the flames shot around them. The rug was plush

and soft, and the pillows seemed to surround them, along with the crimson light and warmth of the blaze.

Moments later, he could barely remember their having shed their clothing.

The minute Daniel entered his apartment, he knew he wasn't alone. His visitor didn't move at first, nor was there much light. But he knew he wasn't alone, and he knew who had come.

He pulled his scarf from around his neck, irritated, as he walked in. "What are you doing here?"

"I came to see you."

"Why? I told you not to come here."

"Why?"

"Because this is my home."

"Surely one friend can visit another in his home."

"Not mine."

"Does that mean that we're not friends, or that your friends don't come here?" his visitor taunted.

Daniel walked to the bar on the left side of the room, casting his visitor a wary glance as he poured himself a stiff Scotch. "Go home, go away. There's nothing else to get from me. Not here. Not now."

"I didn't come to *get* things."

"Then, why?"

"I'm trying to figure out just what it is that *you* want to get."

Daniel arched a brow, lifting his glass. "And why do you care? Money is your motivator. You always told me so."

"How many people tell the truth, the whole truth, and nothing but the truth?"

Daniel swallowed his drink in one gulp. "Go home."

"You don't know the half of what I've done for you, or what I'm willing to do."

"I don't want anything."

The visitor moved close. Looked into his eyes.

"Oh, Daniel, you liar. You awful liar."

"Don't—"

"Don't send me home, Daniel," his visitor said softly, very softly. "We have so much to talk about."

Her words trailed off as she reached up and delicately touched his cheek.

Then she walked past him.

Waiting...for him to follow.

He poured another drink. Stood shaking his head. With grim determination, he tossed the drink down.

Then he turned and followed.

Just as she had known he would.

The first thing Jillian saw when she opened her eyes was one of her shoes.

Then she remembered where she was. And why. She blinked, not sure that she hadn't been dreaming, that she hadn't totally lost her mind.

It had been a wonderful night. Wonderful. Incredible. Beyond imagination. He was... Wonderful. Incredible. Beyond imagination.

Her mind didn't seem able to function beyond those words of assessment. She still felt warm.

And insane. Totally insane. But last night it had felt as if she'd been...compelled. Obsessed. On fire. And as if staying was not only totally natural but inevitable.

The fire had died down, and she would have been cold, if not for him. Stretched out beside her, he provided enough body warmth to dispel any sense of chill. But time had passed, morning had come, and with it, some sense of reason. She jerked up, then realized that he had been awake, lying beside her, not moving lest he disturb her.

Those dark blue eyes were on her looking grave. He seemed far less the corporate man she had surveyed from a distance. Instead, literally stripped down to the essentials as he was, he was incredibly real and down to earth.

The insanity of the situation washed over her, and she scrambled to her feet searching somewhat awkwardly for her clothing. "I—I can't believe I did this."

"You didn't rob a bank or commit murder," he told her, still watching her.

"No, of course not, but..."

"But?"

She paused at his tone, looking at him.

"You're sorry about last night?" he asked.

She smiled, aware of the awful tumble of her hair, her arms locked around her chest. "Not at all. I haven't had such a wonderful...well, I haven't had such a lovely evening in a long time. Thank you very much. But neither have I ever been so completely irresponsible."

"Irresponsible?"

"I'm well over twenty-one, of course, and I've always done what I've chosen to do, but I live with Henry and Grandfather, and they're both like a pair of old women. They worry if I'm late and don't call."

"Oh, that."

Sleek, confident, he was rising, stretching. She caught her breath. He was perfect, and she was losing her mind. She barely knew him. He was the shark brought in to devour them all. After an evening of, well, perfect, total decadence, she was in love. Or wild infatuation. Or something.

"I should have called."

He stood before her, smoothed back a lock of her hair, and studied her eyes, as if he were even more surprised than she was that these strange, gripping emotions should have survived the sunrise.

"I called."

"What?" she asked sharply.

"I called the house and told Henry we'd stopped for a drink, that the snow was coming down hard, and that you might be staying. He agreed that you should stay here, rather than brave the weather."

"Oh." He'd taken an awful lot into his own hands.

"I'll put coffee on."

"Sounds good."

"There are two showers. The guest room has everything you'll need."

"Ah, you entertain frequently," she said, trying to make the words light.

He shook his head. "No. Not frequently." He turned from her, walking toward the kitchen.

When she emerged, coffee had perked. He joined her in the kitchen a few minutes later, Mr. Corporate America again, perfect in Calvin Klein today, she thought.

He did wear a suit well.

Still, that extra length of hair over his collar would always mean something special to her now, as would knowing where he lived. There was nothing stark or impersonal about his surroundings. She loved the feel of the place, loved knowing that his reading interests were many and varied—despite the fact that the expected sports and business magazines were in the rack by the leather sofa, and that she had found the *New York Times* just outside his door after she had poured her coffee. Antique volumes elbowed popular fiction and contemporary literature along his shelves.

"Fruit, bagel—or a great doughnut?" he asked her.

"Ah, you're expecting me to say 'Just a bit of fruit, please,' aren't you?" she murmured.

"No, I think you should go right for the doughnut today."

"How about the fruit *and* the doughnut."

"Sounds good to me."

He produced both. They sat at the counter in the kitchen and ate together, sharing the paper. It should have been at least a bit awkward, Jillian thought. But it wasn't. It was fun. And then, as he poured her more coffee, she set the paper down and looked seriously into his eyes.

"Robert?"

"Yes?"

"I wasn't lying when I said, well...last night was the most wonderful time I've had in forever. Maybe in my whole life. But..."

"But?"

"Will you understand if I want to back off?"

He hesitated, looking at her. "I'll try."

She ran a finger around the rim of her coffee mug. "You said you don't believe in 'strange.'"

"I—"

"Wait, please. Okay, suppose the tarot reader *had* been set up to tell us both specific things? How do you explain the way I reacted when I saw you? I never, ever pass out."

He set the coffeepot down slowly, leaned on the counter and studied her seriously. "Most things, they say, are psychological. The human brain, we all know, is the most incredible computer ever. Okay, so I'd just come into the company. You heard wild and ridiculous rumors. Somehow, perhaps, I became something really awful in your mind. And after the whole bit with the tarot reader, the drinks, the whole Halloween thing..."

"I still say it was genuinely strange," she told him softly. "And then...how do you explain last night?"

His eyes met hers. "I say that every once in a while we're just incredibly lucky and come across someone else in this world who is unique, so wonderful and exciting, so beautiful and sexy, it's almost unbearable. And sometimes, by the grace of God, that person feels the same way about us. That's how I explain it."

She exhaled slowly.

"Well?"

"I say it's a darn good explanation. But I've still got to ask you to let me go slow. It's very strange for me in a different way. Friday...Friday marks the anniversary of my husband's death."

"I know. And I'm very sorry."

"I knew he was dying when I married him."

"So I've heard."

"You don't want to know why?"

"I'm assuming that you loved him and were willing to take whatever time you might have."

She smiled. "Well, yes. But I thought...I thought I could make him better. Rather arrogant of me, huh?"

"No. I think it was rather great of you. And I'll tell you what. I won't call you. I won't see you. Except for work. When you're ready, you let me know. All right?"

She walked around the counter, wrapped her arms around him and kissed him. He held her and kissed her back, and the world began to recede. She wanted more.

He eased back, lifting her chin. "Are you calling me already?" he whispered.

She shook her head.

"I'll be here. When you need me, I swear, I'll be here," he told her.

When he released her, a chill swept through her. She shouldn't have let him go. The sense of discomfort stayed as they left his apartment, went down and called for his car.

The snow had turned hard and heavy, but the city workers had done a good job. Heavy piles had been pushed aside, leaving the roads and sidewalks clear.

As they drove, Jillian was thoughtful. "So you really don't believe in 'strange'?"

"No."

"Or in miracles?"

"No, I'm afraid not."

She smiled and looked at him. "How about a bit of magic?"

"Nope."

He drove into the parking garage at Llewellyn Enterprises.

"But," Jillian pressed, "you did say it was incredible when you found someone and, 'by the grace of God,' that someone felt the same way about you."

"I did," he agreed.

She opened her door, exiting before he had cut the engine, then leaned in and looked him straight in the eye. "Then, you already believe in miracles and magic," she told him.

Then she turned and left.

CHAPTER 6

On Friday morning, Eileen came bursting into Jillian's office. "We're off to the house in Connecticut for some stills and filming on the ad campaign. All of us. We'll take Monday if we need to. I suggest leaving work a little early, since we'll start with the light first thing tomorrow morning."

Jillian inhaled. Eileen was a few years older than she was, and ever since they were little kids, Eileen had always seemed to think that made her boss.

"Eileen, I can't leave this afternoon."

"Why not?"

"I'm going to the graveyard. It's the first anniversary of Milo's death."

Eileen let out a breath of air. "Oh, Jillian, I'm sorry. I knew it was coming up, but I forgot it was today. You had that memorial service a couple of weeks ago, so..."

"Yeah, I know. And it's not that I think any one day really makes a difference, but I do want to go by the graveyard."

"I'll go with you, then we'll drive up together."

"No, Eileen, it's all right. Really. You'll want to drive with Gary, and I want to have a car if we're going to be there through Monday."

"There are cars up at the house. I don't think you should be driving alone."

"Don't be silly. Besides, I have to head home, too, pick up some clothes for the weekend."

"Henry can send them to the office for you. Jillian, I don't want you going to that graveyard alone, all right?"

Actually, she'd really wanted to be alone. But Eileen seemed awfully concerned—and persistent. And the drive to Connecticut could be long.

Besides, since Robert Marston had kept his distance, as she had asked, it wasn't as if she had other plans.

"I guess. But—"

"I could go with her, Eileen," Connie supplied from the doorway.

Eileen whipped around. "It's no problem for me, Connie. And Daniel said you and Joe weren't planning on coming up until tomorrow morning—he said he knows you don't want to leave the kids any longer than you have to."

"Why don't they just bring the kids?" Jillian suggested.

"We're going to be working," Eileen said firmly, looking at Connie as if having children had been a direct violation of the work ethic.

"Agatha will be there. She can watch the kids while we're busy."

"Agatha has the whole house to look after, and she's got to be seventy, at least," Eileen reminded them.

"And she employs a bunch of people. We'll be fine if you choose to bring the children, Connie."

"Thanks," Connie murmured, but she looked uncomfortable as she started to turn away.

"Let's head out at lunchtime, shall we?" Eileen suggested, turning to go, as well.

Jillian rose from behind her desk. "Hey, wait, both of you. I still can't find Jeeves, and I'm getting really worried."

They had both stopped in their tracks, but neither of them turned to look at her.

"Eileen?"

"No, haven't seen him," Eileen said, and hurried out of the office.

"He must be somewhere around," Connie muttered, and hurried out, as well.

That Connie hadn't looked at her seemed strange. With determination suddenly ruling her completely, she walked out of her office, past Connie and down the hall. She burst in on Griff, who actually appeared to be working, deep in study over some financial document.

He looked up.

"Griff, where is Jeeves?"

He folded his hands on his desk. "Jillian, don't worry about old Jeeves, especially not today."

"Today—"

"It's the anniversary of Milo's death, right?" He smiled. "No, I didn't forget. I'm going by the cemetery before heading north. Want me to go with you?"

"Eileen just offered, thanks. And thanks for remembering. But we've got to find Jeeves."

"We will." He stood, walking around to her and escorting her to the door to his office. "Maybe he got out. Maybe he found a girl. You know how cats are."

He kissed her on the cheek. She wasn't sure, but he seemed rather eager to get her out of his office. "Even I have to clean up my desk a bit if I'm going to leave early for the weekend," he told her.

His door closed. Curious, she walked down the hall. She was about to stick her head into Daniel's office, but Gracie Janner stopped her.

"He's not in there, Miss Llewellyn."

She could have told Gracie that her legal name was Anderson, but she didn't bother. No one remembered to use it even when Milo was alive. Llewellyns seemed to stay Llewellyns, no matter what.

At the far end of the hall was the plushest office, her grandfather's domain. She started that way, but then, as she passed Theo's, she saw that Connie, Daniel and Joe had gathered there. She poked her head in. "What's up?"

They all stared at her.

"Nothing," Daniel said, walking to the door to meet her. "Weekend driving plans, that's all. You're going with Eileen?"

"Yes, I guess, but—"

"Nothing. Nothing is going on," Connie said quickly.

Once again Jillian had the feeling that either she—or her entire family—was going crazy.

"Nothing," Joe repeated.

"Nope, nothing at all," Connie said.

Daniel was staring at the group with something like disgust. He shook his head. "Excuse me. I've got to get moving."

"Is everyone going to Connecticut?" Jillian enquired.

"Just about," Theo said, starting to follow Daniel out.

"Theo?"

"What?"

"This is your office," she reminded him.

"Yeah, yeah, but I have some...papers. Papers in Daniel's office." Theo sped by her.

"Jillian, you should call Henry," Eileen offered. "I'll get hold of Gary. Excuse me." She sailed on by.

With a shake of her head, Jillian turned away herself and

headed down to her grandfather's office. Amelia Yancy had her desk—a huge oak affair, like a guard tower—dead smack in front of the double doors that led to Douglas's office.

"Is he in?" Jillian asked.

"Yes, but—"

Jillian had started around the desk.

"He's in a meeting with Mr. Marston."

Jillian hesitated. Since the night she'd spent with Robert just two days ago, she'd needed perspective. A slowdown. But though she hesitated, she didn't want to avoid him. Not completely. She didn't want to be ridiculous about any of it. Or feel...possessive. As if there were really something deep there, going beyond the accident of two people meeting and feeling such an instant attraction. It was scary. And she didn't want to cling to him, which would be far too easy to do. She knew so little about him.

Still, she just smiled at Amelia. "I'll burst in on them. My fault. Don't worry, I won't let Grandfather yell."

She tapped on the door and could envision her grandfather's frown as he called, "Come in."

She entered. Robert was seated in front of Douglas's desk, relaxed but wearing a slight scowl. She wondered what their conversation had been about. Both men rose as she entered, and as she drew closer to Robert Marston, she felt again a strange sense of déjà vu, and wondered why she was being such an idiot, trying to keep any kind of distance between them. He made her tremble, made her feel warm. She wanted to walk over and slip her arms around him, ride off with him into the sunset, into the snow, to a glowing fire and surroundings of pure warmth.

She stopped short, remembering that she was going by a cemetery, that the man she had known and loved for a very long time had been dead just one year today.

"Excuse me for interrupting, but, Douglas, why didn't you tell me this morning we were heading for Connecticut?"

"Because we just discovered at nine-fifteen that all the arrangements could be made so quickly."

"The arrangements?"

"Cameramen, lighting, all that. We've given the project to Brad Casey—right beneath Eileen, of course—and since we're making such a big deal out of it, we had to clear the calendars of everyone involved."

"Interesting. Everyone forgot to clear it with me."

"I poked my head in this morning and asked if you had weekend plans," Douglas said.

"But you didn't ask me if I was available to go to Connecticut," she explained.

He looked truly mystified. "I'm sorry. You said you were free, and frankly, it's not as if...well, it's not as if you have a husband, children, or...well..." His voice trailed off. His steady old eyes were on her, and he smiled slowly. "You have me. And I'll be in Connecticut."

"Is there a problem?" Robert asked.

He was watching her, but she was careful to reveal no emotion in her eyes. "No. Not after I go to the cemetery."

"Naturally," Douglas said. "Is everything all right with you then?"

"Yes, I guess so."

"Well?" Her grandfather spoke softly, but he was clearly implying that she should leave.

"Fine." With little choice, she turned and walked out, still wondering about the subject of their meeting.

She had barely sat down at her desk before Connie came rushing in. She stared, opened her mouth, shook her head and rushed out.

"Connie?"

Connie pretended not to hear her, so Jillian walked out of her office and into Connie's. "What is going on?"

"I—I—nothing."

"Connie, I've known you for years. What's the nothing that's going on? And what is Robert Marston doing in my grandfather's office?"

Connie's eyebrows shot up. Then she looked vastly relieved. "I haven't the faintest idea. Work, I guess."

"Connie, why did you just come into my office?"

"I—I—I—"

"Connie, don't *I—I—I* me."

"He's dead!" Connie blurted.

"What?" A chill seized her. "Who's dead?"

"Jeeves," Connie whispered. "I'm so sorry, but we just didn't want to tell you. You were so upset about the tarot card reader yelling at you and all, and he was a black cat, and it was Halloween...."

"The cat is dead?"

At the deeply voiced question, Jillian spun around, and Connie leapt to her feet. Robert Marston was standing in the doorway.

"Why is everyone lying about a dead cat?" he enquired.

"We weren't lying—we just didn't want to tell Jillian. We didn't want to upset her," Connie explained quickly.

"Connie, that's ridiculous. I'm very sorry, of course, but...why lie to me?"

"We just...we just didn't want to upset you," Connie repeated.

"How did the cat die?" Robert asked sharply.

"We think it must have been old age," Connie said. "He was just...dead."

Robert Marston turned around and left, a thoughtful look on his face. Connie was pale and still very upset. Jillian shook her head. "Connie, it's all right. I just wish someone had told me. I wouldn't have gone crazy looking for him."

"I'm sorry. We meant to tell you, of course. When the time seemed right. Today...well, you know, today being the anniversary of Milo's death, it didn't seem like the right time."

"It's all right. I'm a big girl." Jillian started back to her own office. Then she paused, looking back. "What did 'we' do with Jeeves?"

"I don't know," Connie said. "Either Daniel or Griff took care of...the remains."

Jillian walked back into her own office, far more disturbed than she had let on. There was something Connie wasn't telling her. She was sure of it.

She tried to work, but she couldn't seem to concentrate. She put down her pencil and folded her hands in her lap. Douglas had told her that morning that she shouldn't come in today, but she hadn't wanted to sit home alone or spend the day brooding. But now...

A year. A full year.

And the cat was dead, too.

And she was having terrible dreams about fires....

She got up and walked to Daniel's office, waving a hand impatiently as Gracie started to rise. She walked in without knocking.

Robert Marston had preceded her here, as well. He didn't see her when she first slipped in, because he was talking to Daniel and his back was to her.

"I don't understand why you just cremated the creature without knowing what had happened."

"For God's sake, Robert, it was a cat."

"And it died in Jillian's office."

"Are you suggesting that—"

"I'm suggesting that it might have been important to find out just exactly what happened to it."

"Jeeves died in my office?" Jillian demanded.

Both men turned and stared at her. Robert flushed, gritting

his teeth, looking away. "Don't you ever knock?" he asked somewhat harshly.

"Daniel?"

"He died of old age, Jillian. He liked you, he was comfortable in your office, so it was where he went to die."

"We should have found out exactly why he died," she said. "We have no idea how old he was."

"Jillian," Daniel explained patiently, "you'd had an episode the night before."

"An *episode?*"

"You passed out after that fortune-teller played some kind of hocus-pocus on you. It was Halloween night, and a black cat died on your desk. We decided not to tell you," Daniel explained patiently. "I'm sorry," he added. "We did what we thought was best."

"Out of love," Robert murmured, still not looking at her.

"Of course," Daniel said, though she had a feeling Robert had been speaking sarcastically.

"Please don't hide things from me again. For any reason," she said, and turned around, leaving them both.

Back in her own office, she closed up her desk. Then she stopped by Eileen's office and told her cousin she would be in the coffee shop downstairs.

"Mr. Marston."

The voice that came through on his private line was hushed. The woman had refused to identify herself to the temp, and he had almost refused the call. But now something in the hesitant urgency touched him, and he was glad he had taken it.

"Yes, this is Robert Marston. Who is this? And what can I do for you?"

"It's Mary. Mary MacRae. I work at Hennessey's. I'm the one you gave the money to that day. The ex-junkie," she added so quietly he almost didn't hear her.

He frowned. "Are you all right? Do you need something?"

"No, no, I'm fine, thank you. I found Madame Zena."

"Oh?" He leaned forward, wondering why his heart had suddenly jolted. He was angry with the fortune-teller; all he wanted to know was who had put her up to her shenanigans.

"She'll see you downtown in an hour, the Voodoo Café, off Hudson."

"But—"

"I have to go."

The line went dead.

An hour later, as he parked his car, he wondered if he was going a little mad himself. The Voodoo Café?

But the place was a neat little establishment, no darker than many trendy restaurants. The place was decorated with fine African and island art, and it offered Haitian, African and Creole dishes. He hadn't eaten, and he didn't see Madame Zena anywhere, so he sat in a booth and ordered coffee and the seafood specialty.

Right after his coffee arrived, a woman slipped into the booth across from him. Madame Zena. She looked quite different. She was stunning, with her hair short and expertly styled to emphasize the clean lines of her features. She was wearing a knit suit and gave the impression of cool competence and confidence.

"Madame Zena," he murmured. "Thank you for coming. May I buy you something to eat?"

"Sure. Did you order the special?" she asked.

He smiled. "Don't you know what I ordered?"

She met his eyes, then turned to the waitress coming toward her. "I'll take the special, too, Kia, thanks. And coffee."

He leaned back.

"Impressed?" she asked him.

"Because you knew I ordered the special? It wasn't a bad guess."

"All right, fine."

"Look, I'm worried about Miss Llewellyn."

"She isn't Miss Llewellyn. She's Mrs. Anderson. I remember the write-up in the paper when she was married."

"I'm worried about Jillian," he said.

"You should be."

"Why?"

"Because she's in danger."

"From whom?"

"That I can't tell you."

He lifted his hands. "But you can help me. Who hired you?"

"Hennessey's hired me."

"No, no, I know that. Who hired you to—"

"You *know*," she said, shaking her head. "That's just the problem. You *know*." She lifted a hand to summon the waitress. "This isn't worth my time."

"I'm sorry. I'm a realist. I've seen very bad things happen in this world, and I've seen them happen because of other people's actions. People hurt people, Madame Zena—"

"Yes, people hurt people," she said. "We agree on something."

"So if you would just tell me who—"

"No one put me up to anything, Mr. Marston. My name is Shelley Millet, not Madame Zena. But I am not a charlatan, and I am not playing cruel games. I think that Jillian is in danger. There was something...something in the past. A great tragedy, a terrible force. You were part of it."

"I'm telling you, I didn't know her before."

"The past is as great as time itself, Mr. Marston."

"You're talking in riddles. I never met Jillian before. I went to school with Theo Llewellyn, but I never met Jillian until I came to work at Llewellyn Enterprises. Until the other night. I never hurt her, and I never would. Don't you understand? I'm trying to help her."

"Why are *you* so sure she needs help, Mr. Marston?"

He hesitated. "I can't answer that."

"A feeling?" she enquired.

"No. I'm simply not at liberty to say." If there was something sinister going on, the last thing he wanted to do was give her fuel to add to the fire that someone at Llewellyn had lighted.

"You're an ass, Mr. Marston," she said softly, leaning back.

"What?"

She smiled. "Sorry. That was rude of me. But there you are—educated, young, powerful, built like steel, full of sense and logic. An intelligent man. But you must see, and if you don't, you are in trouble. The world is full of good and evil. *Yin* and *yang*. Forces. And chances. Karma. Call it whatever you will, Mr. Marston. But if you can't open your heart and your mind, you will fail again."

"Fail? Again? At what? How did I fail before?"

"You were arrogant then, you are arrogant now. You believe too strongly in your sense of purpose, in your belief in the power of the mind and the body."

He shook his head. "I came to you for help. You're playing word games."

"I'm trying to help you."

The food arrived, but he hardly noticed what he was eating, too lost in the frustrating conversation to give his mind to the meal.

"So...you recognized Jillian psychically, not by sight. And you knew me the same way. Then something made you start screaming, 'Witch!' at her, and your eyes just happened to roll back in your head when you met me?"

To his surprise, she hesitated, looking slightly disturbed. "I knew who you were."

"Who told you?"

She ignored him and said instead, "I knew her husband. Who is dead a year today."

Robert felt a strange chill. He gave himself a mental shake, annoyed, and reminded himself that he didn't believe in psychic phenomena. "Did he read tarot cards, too?"

"No. He was a teacher. As I am. We taught at the same inner-city school."

"So you knew Jillian then?"

"No. He had quit teaching by the time they were married. He was very ill already." She had eaten a large portion of her food, and now she glanced at her watch and sighed. "We don't get much time. I have to get back. I'm sorry if you feel I'm not trying to help you. I am. But I'll never be able to do anything for you unless you open your mind." She rose, a slight smile on her lips. "You're a good man, a decent man—even if you are being an ass."

"Oh?" He leaned back, crossing his arms over his chest.

"You want to help her? Stay with her. Watch out for her. Don't leave her this time, thinking that you are all powerful and your name will be enough to protect her."

"This time. *This* time?" he said angrily. "There you go again."

"Good and evil, Mr. Marston."

"Yes, we agree, good *people.*"

"Christmas. The season is approaching quickly."

"What? Is she going to be run over by a reindeer? Miss Millet—"

"It's a time to believe, Mr. Marston. A time when goodness should win out, a time for miracles. But I promise you—miracles never occur for people who don't believe in them."

"And what is the miracle I'm looking for, Miss Millet?"

She stared at him with her curious golden eyes for a moment. "Life, Mr. Marston. Life itself is the miracle. Now, if you'll excuse me...?"

She turned and headed for the door, then stopped, looking slightly puzzled, and turned back. "By the way, the cat was poisoned."

"What?"

He was standing before he knew it, but she was already leaving.

He dropped several bills on the table and chased after her, catching up with her halfway down the street. He grabbed her arm. "How do you know that?" he demanded. "How do you even know about the cat?"

"What difference does it make? You won't believe me if I tell you."

"Give it a try."

"Milo," she said.

"What?" He released her arm.

"Milo, Mr. Marston. I don't know how, or why. I don't usually get messages from the dead. Strangely enough, he's also the one who says you're a decent human being. I really have to get back."

She tried to turn, but he caught her arm again.

"Wait. If you know all this, if Milo is telling you things, surely he's told you who's doing it," he taunted.

"No. He doesn't know."

"Milo—the deceased Milo—talks to you, but he doesn't know what's up. He warns of danger but he can't tell you what it is?" His voice dripped deep, harsh skepticism.

"If you don't want to listen to me, don't try to find me anymore. What I do know is that energy is never destroyed. There will always be good and evil, and now the evil has come again. Jillian is in danger. Maybe you're even the cause of the danger. Now, if you'll let me go..."

"But—"

"If you're ever willing to really listen, Mr. Marston, you can call on me again."

"One of them put you up to this. One of the Llewellyns. Griff? This would be his idea of a practical joke. Daniel? Maybe he's all show—maybe he hates Jillian for being Douglas's favorite, and for being a direct heir. But this has gone too far. Whatever you've been paid, I'll up it. This has turned serious. And if I find out you're an accessory in any way, if you hurt her—"

"I'm not about to hurt her, Mr. Marston. But don't you see? You're being a blind fool. No, Mr. Marston, I am no danger to Jillian. I am not about to hurt her. But you—if you continue to be so damn sure of yourself, you will."

She jerked her arm free and stared at him indignantly.

He shook his head and, totally frustrated, let her go.

CHAPTER 7

Jillian was touched when her entire family arrived at the cemetery.

Of course, they were all heading to Connecticut, anyway, but they were there all the same. Connie and Joe were there, too, which wasn't surprising, since they were her best friends. Connie told her that they had decided to drive up that night and not take the kids, since her mother didn't mind staying with the girls for the weekend. Henry, who was like family, was also there. Again, no surprise. Even Amelia, her grandfather's right hand, was there. Gracie Janner was there, as well, as always the dedicated assistant.

She *was* somewhat surprised that Robert Marston wasn't there, but then, she had told him to give her room.

Father Hidalgo, who had conducted the services at Milo's funeral and memorial, was there, greeting her with a warm smile, a hand squeeze and a kiss on the cheek. They chatted, and she assured him that she was fine—moving on. It *was* what she was doing, wasn't it? Moving on? She was just trying to do it slowly. Intelligently. With a measure of sanity.

She thanked them all for coming and stood by the gravesite, while Father Hidalgo read the appropriate prayers.

It wasn't that she believed that the essence of Milo was really there, in the ground. And she didn't think that it was necessary to pray directly at the gravesite of a loved one who had passed on. It was simply a matter of respect, done in memory. Loving memory. He had been a best friend. And she missed him. He had loved to read, and they had talked about books constantly, arguing about plots, motive and characterization. They were both movie buffs and art fanatics, too. She had gotten to know him their senior year of college, when they had both joined the study abroad program and ended up arguing over the relative merits of the Italian and French masters. He'd had sandy hair, always a bit too shaggy, powder-blue eyes, and a tall, lanky appearance. His smile had been quick, even when he was dying. He had told her that all the drugs made him smile, but she had known that he smiled only to make it better for her.

At the end of the casual graveside service, Robert Marston arrived. He had changed from his business attire to a sweater and black leather jacket. Dark glasses—worn against the glare of the newly fallen snow?—hid his eyes. He stood a small distance away from the family, hands shoved into his pockets, watching. Rock still, yet she had the feeling he was ready to leap at the slightest sign.

Sign of what?

Hidalgo finished speaking. Jillian placed a lone red rose on Milo's grave, dusting snow from the angel she'd ordered to go with his marker.

As she started away from the grave, the others followed. She thanked her family for coming. Everyone tried to be light and at ease. Gary remarked that he was starving, and Eileen said she wanted pizza, while Griff argued that they should stop at the great Chinese place off the highway.

Douglas suggested a vote, and pizza won out.

Jillian had known that Robert was standing to one side, watching her, as they made their plans while standing by the road that ran through the huge cemetery. They were surrounded by stones, angels, kneeling Virgins, winged victories and more. Oddly enough, there was a sense of peace here that she hadn't felt in a long time. But Robert's presence seemed to shatter that peace.

When she slid into the back of Eileen's Audi, she was startled to find him following her. As always, his proximity created a flux of emotions within her. That strange sense of fever.

Happiness. Fear.

Fear?

Yes, and she didn't at all understand why.

"You're riding with us?"

"Do you mind?"

"Of course not. I just...well, you seem to like having a car available."

"I do," he said. "I've been assured there are a number available at the house."

"There are."

He shrugged.

"Thank you for coming," she said, still watching him.

"Of course."

"You were late," she said.

He shrugged. "I had a few things to tie up at the office."

"Oh."

Eileen and Gary entered the car. "Thank God everyone voted for pizza," Eileen said.

"They were afraid not to," Gary told her.

"Why?"

"They all know you like to win."

"Gary!" Eileen protested.

"Just kidding." He brushed her cheek with a gloved hand, turned back to Jillian and winked. Then he asked softly, "You all right, kid?"

Jillian felt a flush touch her cheeks, and she knew Robert Marston was watching her. "Yes, of course."

The pizza place was near the highway, but still in New York state. When they stopped, Jillian stalled, watching as Eileen and Gary went on ahead.

"I thought we'd decided to back off," she told Robert. It was a year—exactly a year—since Milo died. She should be, at the least, reflective. But instead she was glad to be with Robert, glad that he had come in Eileen's car, and feeling guilty that she was so glad.

"We did."

"Then why did you come in this car?"

"Because you shouldn't be alone."

"I'm not alone. I'm with Eileen and Gary."

"You shouldn't be alone with your family."

Puzzled, she frowned, staring at him. "Robert, what is wrong with you?"

The others were standing at the door of the pizza parlor, waiting, exhaling clouds of breath. Eileen stamped her feet to warm them. It was cold. Winter had come early, already bringing snow that stayed on the ground.

"Let's just go in," he suggested.

She balked, tightening against his touch on her shoulder. "No. I want to know what you're talking about."

"I saw the fortune-teller."

"I thought you didn't believe in fortune-tellers?"

"I don't."

"Then..."

"I believe that someone is putting someone up to something, and that you may be in danger."

"Someone in my family?" she asked incredulously.

"Humor me?" he said, his eyes a cobalt blue against the bronze of his features.

"Jillian!" Griff called. "We're turning to snowmen here."

"Well, go in, you idiots, we're coming!" she called back.

They filled three big tables in the pizza parlor, which was warm and welcoming. Already the place was dressed for the holidays. One window had been decorated for Hanukkah, one for the African and island holiday of Kwanzaa, and the rest of the place had been done up for Christmas. Garlands were strung everywhere, red, green, gold and silver. Tinsel decorated every possible surface. The cheese shakers on the tables were in the shape of ceramic reindeer. A beautifully decorated artificial pine stood in the far corner near the kitchen. JOYOUS NOEL was proudly proclaimed in block letters above the open counter.

"Jillian, see the strings of holly on that tree?" Henry, at the next table, called to her.

"They're great," she replied.

"We'll get some," he said.

"Sure. We'll go hog-wild and start the whole Christmas thing this weekend," she called back.

Eileen, across from her, wrinkled her nose with a sigh. "If you start now and insist on a real tree again, it will be dead as a doornail by Christmas."

"Bah, humbug," Gary teased.

"Nice way to talk to your almost wife," Eileen told him.

"It's the 'almost' part that makes me crazy."

"We won't get the tree yet—we always go and cut down a tree for the house in Connecticut, anyway, and it's too early for that," Jillian said. "But Henry loves to decorate for Christmas."

"So do you," Eileen charged.

Jillian smiled. "Guilty."

Griff was across from her. "It's as if you're still waiting for Santa Claus."

"Maybe I am."

"Anyone want kitchen sink pizza?" Theo asked, sliding into the chair on Jillian's right side. Robert was to her left.

"I'll take anything but anchovies," Jillian said.

"They're the best part," Theo complained.

"I'll do anchovies with you," Gary told him.

"Fine. You have your pizza, I'll have mine," Theo teased Jillian.

"If that's the way you want to be," she teased back.

Robert had been quiet, watching them all, Jillian noticed. The thought made her uneasy. "What do you like on your pizza?"

He shook his head and shrugged. "Whatever you like."

"No, seriously."

He smiled. "Seriously. Whatever you like."

She turned away from him, aware once again that he was watching them. She ignored him, disturbed by the comments he had made outside. This was a pleasant occasion, especially considering the circumstances. Still, she was uneasy, and it lasted all through the meal and the drive to Connecticut.

Agatha heard the cars arriving. The great double doors to the house swung open, and she stood there, tall, slim and shivering, beckoning them to hurry on in. "It's simply frigid out here. Come in, come in. I've put tea and hot wine on, some sweets, everything warm and toasty. Hurry."

There was a great deal of confusion as everyone entered the old mansion, greeting Agatha, distributing overnight cases. Jillian found herself watching Robert as he surveyed the house, which she had always thought was magnificent. The original structure—now just an office off to the side—had been built in the late sixteen hundreds. The newest addition had been built in 1845. Her grandfather had bought the home when he first became successful, and through all the years since, it had been a labor of love. He had always restored rather than redone. The huge colonial porch was much as it had been when the country had declared independence. The huge dining room remained, with its double fireplace banking the wall into the left parlor. Though modern appliances had been purchased, the old brick ovens remained in the kitchen. A beautiful stained-glass window had been added above the staircase sometime just after the Civil War, but every square foot of the house retained a special ambiance. If there was anything in being a Llewellyn that Jillian had ever cherished, she supposed, it was her right to be in this house.

She and Milo had been married here.

And he had died here, as well.

"Jillian," Agatha said, hugging her fiercely. Despite her age and diminutive size, she had a fierce strength. Jillian gasped, then hugged her back and kissed her cheek.

"I've all the Christmas boxes down," she told Jillian delightedly. "I thought you might want to begin with the windows or the mantels this weekend."

"Sounds great."

"We have a great deal of work to do this weekend, Jillian," Daniel said, hanging his coat in the closet just off the richly tiled mudroom.

"I'm sure we'll have time for some Christmas," Agatha said.

"But, Aggie, dear," Griff told her, stopping to give her a hug, "it isn't Christmas yet."

"It's never too early for Christmas," Agatha said. "Is it Douglas?" she asked.

Jillian looked to her grandfather, who shrugged, then smiled slowly. "Not at our ages, Aggie. We never know when we're going to see our last, right, old girl?"

"Aye, and that's the way of it," Agatha said, her old eyes meeting his.

"Both of you, stop it! We're going to have lots of Christmases," Jillian protested.

"It's not one's age, is it? It's one's health," Robert Marston said softly.

Jillian spun around. He was watching her. She felt uneasy again.

"I think I'll grab some tea and run on up. I'm very tired," Jillian said.

"Try the mulled wine," Agatha told her as she headed into the huge brick kitchen. "It's my best, filled with honey, cinnamon and a dab of lemon."

Jillian did, using the huge dipper to scoop out a cup from the cauldron that sat over the open fire. It was very hot; she blew on it. She took a sip. "Delicious, Agatha. Henry, you'll love it."

As the others trailed into the kitchen, she slipped out, returning quickly to the foyer to get her overnight bag. When she reached the entry, though, she was startled to hear a loud mewing sound.

She hesitated. The wind?

The sound came again, from the entry doors. She walked into the mudroom, instantly feeling the chill from outside. The mewing came again. She opened the front doors and looked around. Nothing. She heard the sound once again and looked down.

A huge, furry black cat was on the porch. As she looked, he mewed again, rubbing against her legs.

"You poor thing. You must be freezing." She reached down for the cat. "My goodness, but you do look like Jeeves."

She held him close to her, reentering the house, closing the main doors and locking them, then leaving the mudroom.

"Jillian?"

It was her grandfather, and he sounded concerned. She walked into the kitchen with the cat.

Connie leapt up, gasping. Eileen, who had been facing the fire, turned, then screamed. "Jeeves!" she cried out.

"Can't be," Griff protested.

"Of course it's not Jeeves," Jillian said quickly. "It's all right, it's just another poor cat. The creature was crying, freezing outside on the porch. Agatha, have you seen him before?"

"Never," Agatha assured her.

"Well, he's got to stay, at least tonight. Maybe he belongs to a neighbor."

"Jillian, the nearest neighbor here is nearly a mile away," Daniel reminded her.

"Then, he's my cat now," she said.

"I'll get him some milk," Agatha said, rising.

"Give him some of this warm mulled wine," Griff said cheerfully. "That'll knock him out. Aggie, this stuff has a punch to it. What do you think the alcohol content is?"

"Bosh, now, it's a bedtime drink, to help you sleep," Agatha told him.

"I'll sleep. Like a rock," Connie said.

"Even if a Jeeves look-alike has come to town," Joe muttered.

"The world is full of black cats," Jillian told him, somewhat amused that big tough Joe was spooked by a cat just because it looked like one that had died.

"Yes, but that one..." Eileen murmured.

"Looks exactly like Jeeves," Theo finished.

"Exactly," Eileen said, so softly that the word sounded unintentionally spooky—and funny.

"Maybe Jeeves wasn't really dead," Theo suggested.

"He was dead, all right. Cold, and stiff as a poker," Griff murmured.

"It isn't Jeeves," Robert Marston said suddenly. He had been sitting at the kitchen table, sipping mulled wine, but he stood, then, and walked over to Jillian, who was still holding the cat, which he studied carefully.

He still seemed electric, Jillian thought. Dark hair falling slightly over one eye, his gaze very deeply blue, very intense. He had shed the leather jacket and now seemed like energy and fire in his navy pullover sweater and dark trousers. She held her breath when he was near her, afraid to reach out and still uncertain whether what she felt for him was right.

Especially tonight.

"Are you so sure it isn't Jeeves?" she murmured.

His gaze met hers. "Yes, I'm positive," he said. "He was cremated, remember."

"Jillian, come on," Griff said softly. "We were worried. A black cat dying right on your desk on Halloween? After what had happened at Hennessey's?"

"He died *on my desk?*" Jillian said.

"You said you told her," Griff accused Connie.

"Forget it," Jillian said. "We've got this guy to think about now. Agatha, we have a litter box around somewhere, right?"

"We do."

"I'll keep it up in my bathroom, and keep him with me."

"What will we call him?" Griff mused. "Jeeves Junior?"

"That's horrible!" Eileen cried.

"Why? We all loved Jeeves," Jillian said. "Jeeves Junior has a ring to it. Well, good night, all. If you'll excuse me..."

She walked past Robert Marston. He smelled wonderful. She wished that...

No.

He'd said she was in danger. Well, he was definitely dangerous. It was far too easy to forget everything, absolutely everything, when she was with him.

She had to be careful. Because he had been watching them

all again, she was certain. Especially when he announced that
the cat had been cremated.

As she kissed her grandfather good-night, she realized that
he had been awfully quiet.

Watching as well.

It was a fantastic old house, Robert thought. Douglas was
rightfully proud of it. He stayed up with Douglas, despite knowing it was going to be an early morning. The film crew and photographers were arriving at eight a.m. And though he had
offhandedly assured them at the meeting that he was willing to
do whatever they wanted for the ad campaign—an exceptional
idea, since it kept him close to Jillian—he was a little edgy about
what to expect. He had always been good with figures, concepts
and management, he was an accomplished history buff, and he
had played sports in school, making a good tackle because of
his size and speed. But he'd never envisioned himself as an
actor, and he had to admit to a fear of making a fool of himself.

That wasn't going to stop him, though. He had started off at
Llewellyn with more curiosity than anything else—not believing seriously that Douglas's dream meant there was any real
danger to Jillian. But now he was feeling an *urgency* to be with
her. It seemed ridiculous to be away from her; in fact, he felt
absurdly as if he had every right to be with her, and it was alarm-
ing to feel such real emotion. He was already in love with her,
but more than that, he felt oddly as if it were the deepest emotion in the world, as if he'd felt it for years, as if they'd weath-
ered many storms together. And yet he completely understood
and respected her feeling that they had to slow down. That...

That it was all crazy.

But today, after seeing Shelley Millet, aka Madame Zena, he
felt as if he had a real reason to worry, as if there really were
something going on. Forces. Good and evil.

No, he didn't believe in forces, he told himself.

But evil surely lived and thrived in the minds of men.

And there was the whole thing about the cat. He had been late to the graveside service because he'd taken it on himself to do some investigating into the death of the animal. Through Daniel's secretary he had found out that the cat had been taken down to one of the building maintenance men and cremated in the furnace.

The maintenance man must have thought he was insane when he insisted on sifting through the ashes, but he'd bribed the fellow to silence and could only hope that the man would keep his word.

He had brought the ashes to a friend at an uptown police precinct. He wanted them analyzed. He was pretty sure that if any foul play had been done to the cat, there would be some evidence in the ashes. Jeeves had died on Jillian's desk. That seemed an unlucky circumstance, with everything else going on—

"Don't forget to take a look while you're here," Douglas said.

"I'm sorry?" Robert looked questioningly at Douglas.

Douglas smiled ruefully. "You're worrying, eh?"

He shrugged. "I'm taking your concern seriously, sir, that's all."

"Even if it came from a dream?"

"Well, I don't actually believe there's meaning in dreams."

"Maybe dreams warn us of what we see by day but don't really want to admit we see," Douglas murmured.

"Maybe."

"You watched everyone when Jillian brought that cat in, didn't you?" Douglas demanded.

"So did you."

"Aye, that I did."

"And?"

Douglas shrugged. "Well, everyone knew old Jeeves had died. So I couldn't really tell too much."

"You think someone in the office *killed* Jeeves?"

"You do, don't you?"

"I have no idea."

Douglas nodded in reply, staring at the flames that burned low in the kitchen grate beneath the cauldron of mulling wine. "Well, I'm afraid I have no idea, either. I found a pretty good replacement, though, eh?" he said, looking up with a wry smile.

"*You* brought that cat?" Robert said.

"Aye, and shush. Only Henry knows. Do you think I'm an evil old man?"

"Hell, no. I think you're damn clever. And I wish I'd thought of it."

Douglas laughed and rose, shaking his head as his back creaked. "Old age. It's brutal on the body. Well, as I was saying while you wandered off, don't forget to look in the library while you're here. I understand you like books."

"I do."

"Good night, then. You're all settled?"

"Yes. Agatha showed me my room earlier."

"You're next to her."

"Pardon?"

"You're next to Jillian. I arranged for it. You will keep an eye on her?"

"Yes, of course."

Douglas nodded again. "See you in the morning, then."

Robert watched Douglas go up. Then he rose, drained the last of his wine and set their glasses in the sink. He looked around the kitchen, then instinctively walked around the house, checking the locks on the doors.

At last, he walked up the stairs to his assigned room. There he found another concession to contemporary times. The bathroom was pleasantly modern, and the shower ran very hot.

After showering he toweled dry, slipped into a pair of flannel pajama pants and crawled into bed. Despite the heat of the shower he'd taken, his head seemed to be spinning. The mulled wine, he thought, idly remembering Griff's comment. Man, that wine must have some mean alcoholic level. He hadn't felt the effect of a few glasses of wine in a long time. Maybe it had been more than a few glasses.

He started to doze, then was surprised to hear a door open and close near his own. He crawled from the bed, slipped on a robe and opened his own door. Jillian was just starting down the hall, the black cat in her arms.

He followed her, calling her name quietly in the darkened hallway, lest he startle her. "Jillian?"

She swung around. She was clad in a white velvet robe that hung beautifully on her long, slender frame. In the dusky light, her hair curled over the velvet like a sea of flame. Her eyes seemed huge in the night. He felt a fierce tugging somewhere within him, wanting to reach out and pull her against him. He wanted...

Christmas. The Christmas of a thousand days together, laughter, comfort, the complete knowledge that they belonged together. He wanted to trim trees and dress a house, talk about PTA meetings and even groceries.

"Are you all right?" he asked politely.

"I'm fine. He just seemed hungry."

"I'll go down with you. I could use a drink of water."

"Too much mulled wine, huh?" she queried, smiling. "It's potent."

"It is."

"According to Agatha, it will allow you to see leprechauns."

"Only leprechauns?"

"Well, banshees, maybe a few pixies or the like. Ghosts."

"I'll drink a lot of water."

They reached the bottom of the grand stairway. Jillian made a right, through the huge paneled parlor to the kitchen beyond. She set the cat on the floor, went to the fridge, and poured a bowl of milk for the cat and a glass of water for Robert.

She leaned against the refrigerator, watching the cat.

"He is a lot like poor Jeeves, isn't he."

"Yes." He drank the water, watching her. "You all right tonight?" She looked at him. "Yes, of course."

"Well, it's been just a year," he murmured.

She smiled slightly and nodded. "You would have liked Milo. He was so bright and interested in everything. He loved books, just like you." She hesitated. "He was a friend from school, like Connie. When he first got sick, I went with him one day to the doctor's office. It was horrible, going to oncology. There were so many people there. Older people, many of them in wheelchairs. Some children. And some young people, like Milo. I was so upset because...I don't know, it seemed so impersonal. So cold, and sometimes so pointless."

"You thought you could change it all if you married him?"

"I did change some of it," she murmured. "And I learned that money does talk in America."

"So you made his life better," he said.

"He made mine better, too." She turned back to the refrigerator, ready to get him more water. She paused, pointing to one of the small pictures stuck to the refrigerator with a rose magnet. "That's Milo."

He moved to stand by her to look at the picture. Jillian and the young man were sitting together, wearing winter sweaters and sharing a bowl of popcorn, in front of a roaring fire. They were both smiling, as if they had been caught in a private moment of laughter and warmth.

Milo had a slender face, blue eyes and curly, dark blond hair. He was wearing a gold-colored sweater and brown pants. Nice looking. He had the look of someone who liked books, movies and art museums.

"You look very happy together," he said.

"He was the world's best friend," she said softly.

"I'm sorry. Very sorry. I'm sure I would have liked him very much, if I'd ever had the opportunity to meet him."

"Thanks," she said. She had turned away from him. "I think he would have liked you, too." She turned back to him, her eyes serious. "I don't care what that Madame Zena said to you, Robert. We're all a little eccentric, but I love my family."

He decided not to tell her that it had been Douglas who first voiced fear regarding her safety. "It's just good to be near you—even if I am keeping my distance," he said huskily.

"You're awfully good to be near, too," she said, then cleared her throat. "Too good." She laughed. "Well, I'm taking Jeeves Junior and heading on up. Early call tomorrow."

She picked up the cat, which purred with pleasure.

I understand completely, fellow, he thought. *Wish I were you.*

Jillian started out, and he followed her. They walked up the stairs together.

"You're comfortable?" she asked him.

"Great room. I'm right next to you."

She looked at him strangely.

"Do you mind?"

"No, I, uh...well, it was Milo's room."

"Milo's room?"

"When we came here...he was very sick, you know. He—he died here. There's actually a connecting door between the rooms, but I think there's a wardrobe blocking it now."

"Ah."

They reached the landing.

"Well, good night," she told him.

He thought there might be regret in her words. He hoped so.

"Good night," he said. He turned away quickly, walked into his room and closed the door. The light from the bathroom still burned. He left it on, closing the door so the room wasn't pitch dark.

He crawled into the bed. The water had helped. His head

wasn't spinning quite so badly. He hoped to hell he wasn't going to have a major headache come morning.

With the spinning stopped, the wine quickly went to work to make him doze off. But just when he had fallen asleep, he suddenly tensed, waking himself.

He was certain he had heard something.

He opened his eyes.

There was someone in the wing chair by the bed. He froze, blinking.

Yes, there was someone there. A man, just sitting, stroking a cat.

His surprise was so great that he let out a gasp.

At the sound, the man in the chair gasped back. "Damn!" his visitor exclaimed.

Robert blinked again, his eyesight improving in the murky light.

"You scared me to death," the man continued.

"*I* scared *you?* Who the hell are you, and what are you doing in my room?"

"Oh, I think you know who I am. And actually, you're the one in my room, you know."

He was dreaming. It was the wine. Definitely that damn mulled wine. Because the man seated in the chair facing him looked like none other than the deceased Milo Anderson.

Robert rubbed a hand over his face, groaning. "That stuff is wicked," he muttered.

"Yes, it is. But you should follow me. To the library. That's where you'll find what you need to know."

Robert looked into the darkness again.

The chair was empty.

He jumped up and turned on the light. There was no one in the room. He felt like an idiot. A cold idiot. The temperature in the room had dropped ten degrees at least, he was certain.

He looked at the bedside clock and groaned. Almost three a.m. He needed some sleep. Badly.

He crawled back into bed. Milo had appeared because they'd been talking about the man after imbibing killer wine. His dream apparition had told him to go to the library because Douglas had been suggesting he make sure to browse the library while they were there.

He punched his pillow, closed his eyes.

In a short while, he fell asleep again.

His imagined nocturnal visitor did not return.

At seven a.m., his alarm clock blared. Morning had come.

CHAPTER 8

The old house was crawling with people.

Douglas had always loved to entertain, so through the years the house had often been full. But never as it was today. Brad was there, of course. And there were still photographers, videographers, lighting men, a director, a woman who was responsible for continuity, wardrobe and makeup people, and a set designer. Jillian had been to ad shoots before, but she'd never seen anything this complicated. Nor had she been the object of such attention before.

The gown for the first shoot was beautiful. A deep dark crimson with a brocade bodice, flowing sleeves and a silk skirt. She was posed on one of the old carved wood entry benches that might have come from any century, from medieval times to the present. She posed once with her hair done in braids, then free, with stockings and shoes, without shoes, even barefoot. They shot stills first, with just her. A young man continually dabbed powder on her nose and cheeks. Snow lay deeply on the ground outside, but beneath the lights, it was hot.

Brad, Daniel, Theo, Griff and Eileen stood in a little huddle, with Eileen directing the photographers, Brad directing her, and the group of them discussing every little movement. Douglas was there, the faithful Amelia by his side, but he kept his distance, letting the others take the bit for this campaign and run with it.

Robert wasn't there—not until he appeared in black, form-hugging leather pants and a puffed sleeve, V-necked shirt. He, like the carved wooden bench—and herself, she imagined—were suggestive of the magic of a distant past. He smiled at her awkwardly, clearly uncomfortable with his role but game to try it. She smiled, seeing him arrive.

Brad directed Robert into a position on his knees in front of Jillian. The photographer moved him. Eileen moved him. The photographer moved him again. Shots were taken, he was adjusted, she was adjusted. More powder was puffed on their faces, they were moved yet again, Jillian's hair was smoothed; the makeup woman fussed over Robert.

They took a break while the video cameras were set up. They were both given a line, the same line, since it had been decided that the commercials, each thirty seconds, would be a bit different, but all with the same look, the same feel. The line was "Llewellyn jewels, as timeless as love itself."

The first commercial had Robert walking into the room with a locket, saying the line as he approached Jillian, and slipped the locket around her neck. For the second spot, he set the locket around her neck, and she looked into the camera and said the line.

Simple.

It took most of the afternoon. First Robert gave a perfect reading, but something was wrong with the placement of a light and their faces wound up in shadow. The second take, he tripped over a wire as he entered. The next time, Jillian found herself blowing it, nearly sliding off the sofa as she leaned forward to receive the locket. She nearly landed on top of him. They looked at one another and laughed; Eileen sighed with impatience.

They started again.

Jillian didn't mind. It was tedious. Hot. Difficult to hold certain positions. But it was fun, as well. Fun to work with Robert. To see the light in his eyes as they patiently waited, while Griff and Eileen argued a point. Each time he fitted the locket around her neck, she felt the brush of his fingers, the warmth of being near him. At times the room seemed to fade away. She forgot what they were doing. It seemed to be something that had really happened, his eyes on hers, that touch around her neck. The sensation when he touched her....

Deeper than time.

"As timeless as love itself."

It had been his turn. She frowned, certain he had said something else.

I will always be there for you.

"That's not it—" she began.

"Cut! Jillian," Eileen said, aggravated, "he was perfect."

"What?"

"He was perfect."

He was looking at her, puzzled, as well, deep blue eyes studying her. So close. Apparently he hadn't said anything wrong, after all.

Suddenly she felt like drawing in. Getting away from him.

He had lied to her, made promises, failed her....

"Can we please start over?" Daniel called.

"What's wrong?" Robert asked her softly, while the makeup people performed yet another touch-up.

She shook her head. "Nothing. Sorry. Really."

She felt again the deep tremor of his voice against her senses, the touch of his fingers on her flesh, and it was disturbing. She felt the fierce desire to be with him, that it was right to be with him, while also feeling that she should run. Far and fast.

The day wore on. She didn't imagine the wrong words coming from his lips. Once again she fell into the mood of the work, and her every movement with Robert seemed nearly perfect, as they willingly tried everything the director suggested.

At last they broke. A round of applause went around the room, started by Douglas himself.

"We're done?" Jillian enquired.

"For now," Daniel said. "We've got some recording to do. And I'll need to take a look at the stills and see the film when it's been edited to make some final choices—but you're done."

"Great," Jillian murmured.

"Eileen, Griff, you're up now."

There were to be two voiceovers, Jillian discovered. She watched as the sound men went to work. Eileen did the first. "This Christmas, make it a gift that lasts forever." Griff did the second, so they could mix the male and female voices.

Jillian watched for a while, then murmured that she was going up to take a shower.

She ran the water very hot and scrubbed studiously. She had never felt her face more packed with makeup. The shower pulsed down on her deliciously, and she stood beneath the spray, wondering why she was trying to find something wrong when it felt as if everything should be so right.

"I need a psychologist," she murmured. "Or a psychiatrist. I can just lie on a couch and say, 'I've met the most perfect man, and it's the most wonderful, complete feeling in the world to be with him. He's the greatest Christmas gift ever, and still...he makes me feel as if I should run. Guilt feelings, you say? Because my husband has been dead only a year? No, I don't think so, you see, because he was my best friend and a truly generous person, and I know he would want me to be happy. No, that's not just something I'm saying to convince myself. But I do think I'm a bit crazy, totally losing my mind.'"

She turned off the water, really worried for a moment. *She could have sworn he'd said words he didn't say. A roomful of people had heard the line correctly, and she had heard something else entirely.*

She dressed in comfortable jeans and a sweater, and headed downstairs. To her amazement, the parlor where they had been working was almost empty, except for Henry and piles of boxes. He was opening them, the look on his old face pleased and peaceful.

"Ah, there you are, Jillian. It's a good thing the water heaters here can supply an army."

"Where is everyone? Was I that long?"

"You were. And, let's see...Agatha is seeing to the roast, your grandfather is resting, the camera crews have gone home, and the young folks, most of them, I believe, are out sledding."

"Down Dead Horse Hill?" she asked. The hill behind the house was so named, they all assumed, because the climb was steep and might just kill horses trying to reach the top with a heavy load. Not that horses had been used to climb the hill in many years, although a few cars had been known to slide back down it when reckless drivers ventured out too quickly after an ice storm. It was a wonderful place for sledding; they had all gone there ever since they were little kids. Growing up hadn't changed the pleasure of sliding over the snow with the wind in their faces, freezing their noses.

"Dead Horse Hill," he agreed. "Ah, here's the box with the singing ducks."

She gave a little cry of delight, diving in to help Henry. They carefully took out the ducks. Carved of wood and dressed in Dickens fashion, they had songbooks held in their little duck hands. There were ten ducks, and they stretched across the mantel. When wound, they played ten different Christmas carols, with a different duck taking the solo each time. It was one of her favorite pieces.

"Let's set these guys up first," she said.

"You should join the others and do some sledding before dinner," Henry advised. "Have some fun."

"I love to decorate for Christmas with you, Henry. You know that."

"You'd have more fun with people your own age," he told her gravely.

She smiled. "We'll do the ducks, then I'll head on out."

Henry helped her, and they arranged the duck band on the mantel. They looked lonely, so she took a few minutes to put one of the beautifully crafted silver wreaths above them on the mirror.

"It's beginning to look like Christmas," she said, pleased. She loved Christmas. She had loved it all her life. As it came closer each year, she felt anxious. Especially when she was a child, she'd been afraid that Christmas would come but she wouldn't...make it.

Last year Milo had been the one who hadn't made it, she thought. She bit her lower lip. They'd been here last year at this time. First, just her and Milo, Agatha and Jimmy, the groundskeeper and all-around manager of the house and the stables they kept for Tangerine, Blossom, Cream, Igloo and Crystal. Douglas had purchased the horses years ago when he had determined that his young progeny should all learn to ride.

Then her grandfather had joined them.

Milo had loved the horses. The weather hadn't been so bad last year; in fact, November had been mild. He had watched the horses from his window when he became too ill to leave his bed. "Strange, isn't it?" he asked her once. "I never rode, but I feel that I know how, that I could leap on old Blossom and ride off into the sunset."

"You wouldn't run very fast," she had tried to joke. "Blossom is pretty old now. And very slow."

He'd curled his fingers around hers. And she had known that he was smiling.

And then...

It hadn't been that much longer, and he had died.

They had all come then. Her family. And Connie and Joe. Even Amelia and Gracie Janner.

"It's nearly dark," Henry warned. "We can do more Christmas tonight. Agatha can make hot chocolate, we'll make popcorn, play Christmas carols...you go on out now. Play. Be young."

"Henry, you're not so old."

"I'm young at heart, like Douglas, but my old bones are beginning to creak, and that's a fact. Go on now."

She kissed him on the cheek and went into the large hall closet for a good snow jacket and pair of boots. Gloved, booted and decked out for the cold, she left the house.

For half an hour Robert had gone sledding with the others. It had been fun. The snow was perfect, fresh and clean. Here, far from the city, it didn't turn to slush so fast. There were plenty of sleds, small and large, but the Llewellyns tended to like to take individual runs. Even Eileen was shrieking like a kid, going for a running start and taking the hill at top speed.

She loved to try to beat Gary, but her fiancé seemed to take it in stride and hold his own.

At the foot of the hill was a small white wooden fence. Daniel mentioned that Douglas had had the fence constructed when he heard of an accident on a similar hill in which sleds had shot out into the road and people had been killed. "This way, if we get too rambunctious, we only break a few bones," Daniel said with a grin.

Both Connie and Gracie Janner seemed more hesitant than the others. Naturally. They hadn't grown up here and didn't know the hill so well. Not like the Llewellyns, who competed avidly with one another.

Gracie rode with Daniel the first time, and Robert wondered idly if Daniel was aware of the terrible crush his secretary had on him. None of his business. Joe had disappeared, so Daniel offered to take Connie down until she got used to the feel of the hill. Gracie watched like a first-grader sent to the corner on a time-out, but Connie was oblivious, shrieking with delight all the way down.

After a few runs, Robert asked about the stables. Daniel told him that there were plenty of horses, all good riding except for Blossom, who was in retirement.

"If you feel like taking a ride, I'd go for Crystal. He's well mannered, an Arab-quarter-horse mix, with beautiful gaits and sure feet in the snow. If you need help with anything, Jimmy handles the horses and the grounds. His apartment is at the far end of the stables. He'll be watching his soaps—he tapes the shows during the week and watches them all on Saturdays. He'll be happy to give you a hand, though."

"I'll try not to bother Jimmy," Robert told him. "But I may just go for a ride."

"Head across from the house. There are miles of hills and fields, and nothing to worry about under the snow."

"Thanks."

Jillian still hadn't come out. He thought about going back to the house to see if she wanted to join him, but he had still more or less promised to keep a distance, so it might be better if he just went out alone.

He had no difficulty finding Crystal, since all the stalls had engraved nameplates for their occupants. He spent a few minutes studying each of the horses—all healthy and handsome animals. Igloo had been named for his slightly mottled white coloring, Robert was certain, just as Cream had been named for hers. Tangerine was a palomino. Blossom was nearly the size of a Clydesdale. Crystal was almost silver, his size had come from his quarter-horse half, for he was well over sixteen hands high. He had a handsome face and bay coloring, and the facial dip and body structure of an Arab. "Well, fellow, want to explore?" Robert enquired.

There was no need for him to bother anyone for assistance—Jimmy could enjoy his soaps uninterrupted. The Llewellyn tack room was like everything else Douglas Llewellyn owned and controlled—perfectly organized. Bridles hung on the wall, and saddles and saddle blankets rode sawhorses, each item neatly labeled to indicate which horse it belonged to.

Crystal seemed eager for an outing, standing tolerantly still while Robert slipped on his bridle and tightened the girth. He led the animal out of the stables and mounted up.

Soon he had crossed the road and come to open territory. Crystal did have smooth gaits, and he was ready to run. For ten minutes they raced, plowing up snow, tearing up the earth underneath. The wind was a wild rush. It felt great.

Still, he slowed the horse after a while, turning back at a smooth lope, trotting, walking. Crystal was a fine animal.

He loved to ride. Living in the city, he had given up on the idea of buying a horse, something he had wanted to do since he was a kid. He'd always loved horses, and riding had been natural for him from the time he'd been very young.

Unlike the Llewellyns, though, he had not grown up in the lap of luxury. He had a great family, had gotten lots of wonderful encouragement, but he lacked anything like the Llewellyn money. His father had told him that the first American Marston had come to the United States with a Scottish regiment in the British Army, fighting against the colonists. When the British had lost the war, they had deserted many of their Scottish companies, and that Marston had become a passionate American. Marstons were proud, and certain of their own lineage—but they hadn't left the old country with anything but the clothes they wore and the weapons they carried.

Robert had paid for college by going into the Service. From both, he'd learned a lot.

But not a lot about the foolishness of riding in unknown territory when it was nearly dark, he told himself ruefully. He had taken the route Daniel had suggested, but the countryside didn't come with streetlights.

Heading back, he crested a hill and paused. He could see the lights of the Llewellyn property, the house lights and those illuminating the grounds. Dead Horse Hill was clearly visible against the coming dusk. He could still see the group sledding. By squinting, he could pick out who was who. Eileen was still at it, challenging someone to a race.

Jillian.

She was bundled up, but her reddish-gold hair was still discernible beneath her hat. She was laughing at Eileen, responding to the challenge. Connie and the others were encouraging the contestants. Their camaraderie made him smile where he sat, watching. They were a close group—a closed group, in their way. He was the outsider.

But he'd been hired to watch....

Something disturbed him about the scene. He wasn't sure what, but as he watched, his smile of amusement faded. His eyes wandered down, and he saw suddenly that there was a huge gap in the fencing at the foot of the hill, right where Jillian would be heading.

She would stop before then, surely. Except that she was racing, building up speed and momentum and...

There was a car coming. No, a truck. He heard the vehicle sweep onto the curving road that fronted the estate and lay between him and them.

Surely Jillian would stop in plenty of time.

But... *Douglas had had the fence built because people had been killed by sledding onto a road.*

"Stop!" He roared out the warning, but too late. Both women had leapt onto their sleds and started down the hill.

He didn't think; he simply kneed Crystal and went flying across the field, the wind whipping by him.

He felt something strange along with the wind. It was as if he had been riding a long time, as if he had been afraid for a long time....

Crystal neared the road.

The truck was coming fast. Far too fast for a night when snow lay thick on the ground, when ice could too easily lie beneath it.

Crystal and he soared over the road. Over the broken fence.

Jillian, on her sled, was sliding toward him at what seemed to be the speed of light. She opened her mouth in warning and confusion.

He raced on, straight toward her. When he was almost on top of the sled, he veered Crystal and made a leap from the horse's back, catching Jillian, tumbling violently with her from the sled and into the snow.

They rolled. Snow packed around him. Ice-cold flakes stuck to his nose, his lips, his forehead. Gasping, shaken, Jillian tried to push him away while dusting snow from her face, blowing it from her mouth.

"You idiot! What in God's name—"

They heard the crash. The awful sound as her sled hit the road and the truck hit the sled.

The driver either didn't see the splintered wood or didn't care. He kept up his reckless speed, roaring on around the curve in the road.

The sled lay in pieces on the ground.

"Oh." Jillian barely breathed the word.

Shaking, he stood and reached down to her. She took his hand and rose, looking into his eyes.

"Thanks," she murmured huskily. "That's why we have the fence.... I guess someone ran into it or something. I—I didn't even realize it was down."

"Neither did I. Earlier," he added.

"Jillian!" Griff was rushing up to her, grabbing her, turning her around, checking her from head to toe. Daniel came behind him, followed by Connie, then Eileen, who had crashed into the fence laughing, apparently unaware of what had happened. Theo came down the hill, sliding, falling, rising to run again.

"My God, Jillian!" he cried. "You could have been killed!"

"Killed?" Eileen exclaimed. "But what—"

"The fence," Gary said, reaching them more slowly. "Eileen, the fence is down."

"Why didn't we see it?" Connie fretted. "We've all come down dozens of times."

"We were over to the side, Mrs. Murphy," Gracie said, reaching them. "We never came down so close to here until the two Ms. Llewellyns decided to race."

"Oh God, Jilly." Daniel took Jillian from Griff, hugging her to him like the best of older brothers. He looked terrified.

He still held Jillian as his eyes shot to Robert's. "Marston," he said huskily, "I can tell you, I had my doubts, but you're one hell of a company asset."

"I was just in a good position."

"A good position?" Connie exclaimed. "It was like Saint George slaying the dragon."

"The truck was nowhere close when he crossed the road, Connie," Griff told her. "You're getting too dramatic."

"I don't know about that," Jillian said, drawing away from Daniel. "I'm awfully grateful. But everyone, please. Not a word to Grandfather about this, all right? 'All's well that ends well,' right? Please. Don't say anything to him. Some idiot teenager with a new license probably ran down the fence."

"Might just have been a woman driver," Gary teased.

"Or a drunk," Griff said.

"Anyway, we'll get it fixed. Please, let's not worry Douglas needlessly." She spun around, staring at him again with her huge beautiful eyes. "I'm truly grateful—you saved my life—but I don't want him upset. Please."

"I don't need a pat on the back from Douglas," he said. "If you don't want him to know, I won't say anything."

"We're all agreed, right?" Jillian insisted, turning again to look at all of them.

"We're all agreed," Daniel said firmly. "It was an accident."

"And thanks to Robert," Theo agreed, "it's over."

They all nodded.

Robert turned, realizing he was missing the horse. Crystal was gone.

"Don't worry," Jillian said, touching his arm. "Crystal just headed back to the stables." She smiled. "He likes it here. Comfy place for a horse. Jimmy will find him and take care of him."

He shook his head. "I took him out. I'll see that he's back in his stall."

He walked away from the group, wondering how something could be so wrong in a family that appeared to be so close.

That night Jillian managed several times to almost forget her harrowing experience. Dinner was delicious. Moods were light. They'd worked hard, then they'd played hard. The snow had been cold, but the house was warm as toast. Agatha and Henry had prepared dinner between them, and even shy Jimmy came in from his room off the stables to join them. The roast was cooked to perfection, deliciously seasoned. They were all starving. There was corn on the cob, mashed potatoes flavored with garlic, peas, green beans, asparagus, broccoli, salad and Yorkshire pudding. Dessert was strawberry shortcake.

They talked about the shoot and argued which charities were the most deserving, especially at Christmas. She saw that Robert was sitting by Jimmy. The two seemed to have a lot to talk about. She felt both a chill and a warmth, watching him, wondering why she could possibly feel such fear, such determination to take a step back, when she saw him. Tonight he was in a plaid flannel shirt. The red pattern enhanced the darkness of his hair. He was very good-looking, and the flash of his smile seemed sincere. He was down-to-earth, despite his appearance.

He had probably saved her life tonight, she reminded herself. And yet...

After dinner, they all gathered to put up more Christmas decorations. Aggie prepared mountains of popcorn to be strung, then made hot chocolate for them all. She gave directions for stringing various garlands, for winding the lights around pillars and banisters, for placing each Christmas novelty and knickknack.

Eileen came upon a box of ornaments. "We can't possibly use these yet."

"We can decorate the pillars," Jillian said, smoothing back her hair. "And we could do popcorn chains if Griff weren't eating it all."

"Hey! There's a fire going, an old flick on the television, and I'm drinking hot chocolate. Of course I'm eating the popcorn. What good will a string of popcorn do? By Christmas, it will be moldy," Griff protested.

"We're not going to eat the strings we make now," she told him.

He shrugged, smiling, throwing up a piece and catching it deftly in his mouth.

"You're hopeless," she told him.

"I can teach you how to catch every last bite," he told her.

She shook her head, turning back to the ornament box and catching Robert's eye. He was watching her gravely from a stance by the mantel. His eyes were far too somber. He was thinking that she was in danger again, she thought.

From her own family.

She turned quickly away, hoping he would keep his word and not say anything to Douglas.

He was quite a rider. Tomorrow, she thought, she would ask him to go for a ride with her. And when they were alone, she would point out how it had surely been an accident. No one could have planned a truck going by at such a precise time. And the fence...

Obviously an accident.

A little while later, when she was reaching up to hang an angel ornament on one of the garlands, she found that he was beside her, ready to help her. She felt dizzy. It would be great to lay her head against his chest. Breathe him in. His aftershave was great. Everything about him was great....

"You liked Crystal?" she queried, annoyed that her voice was so breathless.

"He's a great horse. He's Daniel's, right?"

She shook her head, smiling. "No. Mine."

"Oh. Sorry, I didn't realize—"

"We're not up here enough to lay personal claim to any of the horses anymore," she told him. "And you took my horse to save my life. A pretty good trade, I think. Crystal has the nicest manners. Except for Blossom, who just moves like molasses. She's Eileen's."

"*Eileen* has a slow horse?" he asked skeptically.

"She hates to ride. But the day we went and bought the horses, she followed Eileen around like a puppy dog. She's very sweet. We don't ride her anymore. But she'll still follow you around. She loves to be stroked, given a lot of attention."

"Ah," he murmured.

"And what does that mean?" she enquired.

"I like to be stroked, too. Given a lot of attention," he told her, grinning.

Warmth. Enwrapping her, encapsulating her. How could she doubt him?

But she did.

"I thought you might like to go riding again tomorrow. You couldn't have gone very far tonight. I know Daniel will be working with Eileen and Brad, but I don't have to approve anything until they get further along. I know you want to—"

"They won't mind one less chef tomorrow," he said. "Riding will be great."

"I'll ask Jimmy to see that Crystal and Igloo are ready for us. Is eleven all right? I'm taking Grandfather to the nine o'clock church service in town."

"Fine," he told her.

He was close, leaning against the pillar, dark blue eyes intent on her. She smiled awkwardly. "Well, I'm going on up, then. Full day. I'll see you in the morning."

"You will."

She turned around. Agatha, Amelia, her grandfather and Henry were playing a round of pitch. Jimmy and Brad were deep into a game of chess. She wasn't sure where the others were.

"Good night, all," she called.

"Good night," she received in return.

"Thanks again," she said softly to Robert.

He was still leaning against the pillar, arms crossed over his chest, dark hair falling over his forehead, gaze fathomless as he watched her. "Shucks, ma'am, it was nothing," he told her.

She turned and started up the stairs, she felt him watching her all the while.

As she reached the second floor landing, she hesitated, wondering if she should see if Daniel was in his room and just make sure that she wouldn't be needed during the day and that Robert would be clear to go riding. She walked down the hall to his room, thinking that since she hadn't seen him, he was probably there.

Just as she lifted her hand to knock she heard a woman's voice, hushed. "I can't, I can't. The way we're doing it is so...so...I shouldn't. Oh God, I've got to stop...."

There was a whispered return, much deeper.

The sound of tears.

Jillian realized that she was still standing there. Listening. *Eavesdropping.* When her cousin was obviously entertaining someone in his room.

She drew her hand back quickly and spun around, almost running down the hall to her own room. Once inside, she closed the door.

As she got ready for bed, she felt cold and shocked. Not that Daniel shouldn't have a lover. He was handsome, virile, masculine, and certainly of age. It was just that...

Who?

Gracie? With *Daniel?*

Or someone else? Someone from town, a neighbor...?

She crawled into bed, and only then did she realize that she might have recognized the woman's voice.

Connie.

No! It couldn't have been. Joe was here. He hadn't been sledding with them, not when she had gotten there, anyway, but he had been at dinner.

Connie was with Joe.

And yet...that voice.

C H A P T E R 9

This time, when he awoke to see the figure of Milo Anderson seated in the chair by his bed, Robert didn't even allow himself to be startled.

He groaned, throwing an arm over his face.

"Go away. You're a dream. I'm only dreaming."

"You're not dreaming. And Christmas is coming."

"Great. Christmas comes every year."

The apparition was silent for a minute, then Milo said quietly, "No, not for everyone."

"Sorry. Really. No, I'm not. Hell, this is ridiculous. I'm apologizing to a dream."

"Look, you did well today, but not well enough."

Robert drew his arm from his eyes to stare at his dream visitor with indignation. "Not well enough? I hurtled across a highway, threw myself from a racing horse and caught Jillian before the sled could go crashing into the truck."

"I said you did well. But did you look at the license plate of the truck and get the number? Did you inspect the fence to find out what really happened to it?"

"It was an accident."

"No, not everything is an accident."

"You sound like Douglas."

"Of course. Douglas is involved."

"What are you talking about?"

"Never mind. You're not ready to understand."

"I understand that I'm having a nightmare. What more is there?"

"The book. I've told you, you've got to read the book. She is in danger. It will come again—unless we can change things."

"Great. So someone—apparently in Jillian's own family— is out to kill her. Before Christmas. And I've got a ghost haunting my dreams, a know-it-all ghost. So if you know it all, just whisper the name of the guilty party in my ear so when I wake up, I'll know who it is."

"I don't know who it is," Milo said, looking perplexed, shaking his head.

"You're dead, you're a ghost, you're omniscient—"

"I'm dead, I'm a ghost, yes. But I'm still here because she's in danger. I don't have access to any more information than you do. Except that I've read the book. And I believe."

"You believe in what? Miracles? I don't mean to be cruel, but after all, this is my nightmare. You're dead and buried. There won't be a miracle. Unless you're thinking of making a comeback?"

"Don't be gruesome," Milo said with a shudder. He leaned forward. "I'm not coming back. It wasn't meant to be. But I was part of it, and I left too soon this time around. I guess that had to happen. But you have to wise up, Marston, or you'll lose her again."

"Look..."

In the darkness of his room, Robert sat up. He had spoken aloud. There was no one there.

He groaned and crashed back to his pillow. Why in God's

name was he having such bizarre dreams? He hadn't been drinking tonight, except for a single beer with dinner.

He rolled over, pulling his pillow over his head. He needed to get back to sleep.

He started to drift. *Don't dream, don't dream, don't dream,* he told himself.

But he did dream again, and though he knew he didn't want to dream, he was aware that he was doing it.

In his dream, he was rising, slipping on his robe and padding barefoot out into the hall to the second floor landing.

And he was walking...down to the library.

Inside, on the huge desk that was the centerpiece of the room, was a book. He walked over to it. Ran a finger over it. The book was very old. Hundreds of years old, he thought. He looked at the cover, looked at the spine, at the pages.

Then he sat down to read, telling himself it was a remarkably vivid dream.

January 3rd, 1661

We fled today, though we did not flee so much as a result of the war, the impending death of the King, or the new regime. We fled because of the burning. Because of the horror we inflicted after the burning.

Because we were too late, and should not have been.

He wanted death.

Michael could not endure what had happened, and not even the vengeance he extracted could allow him to stay. We headed to the North Country, and will fly far and fast. He thinks, I believe, that he can outrun the horror.

Who could have known?

I should begin from the beginning.

I will never forget the day they met, though it was long before the tumult began. She was the daughter of Lord Alfred, the kindliest of men. Tolerant of her headstrong ways, and knowing, of course, that she adored him in return. She was a lady, to the manor born, and she used her position *over* Michael, nose in the air, words ever teasing, haughty, yet filled with a laughter that wound him quickly around her little finger, though he would not let on. I warned him when first we saw her by the spring that she was Lord Alfred's daughter. But he paid no heed. She accosted him to do her bidding, and he complied, yet whatever she asked, he overdid, bringing water, helping her to drink so that it spilled over her, setting her upon her horse with such a flourish that she slid from one side to the ground upon the other. She but laughed, promising him that he should pay, and he told her that he would pay forever, that he was forever her servant, spellbound.

They parted ways then, of course. But I saw the way they looked at one another.

They met again the following day, in her father's own hall. For her father would be riding off in support of the King, and Michael, the finest of soldiers, would captain the troops he had raised. Within the hall, she taunted him. He called her spoiled, willful and a silly child. She said then that he should stay away, and he told her that he could never stay away, for he was enamored. Indeed, he was certain he loved her.

There had been some talk of a marriage between her and Sir Walter, distant kin, a man well versed in the way of the soldier, the churchman and the politician, for he had, at one time, befriended the King, and at another time he had sat with Cromwell and agreed with his position that the King and the church had become corrupt. Already there was talk of treason. Alas, the King was arrogant, oh, indeed, arrogant. He was, in his mind, God's anointed, incapable of treason. He was the state, and the state was him. Michael had ridden with his son, had served the Prince, and therein found his loyalty. The King was beloved by his family, was an educated man, with great dignity. His son was charming and more. Brave.

Sir Walter had been appointed sheriff of the county and had come at Lord Alfred's request. Lord Alfred knew Sir Walter to be crafty and cunning, a man to straddle a fence, but he thought that best for his daughter, his heiress. Should things go badly for the King, the fact that Sir Walter straddled fences so well would be in his favor. He had a way about him. He was the law in a lawless time, was judge and jury. This could not be a bad thing in such hazardous days, Lord Alfred thought.

Lord Alfred was a good man, a man who loved his daughter. But it is truth to say that he did encourage a match between his daughter and Sir Walter. The latter was an extremely handsome man, powerful, determined. And he had coveted Morwenna for years by then, waiting, biding his time. He had been her friend; she had, perhaps, cared for him.

Until Michael.

I was not with him the day that love first created madness between them. But I had seen that look in their eyes, and later, being with the two of them, it was impossible not to see the passion that had risen between them. There was a war to be fought, but they had time together. Long days by the spring. Nature made their bed, sky and air were witnesses to their love. Yet, as Michael watched the change of things, he feared for her. He still had to go to war, for that was a soldier's duty. He was her father's man, defender of her father's honor.

Then, when they rode away, when banners were flying and the stirrup cup had been drunk, Lord Alfred so innocently lent fuel to flame, telling Sir Walter that he must guard all in his absence—his home, his law, his daughter. Sir Walter assumed then that she was both his ward and his betrothed. He loved her, in his way. Loved her with a sickness. For he suspected her affair with Michael. She made her feelings evident.

Once, when the soldiers had leave while the conflict raged, I don't remember the date, but it was while hope still stirred in the hearts of all Royalists, Michael took her secretly to wife.

I remember the night. I see it clearly in my mind's eye, and it *was* clear, for there was a full moon, no cloud in the sky. They stood together in a copse of blossoms, she so beautiful, he so tall and powerful, the knight triumphant, the soldier who would not fail. She did not want him to go to war. She was afraid for him, afraid he would fail, because it became more and more evident that Cromwell would prevail. But a man could not turn his back on his beliefs; she would not love him could he do so. And at first, she was merely scornful of her father's warder, Sir Walter, for remember, once he had been her friend. He loved her. She thought herself safe.

They met, through it all, infrequently. He was there for her when her father fell to a grave illness and was returned to recover at his ancient estate. Lord Alfred was wounded in body and soul; many a day he did not gain consciousness. When he did, he was aware only of the past; he did not remember the war, nor the King's plight, nor the soldier who had risked his own life to save him and bring him home.

Sir Walter held power. Tremendous power.

But she ignored the dictates of the man who was now her guardian and thought he would make himself her husband, lord of the castle, and powerful, even in the Protectorate that Cromwell would lead. On the first night of her father's return, she slipped away to be with her husband. It was then that Sir Walter went to her chambers, ready to tell her that there would be a marriage now, that she would be safe with him, whichever way the wind should blow.

She had friends within the castle. Jane, her maid, Garth,

the groom. Jeremy, her father's old assistant. Jane, hearing that he was coming, made a figure in the bed of blankets and pillows, and when he came, she told him that her lady slept, deep in grief at her father's condition. And Morwenna did grieve his illness, greatly, yet found solace in the arms of her husband. Who better to wipe her tears?

That night, Jane's ruse was respected.

But Michael had a few days to tarry, and one night, when Morwenna was gone to his arms again, Sir Walter pushed past Jane, entered the room and found that his ward was gone.

The next day he threatened her.

She would not be threatened. She did not see the danger. She told him that though she cared for him, she would never be his wife.

It was from that night on that he began to call her witch.

Subtly, he spread rumor. Aye, she was a witch. What else but magic could give a maid such compelling beauty that she should so entice men? He was a good man, a Godly man, and she made his mind stray again and again. Aye, it was a pity that so many could be so fooled! There had been a time, a Christian time, when the old ways had been tolerated, when wiccans had still peopled the hills. For though we were a land known as England, we bordered that country which was Wales. The people there were filled with fancy and superstition, and it was a way of life, one that they enjoyed. But when James of Scotland became James I of England, he brought with him a fear of witchcraft, and suddenly, in the midst of war and sadness and bloodshed, the country was filled with witch finders. They were not the King's men, nor Cromwell's, they were the law. It remained the law that a man should not steal, nor commit murder, though Cromwell sought to murder our King. But witches! Mostly pathetic old women, they were tortured into admitting to pacts with

Satan, to dancing with him, bearing his young, selling their souls to kill a neighbor's pig or put a pox on an enemy. They were used most heinously, prodded, broken, dunked, and yet it was all within the ways of the law, or what remained of the law. Sir Walter, you see, was both sheriff and master of the castle, and half convinced himself that he was like God, doing God's work and, when the tide began to turn, doing the work of the country. He was Cromwell's man, and therefore, when the King's cause began to fail, he could accuse her of treason and heresy as well as witchcraft.

It was England, after all. By the law, witches were hanged. Heretics and traitors could be burned.

Morwenna loved her soldier, her knight. She made light of her situation, saying that she would not desert her father. He wanted her to come away; she wanted him to quit the army. He could not desert the King's cause until he was so ordered by the King. She would not leave her father.

But when Michael had to ride to war again, she begged him not to go. She was so fearful. Still, her fear was for him. He promised her that he would come back to her. He swore that when she needed him, he would be there for her. "Always," he said to her. And I heard it myself. "Whenever you need me, I swear, I will be there."

He and Sir Walter had crossed paths many times. Sir Walter claimed only to care for Morwenna's welfare. Naturally, Michael was welcome in the manor. He was Lord Alfred's captain, and his champion. Yet, subtly, Sir Walter warned him away from Morwenna.

"You cannot help our lady in these difficult times," Sir Walter said. "I see that you watch her. You had best forget her."

"Ah, but, sir, she is the daughter of my dearest patron, Lord Alfred. I will never forget her. I will wage any battle for her."

"You think you can fight battles, win wars, that are lost."

"I think that I am steadfast, and I will always serve my lady, as I have served her father."

"You must take care, sir, because the wind begins to blow in one direction now. If Cromwell's forces find victory, you, sir, will be a traitor, and you will not be welcome here."

But as always, his wife slipped out to be with him, and she was angry when he spoke about Sir Walter.

She lay with him, and he with her, and they were man and wife. No matter what the words they exchanged, they were happy with one another. She leaned upon an elbow, watched his beloved face and shook her head. "Maybe we underestimate him."

"Your father still lives."

"Poor father has no mind."

"He would not dare seize power while your father lives. Still, you should come with me now," he told her gravely. "Tonight. We'll ride tonight. Across the snow. The Prince will flee soon to Scotland. We'll follow, adventurers in the night, riders of a fierce storm."

She touched his face. "My love, I cannot, will not, leave my father."

He took her hand, holding it to his cheek. "Is your love for him greater than your love for me?"

"My love is as steadfast as your loyalty—for you both," she told him.

He rolled, taking her into his arms. "If I did not think him a pompous ass, I would force you with me now. Ah, wife, dearest wife. I find no fault with your love for your father, but he is not truly with us anymore. Still, to know that I am loved with that same sweet devotion is something I take with me in my heart, wherever I go."

"Why must you still go?"

"We have argued this—"

"The King loses."

"I will not be the greater cause of his loss."

"And I will not leave my father."

"Stubborn wench," he accused.

"You are the arrogant fool, my husband."

"Still, lady, no evil shall touch you. I am your husband, your fool, and I will let no evil touch you. When you need me, I will be there."

"If Cromwell does take this war—"

"Then he will understand that a soldier has fought with loyalty. When the King disbands us, I will be a good citizen of my country."

"It will be a miracle if we are to be together, to live a normal life, to see a family grow, to love forever."

"There are no miracles, my lady. Just the strength of our wills, our convictions—our love."

She smiled. "I, beloved, will believe in miracles. For us both."

When the cock crowed, it was time to part. She to the manor. He to the war.

It was after that day that Sir Walter began to turn.

He had loved her so much. Wanted her so much.

And he was bitter. Very bitter. He came to her room again one night, demanding that she accept his proposal. She would marry him within the week.

She rejected him flatly. She wasn't afraid. Her father was still alive.

Sir Walter was like a rabid dog. She would marry him. If she did not, he would have her killed. Publicly. That would bring her lover, and then he would kill Michael, as well.

She was amused. He would never kill Michael. Michael was stronger; Michael rode with soldiers. Sir Walter might have a few men in his employ, he might be sheriff, but he wouldn't kill her. And he couldn't kill Michael.

"You mark my words, my beauty," he told her. "You will change your mind. I will see that you burn."

"For what? Despising you?"

"You are a witch."

"You'll hang me, then."

"You'll die for whatever crime I say. I can make it happen."

"Never. Michael will come for me before he'll let you kill me."

"We'll see, won't we, my dear. These things will happen. Unless you determine to love me. I will see you dead by Christmas, unless you change your mind."

"I will not change my mind. You don't understand. I love Michael. I will love him forever."

"I will arrest you tomorrow."

"For witchcraft?"

"For witchcraft, heresy and treason. You will burn. Unless there is a miracle."

"Arrest me. Light your fires. There will be a miracle."

But there was not to be....

"Robert, there you are."

He heard her voice from the depths of sleep. He was cramped, cold, uncomfortable. Too many dreams. They came back quickly. He didn't think he liked sleeping in this house. He opened his eyes and saw his own fingers, lying on wood.

A desk.

Pages.

A book.

"Robert? Are you all right?"

He looked toward the voice. Jillian was there, dressed not for riding but for church. She was wearing a long woolen skirt and a matching sweater, and her hair was shimmering, her eyes brilliant, curious, as she watched him.

"What on earth are you doing in here?"

What on earth, indeed?

He thought he had been dreaming. Dreaming a ghost, a book, a story. The library. If he hadn't been dreaming...

A ghost had come to his bedroom and then told him he had to go read a book.

And here he was.

He shook his head, trying to get the cricks out of his neck. "I, uh..."

Simple, he thought. *Milo on the mind, Jillian in danger, Douglas worried, me keeping silent. I dreamed up a ghost. Power of suggestion. I walked to the library. Picked up a book with a story about star-crossed lovers during the English Civil War. Fell asleep again...*

"Robert? I just thought I'd tell you we're leaving now."

"Now? How about in five minutes?" he queried. "I'd like to come with you."

"Really?"

"Yeah."

She smiled and shrugged. "Great. We'll wait."

Agatha and Henry went, as well. Douglas didn't comment on the others, but he made Robert welcome.

The church was beautiful and very old. The stones in the cemetery in the churchyard dated back to the sixteen hundreds. Robert found himself staring at them, looking for people named Michael or Morwenna.

The sermon was about miracles. Life itself was a miracle. Faith was a miracle. The most important miracles were those created every day, little miracles, miracles of caring. It wasn't a long sermon but short, sweet and uplifting. Douglas commented as they left the church that he liked the priest.

"I always like a guy on the positive side," he told Robert. "Too many fire and brimstone fellows out there. Everything is bad, nothing is good. Hell, yes, we all need help now and then. But life is what we make it. Don't you agree?"

"Definitely," Robert told him. "We're all responsible for ourselves."

"By the grace of God, here I am," Douglas said. "Now, there's a miracle."

Jillian was smiling. "Robert doesn't believe in miracles, Grandfather."

"When there's a miracle sitting right next to you? Shame on you, son."

Robert smiled, amused by the way they teased him. "I stand corrected," he said. "You, sir, are a miracle. You're also an example of hard work and taking the bull by the horns."

Douglas sniffed but seemed pleased. In a few more minutes, they were back at the house.

In the kitchen, they had pastries, coffee and juice, and then Jillian said she was running up to change for riding.

"By the way, Grandfather," she said, speaking a bit hesitantly, "if you see Daniel, tell him that we'll be a few hours. I know he doesn't need me, but—"

"You didn't check with him last night?"

Watching Jillian, Robert thought he saw her flush uncomfortably.

"I was going to. I, um, forgot. I fell asleep."

She was lying, Robert thought. He wondered why.

"Well, I'm sure nothing earth-shattering can happen in a few hours. What do you say, Robert?"

"I'm not involved at this stage. When they have the finished product, I take over," he told Douglas.

"Then, bless you, my children. Go riding."

"Meet you at the stables in ten minutes," Jillian told Robert.

The horses were already saddled and bridled, each in its customized tack, when he reached the stables. He started for the mottled white horse, Igloo, but Jillian stopped him.

"No, take Crystal. You liked him yesterday. And he liked you."

"He's your horse."

"Igloo is a sweet guy, too. Please, I insist."

"Okay. Thanks."

Instinctively, he checked the girth, noted that the saddle and stirrups were the same as they had been yesterday, and mounted. Jillian obviously loved to ride, and was good at it. She leapt easily into the saddle and seemed instantly comfortable. She patted Igloo on the neck. "Behave yourself today."

"Is he known for making trouble?"

She grinned. "He's Griff's horse. He's a prankster."

"Well, now I feel bad. You should ride your own horse."

"I'll be fine. I like a tussle with Igloo now and then."

"Ah, you think I can't handle him?"

"No, I didn't say that at—" She broke off, aware that he was teasing her. "Race you up the hill," she told him.

And then she was gone, snow from her horse's hooves hitting him in the face.

Laughing, he took off after her. They ran for a fair distance. Igloo was strong, but Crystal was faster. He sped past Jillian, her turn to be pelted with snow. She laughed, trotting up as he waited for her.

Then she took off again.

He urged Crystal forward. When he was abreast of her, he leapt from his horse, catching her, bringing them both down into the snow. She laughed, catching her breath.

"Are you planning on making a habit of dumping me in the snow?" she demanded.

He leaned on an elbow, keeping her pinned. "I couldn't resist temptation," he told her.

She stared up at him. Her cheeks were flushed, her eyes incredibly bright.

"I'm falling in love with you, you know," he told her.

She sucked in her breath, still staring at him, not speaking at first. "I owe you my life."

"You don't owe me anything. Besides, you might not have been killed. You might have stopped in time."

"I might have. But you saved me."

He smoothed a reddish-gold lock of snow-covered hair from her forehead. "Saved you, saved myself. I told you, I'm falling in love with you."

"We're going slowly," she said softly.

"Fine. I'm slowly falling in love with you."

"I'm freezing," she said. "And if we don't capture our wayward horses, they'll head back without us."

"Good point," he said, rising, then helping her to her feet. Luckily the horses had wandered only a few steps ahead. They were easily caught.

"Need a hand?" he asked.

"No, thanks, I'm fine," she said, shaking her head. She was quickly up, watching him as he mounted.

"Robert?"

"Um?"

"I'm...seriously, thank you again."

"For?"

"Your daring rescue."

"Well, according to your husband," he muttered, "it wasn't enough."

"What?" she demanded sharply.

He looked over at her, shaking his head. "Sorry. I just..." He shook his head again, embarrassed.

"What?" she demanded again. "Robert..."

"Nothing. I'm just... I'm having dreams in this house. Last

night I dreamt that Milo came into my room and told me I
shouldn't pat myself on the back too firmly, because I didn't do
such a great job. I didn't get the license number off the truck,
nor did I take so much as a look at the fence."

She was frowning. "Why would you?"

"Well, if someone is out to hurt you..."

"Who would be out to hurt me? It was an accident."

"Maybe. Maybe not."

"Robert, don't start in on my family again." She swung on
him suddenly. "You don't even believe in ghosts. And if Milo
were a ghost, he'd be coming to see me, not you."

"Hey, sorry."

"My family is *not* out to get me."

She was angry, but he didn't intend to give in. "I hope
you're right."

She stared at him, then kneed her horse. Igloo took off, and
Crystal followed.

With a lightning change of mood, she suddenly slowed her
horse, turning back to him. "Come on, I'll show you the cottage."

She was racing again. He rode after her. A minute later, he
was thinking that she didn't need enemies, she was reckless
enough with her own life. But she could ride well, and she was
leading him down a trail through thick, snow-covered trees.
Then they burst into a clearing in front of a small, two-story,
raw wood cabin that might have come out of a children's book.

She reined in Igloo, leaping off the horse, starting for the
door. He left Crystal tethered by Igloo and followed her up the
steps to the small porch, then through the door.

"Hey, wait a minute," he called. "Where are we? You can't
just walk into people's houses, Jillian, no matter what last name
you choose to go by."

She was already in, shivering as she stood before a rustic
stone mantel. The place was clean and neat, sparsely furnished

with some old overstuffed chairs, a sofa, brass hearth tools and a few hanging copper pots. Simple stairs were built against the far wall, and the parlor stretched into a dining room furnished with nothing more than a rustic table and chairs.

"Where are we? Who owns this place?" he demanded.

"I do. It was in Milo's family—it was his studio. Come upstairs. I'll show you some of his work."

The cottage was bitterly cold, but he was too curious about Milo's work to care. He followed her up the stairs. The second floor might have been an artist's studio anywhere. There was a daybed piled with pillows, a few chairs, another fireplace. And then there were easels, paint boxes, brushes, charcoal, all scattered in a haphazard yet still somehow organized pattern about the room. She walked over to one canvas, lifted the drape from it. The painting, done in acrylics, was arresting. It was a dining scene, with the characters done in caricature. It was Jillian's family and friends. Griff, his features slightly exaggerated, so he took on the appearance of the perfect dandy. Daniel, so serious and gruff that he looked like Pa Kettle. Theo, in the middle, his midriff bulging. Eileen, trying to be tall. Henry was in the background, looking older than Methuselah, with Aggie, barely a skeleton, by his side. Connie and Joe were in the front, playing chess, staring at one another. Two little girls holding dolls stood on the other side; Jillian was with them. More people, including a few he didn't recognize, were walking in and out of the far background. He recognized one of them as Gracie Janner, and another as Amelia. He didn't see Brad Casey, and at first he didn't see Douglas.

"Where's your grandfather?" he asked.

"Right there."

Douglas was in the center, looking on. "Like God at the Last Supper," Robert mused, wondering how he'd missed the man.

"Hey, I showed you this because I wanted you to see that though he teased us all, Milo painted this with a lot of love."

She was right. Everyone was smiling at one another, as if they had learned to tolerate one another's eccentricities.

"Milo was quite the artist," he said softly, looking around.

"A wonderful artist."

Robert pointed to another easel. "Is that another of his works?"

She hesitated. "No, that's mine."

"May I?" he asked. She shrugged, so he walked over to it, removed the covering. This one had been done in oil. It was Milo, wearing a loose-fitting white shirt, against a blue background. He had the appearance of one of the Romantic poets— Shelley, Byron, Keats, lost as if to art, far too young.

"It's great. You should paint more often," he told her.

"Painting isn't my talent," she told him. "I design jewelry, and occasionally clothing, now. I don't even really like to sketch anymore." She shivered, and he realized how cold the cabin was. There was heat here, along with electricity, but since the place was apparently seldom used, the heat was kept very low, just enough to keep pipes from bursting.

"We should go. You're cold," he said.

She nodded. "I think I'll have Jimmy get some people out here early this year to clean. I dress this place for Christmas, too. Differently, but it's fun. I'll turn up the heat."

"Who comes out here with you?" he asked curiously.

"Well, Milo did, of course," she murmured.

"Milo is gone," he said softly.

"The girls come sometimes—Joe and Connie's girls. They love this place. I have a box of their toys downstairs, but usually I set them up with easels and crayons, or give them finger paints, and they go to it. Children are wonderful artists. They haven't gotten to where they've let others sway them yet, so they just use their imaginations. I still like to come here sometimes.

I sketch out pieces here, and in the corner over there I have tools to work with gold and silver."

"Nice."

"Thanks. It's peaceful here. As if you're alone in the world." She smiled, then shivered again. "I guess we *should* go." She started walking toward the stairs.

"Do you want the lights off?"

"No, that's all right. Leave them on. A beacon in the snow."

"Don't you worry about people breaking in?"

"You can only get here on foot, horseback or by snowmobile in the winter. And anyone that desperate is welcome to come in for warmth or rest."

He paused for a moment at the canvas Milo Anderson had done. "I think you're wrong about the peace in this painting, though. I think Milo saw things in your family that he was afraid you didn't see."

"That again!" She flared. "Lay off my family."

"Jillian—"

But she had already clambered down the stairs. Outside, she leapt quickly and easily onto her horse.

He called her name again, but she ignored him, turning Igloo and taking off.

Fast.

"Jillian!" he called, teeth clenched as he rode after her. "What the hell are you doing?" he roared, nearly drawing abreast.

She turned toward him, her hair whipped back by the wind. "We're racing!"

It was then that he saw her saddle slipping, starting to slide beneath her horse.

"Jillian!" he shouted, but the wind was whirling around them, hooves were pounding, hearts were racing.

She didn't hear him.

He spurred Crystal to greater speed. He'd already pulled this

stunt once; he could do it again. Crystal drew alongside Igloo.
"Jillian, the saddle!"

She turned toward him, still angry, not really listening.
"Leave me—"

He leapt for her, catching her by the shoulders, bringing them
both down into a deep bank of snow. She sputtered furiously at
him, snow in her eyes, nose, hair, everywhere.

"Damn you, enough is enough—"

"Jillian, take a look at your saddle."

He didn't stay down with her but quickly rose. Igloo was trotting off, neighing in distress. The saddle was now all the way
beneath the horse's belly.

As they watched, the girth gave completely and the saddle
fell from the horse into the snow.

"All right," she whispered at his side. "I'm sorry. You rescued me again. You're a handy man to have around in case
of accidents."

"Accidents?" he snapped. He could imagine the conse-
quences if she'd stayed on the horse as the saddle turned. She'd
have been trampled beneath Igloo's hooves.

She was staring at him stubbornly. "Yes, accidents."

He shook his head and started walking. He was shaking,
afraid, and he didn't want her to realize it.

"Robert!"

"What?" He spun back around.

"Robert, it had to be an accident. Think about it. I was riding the horse you were supposed to be riding. Crystal is my
horse. Anyone in my family would have thought I'd be riding
him. So it had to be an accident."

He still didn't believe it, and he didn't answer as he kept
walking through the snow to the fallen saddle.

He hunkered down, inspecting the hemp girth. He wasn't a
forensics expert, and he couldn't tell if the rope had worn away

or if it had been given a little help with a sharp instrument. Whichever, it wasn't going back on the horse.

"Robert." Jillian was standing stubbornly before him. "Accidents do happen."

"Accidents and miracles," he muttered. "Yeah, yeah." He stood.

"Robert?" Her arms were crossed resolutely over her chest.

"What?"

"What were you doing in the library this morning?"

"Reading."

"You were sleeping there."

"Well, yes, then I was sleeping."

"But...why were you there?"

He picked up the saddle and hefted it over his shoulder. "Because I was dreaming about your husband's ghost, and he told me to go there."

"Why?"

"To read a book."

"What book?"

"An old book about the English Civil War."

"Milo told you to read a book about the Civil War in England?" she enquired skeptically.

"It was a dream, Jillian, just a dream. And this thing is heavy. Let's get back."

"Just leave it. I can ride bareback, and we can come back with a snowmobile later to get the saddle—"

"No, I think I'll keep my hands on it. But let's get going, okay?"

She walked past him, waited by the horses. He set the saddle over Igloo's back, and they walked the horses through the snow. Silent and mistrustful.

When they finally reached the stables, she turned and quietly assured him, "If Milo could come back, he'd talk to me."

"It was a dream, Jillian. I don't believe in ghosts, you know that."

"I know. You don't believe in anything. Just what you see and touch and feel. And I'm telling you an accident happened. My grandfather is nervous in his old age. I love my family, Michael. And that's that."

She started to walk away. He caught her arm, frowning. "Robert," he said.

"What?" Her brow furrowed.

"Robert. My name is Robert."

"I know your name is Robert."

"You just called me Michael."

"No, I didn't."

"Yes, you did."

"Oh, for God's sake, I know your name, and I didn't call you Michael. I think you're losing your mind."

She wrenched free from his hold, left her horse for Jimmy to tend and went racing toward the house. He thought she was crying, and he gritted his teeth.

"I'm not going crazy," he muttered. "And I wish your wretched husband *would* haunt your dreams. And you *did* call me Michael."

Michael.

The name of the soldier in the book.

CHAPTER 10

When she returned from their ride, she found most of the group in the kitchen, prints spread out all over the table while comments bounced between them. Jillian had to admit that the photos they had chosen for print ads were wonderful.

"I prefer the one on the left. Jilly's eyes are a little too closed in the first one there," Daniel said.

"There's a stray hair in that picture," Eileen objected.

"That's easily touched up," Brad pointed out.

Theo looked up at Jillian, grinning. "What do you think?"

"I'm amazed."

"Good," Eileen murmured. She exchanged pleased glances with Daniel and Theo, then looked at Brad. "Congratulations. You saw something we didn't. And it's terrific."

Brad flushed. "Thanks. But, Eileen, you were the one who took my artwork and turned it into magic."

"Hey, I had a hand in it, too," Theo protested.

"You can all be proud—you all had a hand in it," Douglas told them.

"Robert?" Eileen asked.

Jillian looked around and saw that Robert had reached the house, as well. He pulled his leather gloves from his hands as he viewed the photos.

"I think they're great. You've captured exactly what we wanted to portray."

Douglas smiled. "Let's crack some of that champagne we ordered up for Christmas," he suggested. "I think the occasion deserves it. And I'd like to make a toast."

"I'll get the glasses," Agatha said. Henry immediately went to help her. When they got back, Jillian accepted a glass, looking around the room. Gracie Janner actually looked cute—flushed, her cheeks a little fuller than usual.

Was she having an affair with Daniel? Jillian couldn't help but wonder. Still, she could have sworn the voice had been Connie's. And only Connie and Joe were missing at the moment.

"Where are Connie and Joe?" she asked, lifting her glass for Henry to fill.

"Joe asked me if it was all right if they took off," Daniel told her. He didn't look at her. He was studying his bubbles as the champagne settled in his glass.

"And here's the toast," Douglas said, standing at the head of the table. "To you all, for making this come together. I have always said there's nothing in life as important as family. I sat back and watched you plunge into this together, and I have seldom been prouder, more glad of what God has allowed me to create, or more pleased with each and every one of you. Salute."

"Salute," they returned in unison.

"To you, sir," Griff said, raising his glass to Douglas. "With our deepest gratitude for the richness you have brought to our lives."

Douglas nodded, accepting the compliment. Then he looked

at his glass and grinned. "Pretty good stuff. Now I'm off for a nap. Aggie, when's supper?"

"Three o'clock, and it's scrod, so be punctual," Aggie warned.

"We certainly will be," Eileen promised. "There's nothing so horrible as overdone fish!"

"But Aggie never overcooks the fish," Theo said.

"The best breaded scrod in all of New England comes from this kitchen," Eileen said quickly.

"The best," Jillian echoed softly.

"Wouldn't miss it," Griff said, and strode from the room.

Jillian quickly exited, as well.

She was feeling fiercely loyal at the moment, after the way Robert had torn into her family.

She found herself heading to the library, where the book he had been reading was still lying on the desk. She sat down and idly turned a few pages. How strange. He'd never met Milo, he was the world's worst skeptic, yet he was dreaming about Milo coming back as a ghost.

She sat back in the chair, suddenly chilled, hugging her legs to her chest. "If you could come back, you'd come to me, wouldn't you? I know that you would."

It seemed as if a breeze drifted through the room. Cool, but not chilling. She hugged her knees more tightly.

She looked back to the desk. It seemed that a page had turned. Curious, she studied the book. It was very old, probably one of her grandfather's oldest volumes. It was in excellent condition for its age, though. It had been published in America and was a collection of letters from the time of the Civil War and Reformation in England. She began idly to turn the pages. The book was by a man named Justin Miller, aide-de-camp to Captain Michael Trellyn. There were a narrative, a collection of legal documents and sections of letters, as well as a chronology, and what was probably a somewhat biased look at the English Civil War.

She scanned the pages, then paused, seeing a section titled, "The Letters and Diary Entries of Lady Morwenna, with Correspondence to Her Captain, While He Was Away at War."

She loved old letters. Douglas had dozens of books filled with correspondences from the American Civil War, World War I and World War II. They were so poignant, creating flesh-and-blood tales that conveyed the sorrow of warfare with much greater effect than any simple recitation of dates and places.

The first entry in the section was a diary selection.

I saw Michael for the first time today. Or perhaps I should say, "again," as I believe he must have been around these many years, though I never noticed him until now. He has grown, gone off to be a soldier, and they say that he is a fine one. What a confident fellow, so sure of himself and so very amused by me. He does not seem to be aware of my position nor of his own lesser status. He calls me "Lady Morwenna," but the way he says it...! He shall learn. He spoke with Father today. They talked and talked. Both admitted that though the King is often wrong, he is the King, and they will stand by him. They were closeted together like very old friends. Naturally my father will raise an army. It appears this man shall lead it. Well, he's a fine enough commoner for that! Tall, sits his saddle well, his eyes very hard and direct, his chin far too stubborn, but he is well made, and it will truly be a pity should a cannonball destroy such a fine physical specimen.

Walter was here, as well. He has a civil position as sheriff now, and he is considered a fair and just man by both the King's people and Cromwell's, a hard road, they say. I say that he tells a good story; he straddles a fence well. But he is kin, and Father will leave him to govern here when they ride away to war. He is well educated and clever, and I suppose it is good that he is here. They say that much of the country is in total upheaval. Order will reign if Walter is here. He has suggested marriage, I know, to my father. He is handsome enough, and has a talent for power, but I pretended I knew nothing and reminded him of our kinship. He reminded me that it is a rather distant kinship, yet close enough that he would be an excellent heir to my father's properties. Since he is kind, I pretend to weigh his suit. But there is something... No matter. If only he intrigued me as does the captain, who is, of course, only a commoner. We are not royalty, of course. I shall pray, at the least, that, haughty as he may be, he does not fall to the fever of Cromwell's men.

The entry ended. The next page began a letter written soon after, when Captain Michael Trellyn had gone on to war. Despite her cool presumption regarding her position in society— she was, after all, the daughter of a lord, and he was simply a soldier—passions had flared. She wrote as the lady of the house, admonishing him to keep his head down, to take the greatest care, to watch out for gunfire. *Though it is my understanding that firing pieces are most sadly inaccurate, it is also my understanding that they are most deadly when aimed by accident or precision to actually strike the human body.*

"Oh, Lady Morwenna, if you could only imagine the weapons we have now," Jillian murmured aloud. She kept reading, intrigued.

The early writings continued to ask after his welfare, to warn him to keep his head low, to care for her father, who was also among the men fighting for King Charles I. Subtly, the relationship began to change. He'd been home, and they had met again by a river or a spring. The words became more intimate, the pleas more desperate and more loving. Then came one that warned of the end.

Dearest...by all accounts it does not go well for the loyal troops of the King. Here, those afraid of Cromwell's retribution have already begun to denounce him. In all honesty, and without disloyalty, I must admit that I do not suppose he has been the best king. He has always been so adamant about the Divine Right of Kings. He believes that God allows him any extravagance he sees as fit. Alas, by God's right, he should have cared more for the plight of his people and less for his own excesses. But these are thoughts I share only with you. My father honors the King, and the man I honor above all others gives his faith, his loyalty, his sword—and is willing to give his life, as well—for the King. Be warned, beloved, as you face the fire and powder and bloodshed of the battles, that the tide has turned. Here, though he often makes me laugh with his presumption, Sir Walter walks the line, though evermore tottering toward the other side. What a righteous man he has become, simple in his wants and desires. He brought in a witch finder the other day before Sunday service. He was very angry when I laughed at such a notion. Only fools, he told me, refuse to see that the devil lives among us. He was so very angry when I laughed in his face. I know the King to whom I give my loyalty is heir to the very man, James I, who came to England believing with the deepest passion in the curses of witches and the work of devils and demons among us. Still, it is just a charade. Such a tragic comedy that a good God would ever allow such things to come to pass. I am well aware that there are laws, that witchcraft is illegal and punishable by death, but there are men, have always been men, sane men, even in the midst of the worst insanity, to refute the persecution of pathetic old women who have done no more than to raise a fist against injustice and mutter an angry curse. Sir Walter shakes his head at me and warns me that wise men, learned men, all recognize and fear the work of the Devil. He says that Satan himself walks among us, tempting us, moving us to acts of heresy and treachery and sin. Ah, but he swears as well that his sole purpose in life is to guard me, and my father's property. His love is the deep love of kinship, he says, and he will see that I learn the ways of the Lord—and of Cromwell, it is becoming apparent. For me, I am well enough. Sickness in the village keeps me busy; fighting with Sir Walter keeps me amused. They speak of torturing the poor old woman who was arrested, and my fight in her defense keeps my mind from the fact that I miss you, my love, body and soul. Ah, well, I must end now, for the soldiers stopping by shall leave, and I am entrusting this to a Private Goodman, who has sworn he will see it through to you. Ride with God, my love, and come home to me.

She did not sign her letter, or, if she had done so, the signature had not been transposed to the book. The next entries were from her diary again.

Jillian went through page after fascinating page. Lady Morwenna wrote about the time in which she lived, interesting facts about farming, and about her land, her home. *There is no place more beautiful than here, on the Welsh borderland, with the mountains, the streams, the rivers, trees, flowers and foliage. All the earth rolls. It is wild, it is verdant, gray on a harsh day, greener than emerald in the midst of summer when the grasses grow deep. How odd it is to think that years ago, an English King came here and brutalized all that he saw. Wales became part of his rule and we forever English, beneath the domination of Edward I, Hammer of the Scots and Butcher of the Welsh, though that was not to be written on his tomb. Yet now a King of England runs, and there is rumor that he runs for his life.*

There were more such entries, along with recipes for cures for wounds, her search for specific mushrooms to make tonics and salves, about the weather, blustering and calm, rain and sunshine and snow.

There came a heart-wrenching entry in which her father came home injured. Terribly sick, his mind wandering, his body was confined to bed. The lady's love for her father was touchingly evident. Along with her father's infirmity came a subtle change to life at the manor. *I have no time for the continual meetings Walter demands. I tend to Father, and ignore him. And yet, I wonder what ill I may be doing, for it has come to my ears, through faithful servants, that this usurper in my home becomes evermore entrenched, and grasps each day with greater strength for power here.*

She spoke no more of Walter for several days. She wrote about her father as he had been when she was little, so tender always, as she had grown. Yet even then, each entry was not finished until she had added in a prayer for her captain, still fighting the war, still commanding her father's loyal troops.

And then...

He should have been far away at battle. I missed him so. I ached for him, prayed for him, and told God that I longed for him to come to me, for my soul was so very distraught.

And then he came.

Aye, he came to me last night. I knew not that he had returned to the village, here where we lie so close to Wales. The moon was full when I awoke, I knew not why, and looked out the window. He was there, as tall as the light, shimmering in half armor, as powerful as the darkness beyond. I said nothing, but rose, and he came to me and he held me, and I felt the strength and the trembling in his arms. He went down upon his knees, his arms around me

*still, his head bowed. I removed his plumed hat, slid my
fingers through his hair and knelt down to join him. He
kissed me, wrapped me in his arms, loved me. And I knew
then that there were indeed miracles in this world. He told
me that in a fortnight I must meet him by the stream. It will
be summer then, and warm. He stayed the night, and there
was magic. But come the morning he was gone, and I was
bereft, afraid that I had dreamed, and yet, the essence of
him lingered, that haunting scent upon my sheets. I can
now scarcely wait for a fortnight to pass.*

There were no more entries until then.

*Dear God, I am so excited, so jubilant, it is near impossible
to keep the secret! That I am so loved, so cherished, is a gift
unequaled on earth. I thought myself insane, for there was
no talk of the armies or soldiers nearby, no Cavaliers or
Roundheads, and yet I believed. He had said that he would
come, and so I went to the river. There, in the moonlight, with
an owl crying out softly above, I found him. He had come with
just a few of his men. I ran to him and I greeted his friends,
and I told them all what I knew of the situation in London and
in the field. At first I wondered why he had come to me with
others to witness the night. Then I knew, for a priest stepped
forward, and my love went down upon one knee, a glimmer
of the moon's refection alight in his eyes, and he most humbly
asked for my hand—admitting, of course, that he was just a
commoner and I, after all, the daughter of a lord.*

*There, in the night, with the sounds of the river flowing and
the owls and the night birds, the scent of summer wildflow-
ers on the air, before God I swore to be his wife, and he vowed
to be my husband. He had brought sweet wine from the King
himself, and we drank and danced in the moonlight. Then all*

witnesses melted away, and we were alone in the soft yellow glow of the fire, surrounded by shadow. There was the comfort of the earth, the beauty of my love, the perfect warmth of his strength. And when at last the dawn itself came, he spoke gravely of the worry that plagued him. I assured him that I was well and strong and could manage Sir Walter and his underlings! He told me that he wished I would come with him, but I again argued that he must stay. I could not desert my beloved parent or my father's home. He swore that he loved me, held me, cradled me, and vowed that he would come, through wind and rain, snow or fire, that he would be with me, if ever I called, if ever there was the slightest need.

"Hey!"

The voice so startled Jillian that she dropped the book, feeling as guilty as if she had been involved in an illegal endeavor.

It was Griff, standing in the doorway.

"Hey back," she said, amazed that she was still trembling.

"You're late."

"Late?"

"For dinner."

"Dinner? It can't be."

"Jillian, trust me, it is. Would I lie to you? Well, would I lie to anyone about something so trivial as dinner?"

She grinned, closing the book. "No, you wouldn't lie about dinner."

"I don't really lie."

"You wouldn't *fib* about something so trivial as dinner."

He bowed gallantly, offering her his arm. She grinned and took it, and they started out of the library together. As they turned toward the stairs, Griff suddenly paused. She saw that he was surveying them in the mirror at the far end of the hall. "Great-looking couple," he teased.

Griff *was* handsome. Tall, blond, with sculpted features, generous lips, large, deep-set eyes. She matched him well, with her light hair, just touched with red, and her own slimness and height.

"You're just gorgeous," she said.

"Not like tall, dark Robert Marston, though, huh?"

"You're my cousin, and you know I adore you," she assured him. On tiptoe, she kissed his cheek.

He sighed. "Scrod awaits. Feathery light, perfectly dusted with bread crumbs. Of course, let me remind you that we're not all that closely related. If Tall, Dark and Overpaid falls short."

She laughed, but she was aware that the sound was just a little uneasy. She really was irritated by Robert's unfair attitude toward her family. Sure they all had their quirks. Eileen was most often sweet, always very talented—but a young woman with a chip on her shoulder, always worried that people weren't taking her seriously. Maybe she had the right. They'd both had to fight for their places with three male cousins. For all Griff's devil-may-care manner, he knew how to deal with buyers and could charm almost anyone into taking a chance. Then there was Daniel, so serious that he seldom knew how to play anymore. And Theo, the most steadfast, but with his own secret world.

But they were her family. All that she had. And they meant everything to her. Robert Marston couldn't change that with his ridiculous suspicions.

She was angry, she realized, especially angry that he seemed all but convinced she was the object of some foul plot, when he didn't believe in anything else. All of this had started on Halloween, with the tarot card reader. He didn't believe in the occult, in the miraculous, in anything beyond what was flesh and blood or tangible. But there he was, dreaming about *her* deceased husband's ghost—and casting blame upon her closest relations.

"Hey, are you with me?" Griff asked. "You *are* in love with him, aren't you."

"Him...?"

"Oh, please. Robert Marston."

"I—Griff, he just came into the company. I would never do anything so...quickly. I hardly even know him." She turned to him curiously. "What do you think of him?"

He shrugged. "He seems to be a good enough guy. Theo thinks well of him, and he should know. They went through college together."

"So you approve?"

He laughed. "Do you care if I approve?"

"Well, yeah, I guess I do. This family means a lot to me."

"Ah, there's Douglas speaking."

"Maybe. Doesn't the family matter to you?"

"More than I ever let on," he said. "More than I ever let on. Come on, let's get down to dinner. I like Robert just fine. As long as he stays out of my office and remembers that I'm a Llewellyn, lord of the castle. Well, okay, one of a pack of lords of the castle, but you know what I mean."

"Hey, up there!"

Douglas was at the foot of the stairs, calling them.

"Coming," Griff responded.

"Race you down," she challenged him.

They were probably lucky they didn't break their necks. Griff was beating Jillian, so she jumped up on the banister and slid down. He jumped down the last few steps and crashed to the floor, and she came sliding down on top of him. They were both laughing hysterically.

She hadn't realized that Robert was talking to her grandfather, that he was leaning against the door frame that led into the dining room. He watched her as she took Douglas's hand and rose, sobering.

"Shall we eat, since everyone is waiting?" Douglas asked pleasantly.

"Of course. Sorry." She hurried into the dining room.

Daniel had been talking earlier about heading back that night, but now, because of a slight warming that day and a freeze setting in, the roads were dangerous. Daniel paused as Douglas entered and everyone sat down. Douglas always said grace. He did so, and as soon as the prayer was completed, Daniel said, "Jilly, pass the potatoes, please. I wonder if I should still get on the road," he went on, returning to his previous topic.

"We'd planned on going back tomorrow," Robert reminded him.

"Yeah, I know. It's just that with all of us here, every exec in the office is out," Daniel said.

"Joe Murphy will be in. And Connie can handle a lot of what comes up," Robert said.

"Oh, yeah, Connie can handle a lot," Daniel murmured. Jillian found herself studying him, wondering what had been going on in his room. Was he seeing Connie? She couldn't believe it. Not here—not with Joe in the same house. Connie loved Joe. And they had those two beautiful little girls.

It couldn't have been Connie. It must have been Gracie.

"As long as someone is in by the afternoon," Theo said. "I wasn't planning on heading back at the crack of dawn—too cold, the roads will still be bad. But if we head straight into the city around ten, that should be all right."

"Sounds good to me," Eileen agreed.

"Can you believe it's this bad in early November?" Gracie Janner asked.

"Which means it will be great when we get around to filming in Florida," Griff commented.

"We're filming in Florida?" Jillian said.

"You didn't know?" Robert asked.

"Artists never pay attention at meetings," Griff said with an overly dramatic sigh.

* * *

Jillian was definitely angry with him, Robert realized as the night went on. Well, she loved her family, naturally, and he had attacked them. However, she was being a fool to ignore the danger.

Too many strange events were occurring. First the tarot card reader. Something just wasn't right there. Then there was the strange incident of the cat, which died in her office. Of natural causes? Of old age? The cat hadn't looked all that old to him. Had the others finding the cat inadvertently ruined the plan for her to find a black cat dead on her desk immediately following the Halloween tarot card reader?

The cat had been cremated, but there was a lot that could be learned from ashes, or so he hoped, because he wanted to know exactly how Jeeves had died.

Then, a fence down, a speeding truck. An accident? Maybe just a hoped-for accident?

Next, a broken saddle girth. On the horse anyone would have assumed she would be riding. Well, he'd taken the girth, and it was going to the cops, too, and he was damn well going to find out if normal wear and tear had been given a hand. A dangerous hand.

Jillian wouldn't listen to him, but at least she was nearby, where he could keep an eye on her.

He was tired, having spent the afternoon with Daniel, going over plans for the new campaign, but he didn't intend to leave her alone to go sliding down a banister again. He stayed up, not participating, but watching as the house was decorated. It was clearly Jillian's project, with Henry her right-hand man, and for once the others seemed willing to be the workforce. They did seem more like siblings than cousins, he had to admit. They joked, teased, argued, scuffled, ruffled feathers, mostly made up.

Daniel gave up for the night first. Soon after, Eileen and Gary gave in, and Jillian followed them.

She kissed her grandfather, then offered a cool "Good night, Robert."

He didn't stall, just bid Douglas good-night, thanking him for his hospitality.

"It was a working weekend—no thanks needed," Douglas told him gruffly.

"Maybe, but I enjoyed myself."

Great house, he thought as he went up the stairs. Great place to raise kids.

From his bedroom, he heard Jillian moving around in hers. Then he heard her settle down to bed. In the darkness, he pressed his temples. No mulled wine tonight, but he felt a slight buzz, anyway. He'd indulged in some hundred-and-fifty-year-old cognac with Douglas. Not that much, but it felt now as if he'd imbibed for hours.

"No ghosts tonight, okay?" he mocked himself aloud. He gave his pillow a punch and settled down, praying for some sleep.

A hot shower had done little to soothe her, and Jillian didn't think she would ever be able to sleep. She was still too bothered by the ride that morning, and by Robert's attitude. He had made no attempt to talk to her that night, but every time she'd looked at him, she'd known what he was thinking. *Fool.*

And still she wished she knew him better, longer. She wanted to argue with him the way she might if they were a real couple. Disagree, but not step away from him. Never let the sun go down on an argument, Milo had told her once. She believed it. And if she were really in love, if they were looking toward the future, they could retire to the same room, hash it out, even keep their own opposite opinions and still curl into bed together.

She reflected on the book she had been reading that afternoon, on Morwenna and her Michael. A war lay between them.

They were on the same side, but it tore their country apart, destroyed her home. And still what they had found between them gave them strength and faith through adversity.

Warmth...

She remembered the words of the diary entry.

He came to me last night....

Had she dozed? She opened her eyes, thinking, remembering, longing for the warmth.

And there he was, standing at the foot of her bed, in a long velour robe. Red, she thought, but she couldn't tell, because the shadows of the night were too thick. It was as if he had been waiting for her to see him; then he came slowly to her, and she sat up in bed, words on her lips but not falling. He hadn't asked her permission to be there; she had said they needed to keep their distance.

But she was glad he was there. So glad. She left the bed, going to meet him. She looked up at him, curling her arms around his waist, laying her face against his chest, where the soft velour of the robe and the bristle of short dark hair teased her nose and cheeks. His fingers moved into her hair and she felt his kiss on the top of her head. She looked up at him again, and once again, words hovered on her lips, but he laid his finger over them, and the deep, uncanny blue of his eyes fell upon her with a brooding depth of emotion that seemed to stop her heart from beating. He never said a word, but she was suddenly in his arms, feeling his kiss, meeting it with her own, feeling a burning hunger, desire that bordered on magic, the essence of dreams.

Then she was in his arms, lying with him, entangled with him. And there she found what was often so elusive in life. A touching beyond the flesh, an intimacy of the soul. She was where she belonged.

The warmth. Warmth she felt as such a sweet and poignant yearning. The feeling she had found in the pages of the book, the feeling she had envied.

Yes, it was just like the book....

* * *

She was alone when she awoke. Silence surrounded her, and a coolness in the room made her pause and think she had imagined the entire fantastic night. Her bed appeared almost completely unruffled, and she was dressed in a flannel nightgown.

Perplexed, she rose slowly, then glanced at her watch on the nightstand and went tearing for the shower. Almost nine. They had been talking about leaving by ten. Showered, dressed, makeup on, hair neatly smoothed, she was certain that she could not have imagined what had been. She stared at herself in the mirror, practicing ways to ask him about it. "What were you doing in my room last night?" she said aloud to her reflection. She cleared her throat and looked very seriously into the mirror. "I thought we had agreed to a certain distance, let some time go by?"

That was it. Just right.

She went downstairs. Voices from the kitchen assured her that the rest of the household had already gathered.

Robert was with Daniel, studying some shots as they separated photos into the pockets of a briefcase. "Down to those—final decisions at the office?"

"As soon as we get in, so we can have them ready to run ASAP."

"Hey, Jilly." Griff met her at the foot of the stairs. "We found one of Jeeves's old cat carriers. Were you taking Jeeves Junior on your lap, or do you want the carrier?"

"The carrier, I guess. If we stop for coffee or something along the way, he'll probably feel safer in an enclosed space. And it's cold. I can throw an old T-shirt in with him."

"Ah, good morning, Jillian," Douglas said.

Gracie came over to her, bearing a cup of coffee. "Just a touch of milk, Jillian, is that right?" She smiled eagerly.

Jillian accepted the coffee, noting that Gracie looked good, not so nervous. The country seemed to agree with her. Maybe she'd had time alone with Daniel.

Jillian suddenly hoped so. She hoped very much that it had been Gracie with her cousin the other night, not Connie. *It couldn't have been Connie!*

"It's perfect. Thank you, Gracie."

"My pleasure."

She sipped the coffee, walked over to Douglas, kissed his cheek and smiled.

"Grab some breakfast. I can see that Eileen is getting antsy," he said.

"I still can't believe it's this cold so early in the year. Makes you want to sit next to a fire and just roast," Eileen said.

Jillian shivered, as if icicles rather than fire danced along her spine. She walked around the table, selecting a scone. They were like a colony of ants in the kitchen, everyone moving about, taking a bite here and there, going for more coffee, packing up papers.

At last she managed to meet Robert at the coffeepot. Business Robert, Mr. Powerhouse in a perfectly cut suit, hair freshly washed and smoothed back, cheeks freshly shaven. He smiled at her as they met there, his eyes touching hers in a way that brought back a sweet rush of the same warmth that had filled the night with magic.

She wasn't insane.

"I..."

"You okay?" he asked softly.

"Yes, I, um...I just, well, I guess I'm a little surprised—though not disappointed—that you came to my room last night. I mean, we'd agreed to let some time go by."

He sipped his coffee, staring at her, a curious frown furrowing his forehead. For the longest time he didn't speak, those deep blue eyes simply pinning hers.

"Dear Lord, please tell me that I *was* with you!" she said a little desperately. Not at all what she had practiced in the mirror.

"Yes, you were with me," he said.

She exhaled a long breath of relief. "Then why...why did you look at me like that, as if I were...way off base?"

He set his coffee cup down, his attention entirely on her as he shook his head. "Jillian, I didn't come to your room."

"What? I don't understand. You just said you were with me."

"I didn't come to your room. You came to *mine*."

CHAPTER 11

They were just getting everything together to leave, when Agatha came out, wringing her hands.

"You can't go," she told them.

Robert was standing by the door with one of Eileen's suitcases in hand. A heavy suitcase.

Given that she traveled constantly on business, it was a bit strange that she didn't seem to have mastered the knack of traveling light, he thought. Especially since she had a room at this house and, according to Gary, a closet the size of a normal room full of clothing.

"Why can't we go?" he asked, setting the suitcase down.

They all stared at Agatha expectantly.

"There's a blizzard."

"A blizzard?" Daniel repeated incredulously.

"According to the news, there are gale force winds and six to eight inches of new snow on the way. It will all be over by this evening. You can't go. And even if you made it in, just who would you be doing business with? The whole city is shutting down."

"Are you sure?" Theo asked skeptically.

"Theodore Llewellyn, would I make up a blizzard?" Agatha said indignantly.

"Well, no, Aggie, but—"

"Come watch the Weather Network," Aggie suggested.

They did. Leaving the bags in the foyer, they walked back into the side parlor and stared at the large screen television.

A freak storm had indeed sprung up. The forecaster was talking about the rarity of such bitter weather so early in the season. "Looks like we can all expect a white Christmas," the weatherman intoned solemnly. "Because this stuff is going to be thick and heavy, and it will be around for quite a while."

"I'm going to go out and see Jimmy, make sure the stables are good and warm and that the generator is in good working order," Douglas said.

"No, Grandfather, I'll go. I want to see the horses, anyway."

"I'm not a doddering old fool, Jillian. I'm not going to trip over the steps," Douglas said a bit indignantly.

"We *are* old, and there's ice everywhere," Henry said. "Good idea, Jillian. Thank you."

"I'll make some calls," Daniel said with a sigh.

"Daniel, we're not losing anything. The city is closing down," Jillian said.

"I know, I know. I just want to get moving on all this. I think we've got a campaign that can add impressive percentages to our seasonal sales, and I admit, I'm impatient."

"I'm bored," Eileen said. "Ready to get back to work."

"It's always good to know that a weekend away with me is so important to you," Gary teased, shrugging philosophically.

Eileen had the grace to blush. "It's just cabin fever," she murmured.

"At least I'm in the cabin," he said.

"I'm going out to see Jimmy," Jillian said.

"I'll put on more coffee," Agatha announced.

"You can put some brandy in mine," Griff muttered. "If I'm going to be stuck in the house all day..." He let his voice trail off, then suddenly slipped an arm around Gracie, drawing her in close to him. "Hey, Gracie. Want to share a cup of spiked coffee with me? Get me through this awful day?"

"Mr. Llewellyn!" Gracie protested, flushing beet red. "Of course not. I'll be with Daniel, ready to take notes, make calls, whatever he needs, as he works."

"Gracie, nobody's going to be working much," Daniel assured her.

Robert noted that Jillian had watched the exchange with more curiosity than it deserved before slipping outside. He decided to follow her. "Daniel, do you want me to take on any of the calls? If not, with this wind whipping up, I think I'll just make sure Jillian is all right."

"Unfortunately, I think I can handle the day's work myself," Daniel said glumly.

Robert went out after Jillian. The wind had come up with a sudden ferocity. He drew his coat collar high around his neck. It wasn't a good day to travel, that much was for certain, and he was glad that no one had insisted on going back. He had dressed to head back into the office, and his low leather shoes were entirely wrong for the snow through which he walked, but his heavy woolen overcoat was decent enough protection. Still, he was glad when he reached the stable.

"Sounds like a banshee's lament out there," Jimmy called to him. "Won't be clearing 'til this evening, so they say." He and Jillian were standing by Crystal's stall.

"I was just talking to Jimmy about the tack room," Jillian said. She didn't seem particularly pleased to see Robert. She had been troubled all morning—ever since he had told her that she had visited him. It had amazed him to see the shock in her eyes. He thought back to how she'd arrived, given him the night of a lifetime, then disappeared back to her own room. He understood her need to go slow, but surely she understood that he was human and not interested in going slowly at all.

Maybe it was this house. Her husband had died here. Maybe her dreams were as insane as his own.

He leaned on the stall door, patting Crystal on the nose. "And what did Jimmy say about the tack room?"

"Same as I told you yesterday, Mr. Marston," Jimmy said. "This is a nice quiet area. Houses are few and far between, mostly owned by folks who've had 'em forever, who live their own lives and stick to themselves. Sure, we've got kids around. Teenagers. Someone busted the fence, right? But I've never seen anyone fooling around in the tack room. And Jilly here is the only one with a real interest in the horses anymore. Well, and Miss Connie. You know how the two of you always went riding together when you were young? She still loves the horses, same as you, Jilly."

"So Connie Murphy was down here this trip?" Robert asked.

"Yup, she was," Jimmy agreed cheerfully. "Joe stopped in, too. And Daniel came in with that skinny girl-Friday of his. Well, now, come to think of it, even Eileen came in with Gary— that Gary is a fine guy. One of his clients just came back from Trinidad, and he brought me some really fine rum. Think she'll ever marry the poor guy?" Jimmy asked with a wink.

"Who knows?" Jillian murmured. "But the point is, the tack room is seldom locked. And there are two seniors from the local high school who come out and exercise the horses a few times a week."

"And you think they might have knocked down that fence?" Robert asked skeptically.

"Our boys? No, sir," Jimmy objected. "They're good kids looking for extra money to help pay for college next year. That fence was run down by some fool going off the road. Go take a look for yourself. You'll see."

"You're still missing the point," Jillian persisted. "Anyone might have gotten in and tampered with a saddle girth." She sighed with exasperation. "I'm going back up to the house."

"I'll walk back with you. Jimmy, are you coming, too?"

"Not at the moment, Mr. Marston. I'll come up for supper later. I'm right fine here. I tend to prefer the company of horses to that of most people."

Robert nodded. "I can certainly see your point at times." He went on out after Jillian. She was obviously trying to escape him, but the wind had already grown stronger, the snowdrifts deeper. She was in such a hurry that she tripped, and he caught up with her.

She was wearing a beautiful gray woolen coat with a warm faux fur lining; it was covered in snow as he helped her to her feet, trying to dust her off.

"I'm all right," she told him.

"No," he protested gently, meeting her eyes. "No, I don't think you are, not at the moment."

"Look, Robert—"

"Jillian," he persisted, holding her by the shoulders. "I don't exactly know what criteria there are for really loving someone, for falling in love. I don't know. I do know that what I feel for you is fierce, and very real. I don't want to push you, but I don't want to stay away from you, either. And I'm afraid you really are in some kind of danger, so is it so terrible to let me be with you?"

"I..." She lowered her head, then looked back up at him. "I'm sorry. I just need a little space. I don't mind you being near me—well, I suppose that was rather obvious last night—but I just don't...I just...need space," she finished lamely.

"All right," he said, releasing her shoulders.

She turned and started back toward the house, then paused, back very stiff. She turned again, facing him. "And it's not that you're not...magic. I've never felt anything in my life like being with you."

She left him then, in the snow. He felt the wind swirl around him with a fury, the cold bite into his cheeks.

Then he followed her back to the house.

The day went well, considering that they were all restless and experiencing a bit of cabin fever.

The electricity stayed on until four p.m. Then the house was plunged into darkness. Aggie worried about the pheasants she was baking, but Jimmy had the generator ready to kick in, so they were fine.

Dinner was delicious, the mood mellow. Robert noted the closeness between Agatha and Henry as they served and cleared. When dinner was over, Jillian suddenly stood up and told Agatha and Henry to get themselves back out by the parlor fire, that they were to do nothing but watch a movie, kick back and sip hot toddies. She was taking over the kitchen.

It was interesting to note the way the rest of the group was ready to kick in. Eileen started scraping plates, while Griff was determined to clean counters. Daniel tackled the pots and pans with the same gusto he brought to a sales meeting. And with the same help. Gracie stood as ever by his side, ready to dry every pot that came her way.

Robert helped Jillian rinse the plates for the dishwasher. When they were done, Griff raided the cupboard for a bag of chocolate kisses, then searched the bar for whatever might be unusual. "Hey, we've got some blueberry brandy," he offered.

"Let's heat some and have it over ice cream," Eileen suggested.

"Cool," Griff agreed. "Robert?"

"Sure."

Soon everyone was seated around the table with ice cream and the blueberry brandy, along with chopped nuts and maraschino cherries that had turned up at the back of the pantry.

"So all of you spent time here growing up, right?" Gracie asked, giggling. She must have been imbibing a bit of the brandy before it had reached the table, Jillian thought. She had never seen the woman anything but completely sober and businesslike before.

"We did. Jillian spent the most time here," Daniel said.

"I lost both my parents when I was really young," she reminded them.

"Yes, poor Jilly..." Eileen murmured.

"Poor Grandfather. He lost his brother, then his brother's son. My mother, my dad, and then Eileen's father just a few years later. I pray I never have to lose a whole generation."

"If we ever have a generation to lose," Theo murmured. They all stared at him. "Well, have you seen any of us rushing into marriage?"

"Jillian was married," Robert reminded them.

"Yes, of course," Daniel said with a wave of his hand. "But we all knew that there would be no next generation from that marriage—" He lowered his head suddenly. "Sorry, Jillian."

"It's all right."

"There will be a younger generation," Gary said firmly.

"I, well, yes, of course—at the right time," Eileen murmured.

"We're so...all-business, aren't we," Griff murmured.

"We're not that old," Theo protested.

"We're not that young, either," Daniel countered. "We're both well over thirty now."

"Still, for a man," Gracie murmured, "that's not old at all. That's the prime of life."

"There has to be a younger generation," Griff said firmly,

"after all the years Douglas worked to create his empire. Hey, maybe that's my real role in life. You all are supposed to work, and I'm just supposed to go off and procreate!"

"Sure, sure," Jillian teased.

"Well, I am good at being suave and charming," Griff said. Then he seemed to grow solemn. "Most of the time," he added softly.

"Sometime in his life a girl must have turned him down," Daniel said dryly.

"With my big brother at the helm, I was always searching. Afraid I'd have to marry for money."

"Right. As if any of us would ever need to marry for money," Daniel said.

"Douglas could leave the whole kit and caboodle to the girls. They're his grandchildren," Griff commented.

"And why not you—for your charm?" Jillian asked.

"And why not Daniel—for his expertise?" Griff shot back

"And why not me, just because I work like a son of a gun?" Theo asked.

"And then we've got the new kid on the block—Mr. Marston," Griff said.

"A stockholder, not an heir," Robert reminded them. "Though Douglas could get sick to death of all of you and leave the whole thing to me," he suggested, sitting back with a grin.

"Or he could leave it all to a home for wayward cats," Jillian said, rising. "What difference does it make? Grandfather is in great shape. There are no guarantees in life. Any one of us could go before he does."

"So true," Eileen said soberly.

"Nope, not me. I'm not going anywhere," Griff said, and they all laughed.

"Well, I'm going off to bed. I assume we're trying to get out of here the same time tomorrow?" Jillian asked.

"Same time," Daniel answered for all of them.

"If anyone deserves the whole thing," Theo suddenly said, looking up, "I suppose it would be Daniel."

"He works the hardest," Jillian said lightly.

"We all work hard. Even Griff," Daniel said.

"And this is pathetic. Grandfather has been as good as gold to all of us," Jillian said, starting to feel offended on her grandfather's behalf.

"Jillian, we're just fooling around," Theo said.

Griff nudged him. "Right. Don't get on her bad side."

Jillian sighed with deep exasperation. "Good night. I am definitely leaving now."

She gave them all a wave and walked out of the room. Robert waited, intrigued by what might be said now that she had left the room.

"Jilly will get it all," Eileen said gloomily, resting her head on the table. "He likes her best."

Griff stroked Eileen's hair. "What's not to like? Let's see, she's beautiful, bright, talented, socially aware, adored by all who meet her—and if that's not enough, we're about to make her famous."

"Yeah. I'm behind it," Eileen said with a grimace. "What's the matter with me?"

"It's excellent work, Eileen," Robert commented, watching her.

"Thanks. I am good, huh? Well, of course..." She studied him carefully for a moment. "You two looking like perfect Ken and Barbie dolls doesn't hurt."

"That's right. The whole world is going to know you, too, Robert," Griff said.

"The whole world knows his name already—*Fortune* 500," Theo reminded them.

"But now they'll know he's great-looking, too," Eileen murmured.

"Hey, get your eyes off him," Gary teased.

"I'm sorry, were you talking to me?" Eileen asked innocently. They all burst into laughter. "Just kidding," she added quickly.

"Daniel is still the hardest working," Gracie commented quietly.

"Gracie!" Daniel protested. He stood. "I'm off to bed, as well. Good night, everyone."

Robert left the room a few minutes later and went upstairs, too. He paused outside Jillian's door. There were no sounds from within. He walked on to his own room. For a long time he stared out the window at the snow. After a while he prepared for bed and slid beneath the covers. He was tired but restless. Tomorrow was going to be a long day. There was a lot of time to be made up; one day at this point was very important, with Christmas so close.

Why wouldn't Jillian trust him? Why did she pull away from him? Was it because of her husband's death, her feeling that she should still be in mourning? Damn, he was worn out. He wished she were there, that he would look up and see that she had come into the room again. But she wasn't coming, not tonight. Still, he was wide awake, staring at the ceiling.

At least, he thought he was wide awake. He heard a noise and looked toward the window, then nearly fell out of bed. His visitor had arrived again. The ghost of Milo Anderson was looking out at the snow, as he had done just moments before. Moments? Hours? He was deeply asleep, dreaming again. God, but he couldn't wait to get out of this house.

The ghost heard him and turned.

Robert groaned.

"Ah, paying attention at last."

"Milo, you're turning into a major pain."

"Sorry, but I have to get you to pay attention. To believe."

"Believe what?"

"You're in danger of repeating the past."

"There is no past."

"You're stubborn. You refuse to see. Hundreds of years ago, men believed the world was flat—they couldn't see that it was round. Let's assume that you believe in God. Do you see him? No. Can any man explain what happens after life leaves the body, when energy is gone, when the heart ceases to beat?"

"Science—"

"Scientists are the first to admit they don't have all the answers."

"Milo, I need some sleep. I'm supposed to be protecting Jillian, and I'll do a much better job if I don't have to spend all night arguing with you. Go haunt Jillian. She loved you. She *still* loves you."

The ghost was strangely quiet. Then he said, "I miss her very much."

"Then, go haunt her."

"I don't seem to be able to."

"Look, Milo, I used to be completely sane, efficient, intelligent, but you're making me crazy. I don't understand this. You say Jillian is in danger, that we're all in danger of repeating the past. What past? I never knew Jillian. And if Jillian *is* in danger, why can't you figure out a way to warn her? Why are you so busy warning me?"

"Well, you love her, don't you?" the ghost said, as if it was a ridiculous question.

"Yes, but you did, too, didn't you? You still do, I suppose. Wait a minute. I still don't believe this. I'm going to wake up and you'll be gone."

"Naturally I'll be gone, I'm a ghost. These appearance things aren't easy, and apparently you're the only one to whom I can appear."

"That makes no sense."

"Maybe it's because you're the most guilty."

"The most guilty?" Robert flared angrily. "Guilty of caring about her? This makes no sense. Neither do you. Suddenly appearing—"

"It wasn't suddenly. I needed all year to get this far, to find out what I was still doing here, to begin to understand."

"Now you've really lost me."

Milo threw up his arms. "There's the problem. Don't you see? Anytime something isn't right there—right before your eyes—you think it doesn't exist. You say you have faith, but you have no faith."

"Yes, I do. I'm not sure exactly what I believe, but who is? Maybe there is a God, one supreme being, and maybe death is just a dark void and nothing more."

"You are one stubborn bastard."

"Excuse me?"

"Sorry. No, I'm not sorry. You're a fool. Everything out there is belief. Love is belief. When it's real, totally unselfish and giving, it's a damn miracle."

"Oh, great, I don't believe in voodoo, so now I'm an evil person incapable of real emotion?"

"Evil? No, not evil. But guilty, yes. You see, she died before."

"Who?"

"Jillian, of course."

Robert felt a chill shoot through him unlike anything he had ever felt before. "She died before? You mean she died and was resuscitated? When? As a child?"

Milo was shaking his head with impatience. "No, no. Robert Marston, there you are again, exactly as you were before. A good man, a sane man, passionate on behalf of what he sees as justice, ready to do what is required of him. Ready to march off to war and lead the troops."

Robert threw up his own hands. "I'm arguing with a ghost. I am losing my mind. Milo, I'm going to force myself into deeper sleep. I will not dream you anymore, do you understand?"

Milo leaned forward. "I don't have all the answers. I wish I did. I'm here because, well, because Jillian shook the snow globe."

"The snow globe?"

"It's in her bedroom in the city. Great piece. I found it at a flea market one day, and I knew I had to get it for her. I got a feeling when I shook it...as if I'd been in that scene before, you know?"

"No, I don't know."

"You're impossible to work with. A facts-and-numbers man. Pity you couldn't have been an artist."

"Sorry."

"Well, we get what we're dealt, right?"

Get what we're dealt. He had an uneasy flashback to the tarot card reader.

"Go away, Milo," he murmured.

"You go away, if you're going to be worthless. This is my room, after all."

Robert jerked up suddenly, staring at the apparition. "*Your* room? You mean, you're in here all the time?"

"No, no, no, don't go getting hot under the collar like that. I wasn't around last night, if that's what you mean. *Please!*"

Robert leaned back. "Then, go away now, will you?"

The ghost paid no attention. "I've tried to get close to her. Even before this weekend. She's why I'm still here. We all come back to...to get it right. And it seems we go in the same groups, similar relationships. And the same instincts are there, which is why she's in danger. She's a threat, but I haven't exactly figured out to whom this time. That's the problem. You have to find out."

"I *am* finding out. I brought the cat's ashes to a cop friend. He's having them analyzed. I have the broken girth in my overnight bag, and I'll take it to the cops, too. I don't have the license number of the truck that went by, but we know that the fence was hit by a car. I'm here. I'll be here. Near her. By her side, when she needs me."

"That's what you said before."

There was a sound from the darkness illuminated only by the thin sliver of light coming in from the bathroom, where he had left the door ajar. Robert bolted up to a sitting position, shivering, giving himself a mental shake. Sleeping. He'd been sleeping. Dreaming. Something in his subconscious tormenting his sleep.

He was awake now, and there were no ghosts with whom to share the questions plaguing his mind.

There had been a real sound.

He looked toward the bedroom door.

She was there again. Jillian. Eyes wide, red-gold hair catching what there was of the light, shimmering down her shoulders, cascading over her back.

She closed the door and walked over to him.

"Jillian..."

"Shh." She pressed a finger to his lips and she crawled in beside him.

He groaned softly, thinking he should resist, thinking resistance would be insane. The perfume of her hair was intoxicating. The sweetness of her flesh was more than he could bear. She didn't want to talk right now. Fine. They would talk tomorrow. And the next day. And the next. He was in love with her. Each time he touched her, he longed to touch her again. The sound of her voice was unique; he could get lost in her eyes. He could no more send her away than he could cut off his own right hand.

Despite her nearness he actually leapt from the bed, strode to the bathroom and looked behind the shower curtain. He checked out the closet.

They were alone. Completely alone.

Even so, when he walked to the bed to crawl back in, he paused instead, then scooped her into his arms.

Her green eyes widened in question.

"I'm coming to your room tonight," he told her.

Hours later, he was still awake, staring into the darkness. She was asleep with her head on his chest, soft hair tangled over his flesh. He held her close, with the deepest sense of tenderness. He'd never known what it was like to feel this kind of commitment to another human being. It was a strange, beautiful and overwhelming sensation.

"I am in love," he murmured aloud. "And I am losing my mind. Absolutely losing my mind."

In a while, wrapped in her arms, he slept at last.

No ghosts haunted him this time.

Just visions of the snow. Of horses, running against the stark whiteness on a winter's day. He could feel a heartbeat, feel the thunder of the horses' hooves.

He was running, running, running....

He had to get there, had to get there.

He just didn't know where.

Jillian's alarm clock rang all too early. It was time to return to the city.

C H A P T E R   1 2

Tuesday was completely chaotic.

They were so busy, in fact, that Robert had done little more than watch Jillian when he could, find out that she was leaving with Douglas when he had to work late himself, and then, when he was back at his apartment, call Henry to make sure that she was home safely. Not surprisingly, away from the house in Connecticut, what had seemed incredibly real started looking ridiculous. There were certainly no further visitations.

One thing really bothered him, though. When he tore through his overnight bag, he couldn't find the girth. He emptied his bag, his briefcase, tried every compartment, big and small. He went over his own actions again and again. When he had left the stables that day, he'd tucked it into an inner coat pocket. In his room, he'd packed it; he was certain of it.

And now it was gone.

He started wondering if he was really losing his mind. That maybe he hadn't packed it. He called the house in Connecticut, asking Jimmy if he had left it somewhere. He talked to Agatha, asking her to search his room.

He didn't have it, and neither of them could find it.

Perplexed, he tried to remember if anyone had been in his room. Not that he knew about. But anyone in the house might have slipped in. He hadn't kept it locked.

It was frustrating. More, it was, in his mind, proof that Jillian really was in danger.

Wednesday, business meetings seemed all-consuming. He barely saw Jillian, and once again he worked late. She left the office with Douglas, so Robert had no reason to worry about her.

Thursday he stopped by her office. No one was there to announce him, so he just walked on in. She was working at her easel, sketching, and she was completely absorbed in what she was doing. He walked over to see the design that was occupying her, but she wasn't working on a design. She had done a sketch. Working with charcoals, she had drawn a woman in a long flowing cape, seated on a horse, reaching down to touch a man who stood beside her. It was a beautiful piece, evocative, every bit as good as the work Brad Casey had done that had led to the new ad campaign.

"That's gorgeous," he told her.

She started and swung around. She hadn't known that he was there. "Thanks. I'm supposed to be working, but..." She flipped over the sheet she had been working on.

She seemed disconcerted that he had interrupted her; her smile seemed forced.

"So...what's up?"

"Want to do dinner tonight?"

"Sure. Sounds great."

"You know we're heading for Florida this weekend, right?"

"Yup. Looking forward to it," she told him.

"Think we can get out of here between six and six-thirty?"

"I'll be ready to go," she promised him.

Not sure why he felt disturbed, he left her.

Jillian didn't know why both Douglas and Robert seemed so edgy, but they were like a pair of overprotective parents, watching her constantly. Wanting her with them as often as possible.

Still, she loved her grandfather, so she took his attention in stride.

And every minute of every day, she knew with greater certainty that she wanted to spend her life with Robert. She couldn't understand why she sometimes shrank from him, why she felt at times that she had to run, when she so wanted to lean against him, to be totally passionate with him, laugh with him, talk to him, lie with him, bask in his scent, in his warmth. Dinner? Of course she wanted to join him for dinner.

She thought, though, that she should tell Douglas her plans, so he wouldn't wait for her. When she walked down the hallway to find him, Amelia wasn't at her desk, so Jillian opened the door to her grandfather's office. Douglas wasn't there, but Eileen and Griff were. They didn't even see her at first, they were so busy reading a paper that she presumed had come from the open right-hand drawer of his desk.

"What's up?" she asked.

Eileen gasped, spinning around.

Griff slammed the drawer shut on his own hand.

"Jillian!" Eileen said.

"Yeah. What's up? What's so fascinating?"

She started walking toward the desk.

Griff produced a paper. "Schedule. For Florida. We get in Friday night around nine. Miami International is a zoo, so they say, but we should make South Beach by ten, ten-thirty. Great place to play. Wonderful clubs."

"And you can just people watch," Eileen said quickly. She frowned. "Well, except for you—you have to get your beauty sleep. We start shooting at eight a.m."

"Don't you have to be there, too?" Jillian enquired.

"Yes, of course," Eileen said.

"But it won't matter what we look like," Griff added quickly.

"Ah."

"Oh, I guess we can let Jillian go clubbing a little bit," Eileen said to Griff.

"Yeah, we'll have a good makeup artist, someone to hide shadows under her eyes, the evidence of a hangover, whatever."

"Gee, thanks," Jillian murmured. "Where's Douglas?"

"Don't know," Griff said. "Do you, Eileen?"

"No, I don't."

Conversation stalled at that point, though they weren't leaving, that much was clear. So Jillian decided she might as well go; she could find out what they were up to later.

As she walked down the hallway, she passed the executive kitchen and decided to slip in for coffee. She poured herself a cup, then smiled when Jeeves Junior walked in, stretched and leapt up on the table as if he owned the place. "Hey, fellow. I'm so sorry about your predecessor, but it's good to have you here." She gave him a stroke and set him down.

Gracie came in just then, humming. She saw the cat, stopped dead and let out a scream, clutching her throat.

"Gracie! It's the new guy," Jillian said soothingly.

Gracie stared at her as if just realizing Jillian was there. "Oh, oh, of course, Ms. Llewellyn."

"Jillian, Gracie."

"Jillian, yes. I forgot. He just gave me such a turn."

"*You* gave *me* a turn. You looked as if you'd seen a ghost."

"Well, I was fond of Jeeves."

"Me, too. I guess we'll have to get just as fond of this guy."

"I'm sure I will, in time."

"Well, I'd better get back to work."

"Oh, me, too. There's so much to do before we go to Florida. Imagine, getting to go to Florida on business in the middle of all this snow."

"Oh, you're coming?" Jillian said, then wished she hadn't.

Gracie's face fell instantly. "It's all right with you, isn't it?"

"Of course it's all right with me. I'm glad you're coming."

"Is Connie coming?"

"You know, I haven't even talked to her about it. I've been so busy."

That was a lie. She *had been* working, of course, but she'd also been sketching, something she hadn't done in a long time. She'd barely noticed Connie, working away in her cubicle. They'd talked, of course. But...well, she had to admit it; she felt uncomfortable after her suspicions over the weekend.

"Connie and Joe have the kids, you know," she said. "We'll see."

She headed for her own office but stopped instead at Connie's cubicle. She knocked and poked her head in. Connie had been busy at her computer, but she quickly looked up. Her pretty round cheeks looked pinched. Her face seemed strained.

"You okay?" Jillian asked.

"Sure. Of course."

"You don't look okay."

"It's nothing."

"I wanted to check with you about this weekend. Are you coming to Florida?"

"You don't really need me, do you? Of course, Joe is going. He's the man, and men work, right?"

"Connie, is something wrong between you and Joe?" Jillian asked.

She thought that Connie waited just a minute too long to reply.

"No, no, of course not. Joe and I are just like Mickey and Minnie Mouse—together forever, with our two adorable little baby mice. We have a terrific life. What could be wrong?"

"Connie, you're talking to me. Your best friend."

"And my boss."

"Connie!"

"I'm sorry. I'm just feeling a little pressured here. I want to go, but I feel like I've been ignoring my kids. That's why we left Connecticut early."

Jillian hesitated just a minute, then asked, "Connie, were you in Daniel's room last weekend?"

"What?" Connie gasped, staring at her.

Was there a flash of guilt in her eyes? Jillian wondered.

"Were you with Daniel—having some kind of argument with him—in Connecticut?"

Connie shook her head vehemently. "No. Why would you think that?"

"I just...I thought I heard your voice."

Connie shook her head again, staring at the computer. "No, although..." She looked up, offering Jillian a smile. "It looks like you and Robert Marston might be dynasty material, after all."

Jillian exhaled. "I do...like him. Very much."

Connie laughed. "Hey, it's me, remember? *Your* best friend. You're doing a lot more than 'liking' him."

Jillian shrugged. "Connie?"

"Yeah?"

"Do *you* like him?"

"Mr. Marston? Sure. He's gorgeous. Good voice—really sexy. And great buns, looks good in clothes—and out of them, I imagine," she teased. Then she sobered. "So what's the matter?"

"I don't know."

"Come on, you can tell me."

"No, I can't because I don't know. Every once in a while, I'm just a little...afraid."

"Everyone is afraid. Falling in love is the scariest thing you'll ever do."

"I don't mean it that way. I don't know, it...oh, never mind." She started to leave, then turned back. "Listen, Connie, no pressure intended. I'd love to have you in Florida, if you can come. I like having you helping me rather than some stranger. But if it causes a problem with the kids, stay home."

"Thanks. I'm just not sure yet."

"When you are, let me know."

"Thanks."

Jillian nodded and left. Glancing at her watch, she decided to head back to Douglas's office. But as she walked down the hall, she saw Daniel striding her way, his expression grim. He was obviously very angry.

He didn't look any happier when he saw her.

"Hey, is there anything I can do?" she asked quietly.

He stopped, staring at her. "What?"

"You look upset about something. Can I do anything?"

"No, no, you can't." He gazed back toward Douglas's office, then stared at her. "Actually, you know what? You can quit being so damn perfect, that's what you can do."

"What?"

He exhaled sharply. "Sorry. Never mind. It isn't your fault. It has nothing to do with you. He just...I won't stay if someone else is going to run my life, that's all. Some things are personal, and I don't give a damn what he's done for us. Look, never mind. I'm just in a rotten mood. I'll get over it."

He walked past her then, striding down the hall to his own office.

The door slammed. Jillian winced, then headed back toward Douglas's office, where Amelia told her he was in a private meeting with his attorneys and had specifically asked not to be disturbed.

"Just tell him for me, please, that I'm going out to dinner, and not to wait for me."

"Sure, Jillian. I'm glad you told me. He worries about you, you know."

"I wish he wouldn't."

Amelia just smiled. "No chance of that, dear."

At last Jillian returned to her own office. And for the remaining hour and a half of the day, she settled down to work.

That night, Robert took Jillian to one of his favorite Italian restaurants in the theater district. She seemed happy and at ease, excited about Florida.

"It's getting better here this weekend, can you imagine? After all this snow, it's supposed to go up into the fifties. But Florida is in the eighties. I can't wait."

Her smile was beautiful, her enthusiasm real. "So you like it hot?"

"Well, I like it cold, too," she responded, grinning. "I love the snow, a fire in a hearth. And Christmas. But, yes, I do love the heat. Swimming pools, a Jacuzzi late at night." She sipped her wine, eyes bright as she looked at him. "Do you like warm weather?"

He nodded. "Fishing, boating, snorkeling, swimming, whatever."

"It will be fun. Different."

"Nice to get away somewhere other than Connecticut," he said, watching her closely.

Her smile slipped a little. "I love the house in Connecticut."

Then she turned the conversation in another direction, and he let her, feeling there was nothing to be learned from her reaction, anyway, other than that, whether she would admit it or not, the weekend's events had made her uneasy.

When they left the restaurant, he asked her to go home with him. She hesitated.

"Look, I'm not trying to push you—"

"No," she said quickly. "I want to come."

"Then..."

"I don't have any clothes or makeup or anything that I need at your place."

He grinned, feeling vastly relieved. "You can't need that much makeup, but we could drive by your house—"

"Then I'd feel too...obvious going back out."

"There's always a shop open somewhere in New York City."

"You have a point there."

So they shopped. They prowled a few clothing stores, then stopped by a deli, picking out fruit together for the morning, plus croissants and bagels. Finally they made their way to his place, where he lit the fire, and they sipped wine and talked and made love.

He was sleeping deeply later when she woke up screaming. Bloodcurdling shrieks sent him bolting from the bed, blinking furiously, looking around, then grasping her shoulders and shaking her. She was still asleep, he thought. She was dreaming. There was nothing—no one—in his bedroom. In a minute, she would wake everyone in the building. She would wake the damn dead.

"Jillian. Jillian!"

She stared at him, shivering fiercely. He could see the terror in her eyes.

"It's burning. The fire is burning. We've got to get out."

"Jillian, there is no fire."

"Out. We've got to get out. We've got to!"

"No." He shook her slightly, trying to wake her. He was breathing raggedly himself, and his heart was thumping. He dragged his fingers through his hair, trying to smooth it back. "Jillian, please, listen to me. There is no fire."

She stared at him. Swallowed. Looked around the room.

Her head fell, and she stared down at the sheets, smoothing them with her fingers. "I—I—God, I'm sorry," she whispered.

"It's all right. You were dreaming. Of course, in a few minutes someone would have broken down my door and hauled me away for attempted murder—but hey, it's all right."

"Robert..."

"Jillian, I'm joking. It's okay, honestly. You were dreaming. You had a nightmare about a fire, and you woke up screaming." He put his arms around her, holding her close, then whispered against her ear, "Jillian, it's all right. It's over."

They lay down together. He loved the way she curled against him, one hand on his chest, knuckles resting against his skin. Hair like a soft web around him. One long leg lightly cast over his. He loved the feel of her, flesh against flesh. He smoothed her hair, still soothing her.

"Everyone dreams," he said softly. "Hell, I told you. I kept dreaming about Milo's ghost up in Connecticut."

"How do you know he wasn't a real ghost?"

"Because—"

"Of course. You don't believe in ghosts."

"Dreams come from the subconscious, Jillian. We talked a lot about Milo, so he appeared."

"So you get to have discussions with Milo, and I get to dream about fire."

"Did you ever burn yourself as a child?" he asked.

"No, Sigmund, I didn't," she replied, laughing.

He smiled, his arm tightening around her. "See?" he asked softly. "You're feeling better already."

"Yes, but..."

"But what?"

"I've had the dream before."

"Before? Recently?"

"Yes."

"And what happens in the dream?"

"Nothing. Just fire. I can smell it. Then I can feel it. It's very real, and then I start to scream."

"But it *isn't* real," he said, kissing the top of her head. "You're safe," he told her with soft vehemence. "You're with me."

She didn't answer.

After a while, he heard her even breathing and decided she was sleeping.

In time, he slept himself.

Maybe there were such things as miracles. Little miracles, anyway, Robert thought, feeling the sun beat down on the bare skin of his chest, wet sand between his toes, and a pleasant breeze stirring the air around him.

Miami was having the perfect winter. Temperatures had softened from deadening heat to a majestic warmth. Skies were clear. Gloriously blue. In fact, it was almost impossible to tell where sea and sky met, the colors of each were so rich, so clear, so beautiful. The days here were simply magnificent. And at the moment, he had nothing to do but enjoy himself. No camera angles to check on, no marketing decisions to be made. He was leaving everything entirely to the others, while he enjoyed the small miracle of Miami and his new job as a male model.

In Connecticut, he had gotten to be the dark-haired guy in the tux.

Now he was getting to be the dark-haired guy in the bathing trunks.

They'd found the perfect location. A white sand beach, palm trees, glorious scenery. This early in the morning, the stretch of sand surrounding them was nearly deserted. It was too early for tourist season to have really gotten going—most snowbirds flocked south just before Christmas, or just after it. So they had paradise all to themselves.

Jillian looked spectacular. Despite the scantiness of her bathing attire, the romantic mood that Brad had so perfectly evoked in his drawings remained. The director they'd hired for the video was very funny, contorting himself every which way to show them how to be sexy and romantic. His antics amused Jillian, and the light in her eyes and the subtle smile that curved her lips each time Robert walked toward her on camera was better than anything any model could have achieved.

He knew, of course, that deep down, she was laughing at him, at herself, at the sheer amusement that, after everything, they were being taught how to be romantic, sensual, totally involved with one another.

It had been a great trip so far. The plane had taken off on time—another small miracle. They had landed, gone to the hotel, then headed out by ten-thirty, which was, by Miami standards, just when things were beginning to heat up. They went to several of the dance clubs, where salsa and the tango were hot. He wasn't much of a dancer himself, but the Llewellyns had all taken lessons while they were growing up, so they were very good. He stood back, watching while Griff and Jillian tore up the floor and all but brought down the house. Later both Jillian and Eileen tried to teach him steps, though to very little avail. Griff was popular, teaching Gracie what he could and making Connie look good when he took her out on the floor, though Connie told Robert she had never been able to dance the way Jillian could.

"I can out-swim her, though," Connie had told him with a grin. "I'll show you—I think we get some beach time tomorrow."

They did. Daniel had scheduled the filming and photo shoots through two. After that, they were free. They had planned on steaks that night at a steak house right on South

Beach, and after that, they were going to go dancing again, then sit at an outdoor café and people watch—something Eileen was dying to do.

They had finished with the stills about two hours ago, and even with the camera setups, the angles, and all the chefs back in the kitchen, they had nearly wrapped up the video. Jillian and he had gotten things down to a rhythm by now. At the moment, she was leaning against a coconut palm, a fan lightly lifting her hair in imitation of an island breeze. She was wearing a crimson print bikini with a flowing serape skirt that caught the breeze and made her look more beautiful than ever. He walked up to her with the locket and she said the line; then they did it again and it was his turn to speak.

The director called for background, places, and then started the countdown. "Five, four, three—" with the "two" and the "one" being silent.

Robert started walking toward Jillian, just as he had done several times already.

"Watch out!" someone suddenly shouted.

"What the hell?" the cameraman protested.

Robert heard a strange cracking sound. Then he saw that a huge palm branch with a cluster of coconuts was coming down—straight for Jillian. He bounded into action.

Jillian heard the sound, but didn't see the danger. She was looking around, tense, ready to run, but uncertain of which way. The others were shouting, starting to surge forward en masse, but they would never make it; he was the only one with a chance, and a slim chance at that.

Seconds...split seconds. He flew toward Jillian, yet it seemed as if she was thrust out of the way even before he reached her and could throw himself against her to push her out of the way.

The branch fell with a whoosh, then hit the sand like thunder.

Sand spewed over the two of them. After a second he lifted

his head and looked at Jillian. She was staring up at him with wide eyes, unable to speak for shock.

The others massed around them, everyone talking, hands reaching out to them. Daniel brushed past them, his eyes on Jillian, reaching for her hands to help her up. "Jillian, are you all right?"

"I'm fine. Thanks to Robert."

Daniel blinked and looked at Robert, who was just getting to his feet. He gripped his hand, shook it. "Thank you, man. Here we are again...in your debt."

"No one is in my debt," Robert said tersely, breaking through the throng. He went stalking over to the downed branch, hunkered low and reached for it, fingering the break.

"Robert?" Jillian was at his side, shaking his shoulder. "Robert, what is the matter with you? It's a broken branch. No one did anything," she added in an urgent whisper. "The wind, maybe. Gravity."

He swore beneath his breath. It looked like a natural break. The branch didn't look cut. It had fallen from fairly high up. Someone would have to have known exactly where they were going to film, where Jillian was going to stand, to have tampered with the tree. And even then, reaching the branch would have been one hell of a feat.

Of course, lots of people had known where they would be filming. It hadn't been a secret. They had permits, they had booked crews, they even had off-duty police to cordon off the area.

The cop hired to watch the traffic was at their side now. "Sometimes storms weaken the branches," he said. "You two all right?" He was an older officer, who spoke quietly, with certainty.

Robert met the cop's eyes. If he persisted with his angry suspicions at the moment, he would find himself locked up—or worse. Jillian would retreat from him, angry that he was casting aspersions on her precious family again. He was tempted to tell her that it was her own grandfather who'd first been suspicious of them.

He didn't say anything, simply nodded at the officer, rising stiffly. "Yeah. Yeah, I'm sure you're right."

"You sure you two are all right?" the officer persisted.

"We're fine," Jillian insisted.

"Good thing Grandfather decided to stay at the hotel this morning," Eileen said. "This might have given him a heart attack."

"It almost gave *me* a heart attack," Theo insisted.

"Let's get this cleared up," Joe Murphy suggested. He paused, looking back at Daniel. "That is, if you want to go on. We can probably get permission to continue tomorrow morning."

"Yeah. I think we should stop," Daniel said.

"Wait," Griff protested. "I have a date tonight after dinner—a late date. Jilly's a trooper. She isn't going to let a little near-death experience stop her from working—right, Jillian?"

"I'm perfectly fine, and more than willing to go on," Jillian said. "That is...Robert, if you are."

He felt like telling them all to stop and get serious—something sure as hell was going on. But they would all just look at him as if he were crazy, and when he needed his credibility, really needed it, he wouldn't have any.

"Sure. Sure, Jillian. If that's what you want."

"So, Daniel, do we continue the shoot?" Gracie asked, turning over her page of notes.

"Yes, Gracie, we're going ahead," Connie said, sounding irritated. She was by Jillian's side by then, dusting sand from her. "Stand still, it's not so bad."

"Hey, Brad, you're the artist," Daniel called. "Help me smooth out this sand."

Brad, who had seemed frozen, his eyes only on Jillian, sprang to life.

The makeup artist had come over to Robert and Jillian, as well. She dusted sand from Robert while she waited for Connie to finish with Jillian, then started on her hair. Joe, Griff, Theo and some of the crew cleared the filming area until there was no sign of the branch or the coconuts.

"Continuity?" the director called.

One of his assistants, looking through the camera, called out, "Clear as a bell. We're back in business."

"All right, then, let's finish up here."

The count came again. "Five, four, three..." Silent two. Silent one. Robert moved, but he was too tense. They had to do it again.

And again.

On the fifth take, he got it right. The others were jubilant. They were done. As they congratulated one another, everyone seemed to have forgotten all about the branch that had fallen. Everyone but him.

They were heading back to the hotel for piña coladas by the pool and water sports on the beach for those in the mood.

Forty-five minutes later, he was listening to a calypso band, drinking a Bud and brooding behind his dark glasses. Jillian was at his side, wearing a floppy straw hat and shades, and sipping a drink out of a plastic, shark-themed take-home glass. She squeezed his hand.

"Robert?"

"Hmm?"

"Please—it was an act of God, not the attack of the killer co-conuts."

Was she looking at him anxiously from beneath those shades? He shook his head, leaning back. "Did you...?"

"What?"

He sat up, swinging his legs around so that he faced her. "Did you feel as if you were pushed before I actually got there?" he asked.

"What?" she repeated, frowning.

"It seemed as if you went flying out of danger before I actually reached you."

"Maybe I jumped," she murmured.

But she hadn't jumped. Robert would have sworn to that. Oh hell, maybe he was losing it. After all, so far he hadn't come up with any evidence of foul play anywhere. Of course, he still hadn't heard back about the ashes he'd taken from the company furnace. That was all he had to go on, since he couldn't find the missing girth.

And even if he were to find out something from the ashes, what could he prove?

That someone had murdered a cat?

A shadow fell over them. "Jillian?" It was Connie. "Race you."

"You can beat me."

"I know. So let me get my ego boosted."

Jillian laughed, rising, setting her drink down and tossing her glasses, wraparound and hat onto her chair. Her long-legged, beautiful stride brought her to the pool. She dived in, taking the lead, but Connie caught up and passed her, just at the end of the large, rectangular pool.

They both laughed. Tried it again. Jillian was smooth and sleek in the water, but Connie was faster. A real swimmer. The two were in the midst of a splashing fight when Joe came up to the pool. "Hey, Griff has rented wave runners, down at the dock by the beach. Come on."

The women climbed out of the water. Jillian came jogging back toward Robert, but he was already rising, anxious about what could happen out on the ocean.

"I've never ridden a wave runner," she called to him. "Come on—it will be fun."

"Jillian..."

She had already turned and was running, arm-in-arm with Connie, down the sand to the water.

He followed behind.

Jillian was already crawling on behind Griff.

For some reason, Daniel had Connie Murphy behind him. Joe Murphy was riding alone, and Theo had Gracie. Eileen and Gary were together; and there was a leftover Jet Ski for him.

"Robert, come on," Griff called.

Robert felt a strange reluctance, but Jillian was headed out there. He hopped aboard. He had used a Jet Ski before, and now he revved his instantly to life and followed after them.

He drew abreast of Griff. He didn't know why, but he remained edgy, his heart nearly in his throat. Griff waved to him. He heard the melodic sound of Jillian's laughter as she waved, too, delighted with the speed, the wind, the sun and the water.

They sped, they dipped, they jumped the waves. Time passed. Griff was fast, as were the others, but he drove safely, keeping well clear of the rest of them.

Finally they went back in. The sun was falling, a huge orange disk draped above the sea. Breathless, Jillian ran over to stand beside him on the sand, slipping her arm through his and leading him back up the beach to the hotel.

Douglas had stayed in all day. Ironically, in sunny Florida he had come down with the flu. Henry had stayed in the suite with him.

Before they had to leave for dinner, Jillian said that she wanted to spend some time with her grandfather. They went together and found Douglas propped up on his pillows, looking his age.

"I hear there was another accident this morning," he said grimly.

"A vicious coconut," Jillian teased.

"Daniel said you pushed her out of the way, Robert."

"I was closest," he said.

"He said it was the strangest thing." He turned toward Jillian. "He said it looked like you went flying before Robert even touched you."

"I don't know about that. It all happened so quickly," Jillian told him. "Now let's forget it. I'm fine. You're the one who's sick. Are you sure you don't want us to stay and have dinner here with you?"

"Jillian, I appreciate the thought, but no. I'm going to have some soup, take a pill that young kid who swears he got through medical school prescribed for me, and then I'm going to sleep. I'm not just sick, I'm old. I love you dearly, but go away, leave me alone." He grinned to take the sting out of the words. "See you in the morning. Nothing makes me happier than when you young people are all out together."

A few minutes later, they left him. Jillian was quiet.

"What is it?"

"I worry about him so much. He is old."

"But in good health."

"He has the flu. He looks sick as a dog."

Robert smiled. "He'll get over the flu. He has a good heart, strong lungs, and his mind's as sharp as a tack."

She suddenly rose up on her tiptoes, kissing his cheek. "Thanks for saying that."

They joined the others in the lobby and decided to walk the few blocks to the restaurant. It was a beautiful night.

Finally, during the meal, Robert began to feel the tension leave him. The steaks were good, the service efficient, the talk pleasant. He kept quiet, watching, noticing certain things about the others.

Daniel still seemed shaken and Brad kept watching Jillian as if he were afraid she would disappear. Eileen only seemed tense when she talked to Gary. Connie and Joe were both extremely pleasant to everyone—except each other. Gracie was, as usual, watching Daniel protectively, and Griff was watching him.

But on the surface, all was well.

When they left the restaurant, they headed back to one of the dance clubs they'd visited the night before. Griff and Jillian started out together again, but when Daniel cut in, Griff walked over to the bar to stand by Robert. He was quiet for a few minutes, then turned on him pointedly.

"Why were you on my tail like that today out on the water?"

"On your tail?"

"Yeah, on my tail. Look, I know things are hot and heavy between you two, but she's my cousin. I adore her. I'd die before I'd ever hurt her in any way."

Robert stared at him in return. "If you say so."

Griff set down his drink. "Well, I've got a date. Good night, Marston. See you tomorrow."

"Yeah, good night."

Griff left them. Connie and Joe Murphy still seemed at odds, dancing with anyone but each other. Too bad. A great vacation...and neither one seemed to be enjoying it.

Robert was surprised when Jillian came to him, ready to conk out a little early. He wondered if she was more shaken by what had happened than she let on. He didn't press the matter, commenting on nothing more than the sand, the sea and the stars, as they walked back to the hotel.

She seemed to appreciate that fact. When they reached their room, her soft silk cocktail dress seemed to melt from her shoulders to the floor. Moonlight poured in through the screen doors leading to the balcony, and the air was beautiful, carrying the fresh scent of the sea. In his arms, she was heaven.

They both slept to the sound of the surf....

Until he was awakened by the bloodcurdling sound of her scream. He leapt up, instantly on the alert, and realized once again that there was nothing wrong. Nothing but her dream.

He caught her shoulders, shaking her. Her eyes were open, but she wasn't seeing him. She kept screaming as if she were in pain. Terrible pain. "Jillian!"

Suddenly there was a pounding on the door.

"Jillian, wake up." He reached for his robe, and hers. "Jillian!"

Her eyes widened, focusing on his at last.

"Put this on," he ordered her.

"What...what...?"

"I think the police are here to arrest me," he said dryly, throwing the door open. Daniel, who had the room next to theirs, was first in line, fist raised from pounding on the door. There were half a dozen others including a member of hotel security.

"You bastard! What were you doing to her?" Daniel roared, ready to lunge.

The security guard stopped him.

Embarrassed, concerned, but also angry, Robert lifted a brow, then backed away from the door, indicating that the security guard should enter. "Jillian, care to explain?"

She was crimson. "I'm so sorry." Her voice was husky, embarrassed. "I had a nightmare. Daniel, I was dreaming. I'm so sorry...."

"So everything is all right in here?" the guard said skeptically.

"Everything is fine. Except that I've awakened everyone and I—I'm sorry."

"This man wasn't beating you...forcing you..." the guard began. He was as crimson as Jillian.

"Good Lord, no!" Jillian gasped.

"Well, then, uh, lady, whatever you ate tonight, don't eat it again," the guard said, then cleared his throat. "Okay, everyone, break it up. Back to bed!"

Everyone left but Daniel, who didn't budge. He was staring at them.

"I had a nightmare, Daniel," Jillian told him, eyes pleading.

"You think I'd ever hurt her?" Robert demanded, his temper shot.

Daniel let his breath escape slowly through his teeth. His eyes were hard on Robert; then he shook his head. "A *dream,* Jilly?"

"A nightmare," she murmured.

Daniel lowered his head, then looked up. "Sorry, Marston."

Robert nodded stiffly.

"About what, Jilly? About what?" Daniel asked.

"Fire," she said.

"Fire? Where?"

"Just...fire."

He nodded. "I guess there was a lot going on today. But you shouldn't worry about a fire. There's a smoke alarm right there, above your head. And a sprinkler system."

She smiled at him. "Thanks, Daniel."

"Yeah. Good night. Good night, Robert."

"Good night."

Robert closed the door behind Daniel, and turned to look at Jillian. He ran his fingers through his hair, ready to tell her that they had to do something, that this was dangerous. He still felt like a fool. As if half the people in the hallway were convinced, no matter what Jillian had said, that he was a terrible human being, a woman beater.

"Jillian," he began, trying to keep the anger out of his voice. But she was just staring at him. And before he could say anything further, she burst into tears. "Jillian..."

He took her into his arms, his anger fading.

"Why?" she whispered miserably, face buried against him.

He ran his hands gently over her hair, cradling her head gently. "I don't know," he said. "But by God, we are going to find out."

C H A P T E R 1 3

The following Friday morning, Robert left the police station and returned to the office, furious. He stalked down the hallway to Douglas's office, ignoring Amelia's warning that Douglas was in a meeting. He let himself in, then closed the door.

Daniel was seated in front of Douglas's desk, and both men looked irate, as if they were trying to calmly discuss a matter about which they held widely varying views.

Robert didn't care. He strode forward, tossing a manila envelope on the desk.

"What is that?" Daniel asked.

"And why are you bursting through a closed door?" Douglas demanded, then sneezed. He had insisted on coming in to the office for a few hours each day.

"You should go home," Robert said curtly. "If you die of pneumonia, you're definitely not going to help anyone."

Douglas's brows shot up, but he seemed as much amused as

outraged. "I'm not going to die of pneumonia—I refuse to. So, what is this?"

"After the cat died, I gathered the ashes from the furnace."

"You what?" Daniel demanded.

"I gathered the ashes from the furnace, took them to a friend who's a cop and had them analyzed."

"Great. Let's bring the cops in here because a cat died," Daniel muttered.

"What did they find?" Douglas asked. His old eyes had remained steady on Robert.

"Rat poison."

Douglas leaned forward. "We do keep rat poison around. For rats," he said quietly.

"Wait a minute," Daniel said. "How do you know there weren't rat ashes in there, too? You couldn't have made this startling discovery immediately following the cremation. You must have waited."

"Yes. And that's interesting, don't you think? Of course, everyone knew about the cat's death—except for Jillian and me."

"What exactly are you implying?" Daniel asked, so angry that he was rising.

"Take it easy, Daniel. I'm not implying anything, except that someone here is careless with rat poison. And that I should have been told immediately about what had happened. I need to know everything of importance that goes on at the office. That cat died on Jillian's desk."

"Did it?" Daniel said, then struck back suddenly, like a cobra. "And who was sleeping with Jillian when she suddenly starting screaming as if she were being sliced to ribbons?"

"What?" Douglas demanded sharply. None of them had told him about the incident. He'd been too sick Sunday and Monday. So sick, in fact, that they'd delayed coming home until Tuesday night, when he was well enough to fly.

"She woke up screaming in the middle of the night. Woke up half the hotel," Daniel said, staring at Robert.

"Did she think there was a fire?" Douglas asked quietly.

"Yes," Robert said. "How did you know? I suppose she's had the dream before?"

"Once that I know of. At the house," Douglas said. "Something's on her mind..." Douglas mused.

Robert leaned over the desk. "Rat poison wasn't on her mind."

"But how do you know that the rat poison wasn't *in* a rat? Maybe the cat ate a damn rat," Daniel said. "Something cats are prone to do."

Robert straightened. He might have Douglas upset and worried, but Daniel was just plain angry.

Or else, he was doing a good job of pretending.

"I want all the rat poison out of here," Douglas said. "If we have any more problems in the building, we'll call in an exterminator. He can set those catch-and-release traps. No more poison."

"I'll take care of it right away." Daniel exited the office as he spoke, but not before casting Robert another fulminating glance.

"Rat poison..." Douglas said. "It had to be an accident."

Robert leaned on the desk again. "You told me to watch her."

Douglas shook his head. "Just because of the dream. An old man's fancy. I'm sure it's nothing."

Robert wanted to tell Douglas that there had been too many accidents for it to be nothing. A fence down, a truck careening, a saddle slipping. Palm fronds and coconuts.

But Douglas looked so ill.

"Yeah, Douglas. Nothing. That's why you dragged me into this."

He left the office, shaking his head. Just outside the door, he paused, suddenly thinking about the tarot card reader. Shelley Millet, also known as Madame Zena. *The cat was poisoned,* she had told him. *How do you know?* he had asked.

Milo.

Milo Anderson.

Maybe it was time to see the tarot card reader again.

He started purposefully toward his own office. Jillian was in danger. And he couldn't allow her to be alone anymore.

Jillian walked into Connie's office and set a package on her desk. Connie sat back, looking up at her.

Jillian grinned. "These are the best 'little artist' sets I've ever seen. I think the girls will love them."

"Oh, Jillian, thanks so much," Connie said. She shook her head. "You do too much for them. For me. For us."

"Connie, it's not that big a deal. I thought they could bring them for Thanksgiving. You're still coming up, right, for the long weekend? It's not a working holiday. And your mom's invited, too, of course."

Connie looked a little pale. "I don't know if we're coming this year. Joe is a little...well, he feels as if we've both been working too much, and..."

"I'll be disappointed if you don't come, but it's up to the two of you. We're friends. You're like part of the family. But I would never want you to jeopardize your marriage."

"Thanks. We'll see. Hey, how about going out with Joe and me for a few drinks tonight? The girls are going to be at a sleepover."

"Maybe. I was going to work late. All this out-of-town stuff has been great, but I'm behind, and it seems like Thanksgiving is just around the corner."

"Come on..."

Jillian laughed. "Like a friend of mine says, we'll see."

She left the package in Connie's office and walked to Robert's. She tapped on the door, then waited for his "Come in."

Then she entered and perched on the corner of his desk. "I'm sane," she told him.

He leaned back, watching her, blue eyes sharp. He'd seemed exceptionally tense since they returned from Florida. Today he seemed like stretched wire. Restless, even though he was sitting behind his desk without moving.

"I never doubted your sanity. But what did he say?"

She had been to see Dr. Alfred Ghaminetti, one of the best psychoanalysts in the tristate area. He hadn't impressed her much. He'd done the right things, she supposed. He'd gotten her to talk. He'd suggested that she look at her own life, at the changes she was experiencing, for the source of her disturbing dream. Perhaps she was just feeling guilty now that she was entering into a new relationship.

"He suggested that maybe I thought I was burning in hell, something like that."

His brows shot up. "You're burning in hell because of me?"

She smiled. "Well, certainly not because of anyone else."

He set down the pen with which he'd been making notes on a marketing presentation, folded his hands on the desk and looked at her seriously. "Then, you should marry me."

The breath rushed from her lungs. She shook her head, sure he wasn't serious. "I should marry you because I have nightmares?"

He looked down, smiling. "No. You should marry me because I can't live without you. Because you won't stay with me more than a night or two when we're here in New York, and because you won't let me stay with you in Douglas's house. God knows, Eileen has spent five years just living with poor Gary, but—"

"Douglas is old. He raised me. I have to stay with him," she said.

He lifted his hands. "So marry me."

A smile curved her lips. "You're not the type of man to live in my grandfather's house."

"For now, I would," he said seriously. "I'd never give up my apartment, but if you're worried about Douglas and you're not ready to leave him to Henry's care, marry me and I'll stay with you until you're ready to move out."

"You're serious," she said.

"Incredibly serious."

"Henry is almost as old as Grandfather, you know."

"So is Amelia—and she stands guard at his office door every day with the strength of a pit bull," Robert reminded her.

She laughed. "Amelia is only in her late sixties. Henry, on the other hand, is almost seventy-five. She hesitated still, feeling a strange tremor shoot down her spine. "You know, there's been speculation that you were brought in just for me, because I was grandfather's favorite but not a male heir."

"And do you live your life by rumor?"

"Of course not."

"So marry me."

"Everyone would make a big deal of it."

"We won't tell them."

"What?"

He sighed. "We won't tell anyone. We'll do the deed on the sly and share it only with Douglas so you'll allow me into the hallowed precincts of your home. And later, when the dreams have stopped, when Douglas is well, when things are moving along smoothly, we'll have a big party and everyone will be pleased."

"But, Robert, why now? Why the urgency?"

"Because I love you," he said simply. "And I want to be with you."

"Are you really so sure that you know me?" she whispered.

"I know that I love you," he said stubbornly. "And can you tell me that you don't love me, that you don't want to be with me?"

"Of course, I love you," she whispered. "It's just that..."

"What?"

She shrugged. How could she explain what she didn't understand herself?

"I'm...afraid."

"Of what? Of me?"

"No, of course not."

"Don't you see? I want to be there for you. I *will* be there for you. Whenever you need me, I'll be there for you."

He was so passionate, so intense. She couldn't help but believe him. "Well, I...maybe. We'll see, all right?"

"We'll see soon," he told her firmly.

That night they went to Hennessey's with Connie and Joe. Mary MacRae, looking healthy, some of the signs of premature aging beginning to dim, was their waitress. She greeted them like old friends, and to Robert's dismay, she told Jillian the whole story about how she had been begging on the street, supporting her drug habit, until Robert's kindness had turned her life around.

"Here, here," Joe said, after hearing the story. "You're a hero. Right out of a storybook. He can probably break through brick walls with a single hand."

Joe had imbibed a few beers. He had been a family friend forever, and Robert knew that he was fairly comfortable with all his employers—except for him. Everyone, of course, had been wary about Robert coming into the business. They had all felt that their jobs were being threatened. No one seemed to believe that he hadn't been brought in to clean house.

Joe had seemed mildly hostile all night. Robert wondered if it had something to do with the angry words he and Daniel had exchanged in Douglas's office that afternoon. Joe was Daniel's right-hand man, as well as Jillian's friend, so if Daniel had said anything to him about the incident, he could be feeling testy.

"I wasn't a hero. I gave her money because of Douglas," he told Joe, watching him.

"Douglas?"

"Uh-huh. I never gave handouts on the street, until I saw Douglas do it."

"Hell, half the time," Joe said, "if you give a junkie money, you're just helping to support their habit."

"Yeah, maybe. Excuse me just a minute."

Mary MacRae was at the bar. He walked up to her. "Mary, can you give Shelley Millet, the tarot card reader, a call for me?"

"Of course."

"Tell her I'm willing to listen." He hesitated, thinking that maybe he was the one who needed the psychoanalyst, not Jillian. "Tell her that my mind is open, that I've had a few visits from Milo myself."

"Visits from Milo?"

"Yes, just say that, will you, please?"

He returned to the table. Everyone, including Jillian, looked curious about his conversation with the waitress.

He had no intention of enlightening them. "Ready to order some food?" he asked.

"Sure. Food," Joe said.

The rest of the evening was pleasant enough. Joe seemed to lighten up the more he drank that night. He'd started out at odds with his own wife, but by the time they left, Connie was laughing and they were cuddling together as they walked down the street to hail a cab at the corner.

Robert looked at Jillian. "Marry me," he said softly.

"Now?" she asked, laughing as if he were joking.

"Yes, it's already November. You're the Christmas fanatic, and I want a wife for Christmas. By then, I want to let everyone know. I want to chop down a tree with you. Have dinner in that house as if I belong."

"I meant, are you asking me to marry you right now?"

"When better?" he asked softly.

"But it's late Friday night."

"You can call Henry and tell him you're not coming home. We'll fly to Vegas. Done deal."

"That's insane."

"Yes, totally. Let's do it."

She inhaled sharply, staring at him. "All right."

Jillian looked at the ring on her finger, unable to believe what she had just done. They'd stopped by the house, where Douglas had been poring over the final edits of the commercial with Henry; Amelia had joined him at the house for dinner, and they were all discussing the new campaign.

In her room, she packed a small bag, feeling odd about leaving with a man, with all of them there, yet not ready to tell them what she was doing.

When she went back downstairs, Robert had joined the conversation as if he'd known them all forever. She noticed that Douglas seemed much better. The doctor had assured them earlier that his flu hadn't taken a turn toward pneumonia.

Jillian had kissed him goodbye, a little uneasy at the way Amelia seemed to be watching with a strange hostility. Then they headed straight for the airport, jumping on a flight to Vegas, where they had chosen the first, tackiest, most awful place for a wedding, but it hadn't mattered. One day they would do it all again in the church in Connecticut, and everyone would be there.

But for now...

She had done it. Married Robert. And standing in the chapel, under the awful fluorescent light in the middle of the night, she had looked up at him, at the strong lines of his face, at the tenderness in the cobalt darkness of his eyes, and she'd been glad.

They spent the entire night making love, sipping champagne and ordering room service. They had chosen an absolutely tasteless and ostentatious hotel room, as well, complete with heart-shaped bed and heart-shaped Jacuzzi. None of it had mattered. They'd had each other. They barely slept for twenty-four hours. They laughed, talked, ate and made love again.

"Do you feel like you know me yet?" he asked her at one point.

She sobered, telling him, "I feel like I've known you forever. Honestly. As if..."

"What?"

"I don't know. As if I loved you before. As if I loved you more than life itself."

To her surprise, he drew away from her and walked to the window. It was daytime. He was splendid, standing there, tall, bronzed, muscles honed to perfection. *Great buns,* as Connie would have said. Jillian did love him. From head to toe, she adored him. There were just these strange moments when...

She was still afraid.

"The tarot card reader told me that we had lived before," he said, looking out on the dazzling sunlight.

"And you believed her?" she asked skeptically. "You don't believe in anything!"

He turned back to her then, coming to her, kneeling down before her passionately. "I believe in you," he told her.

She touched the top of his head, ran her fingers through his hair, moved by his words. "And I believe in you," she said.

He smiled, and then she was in his arms, the two of them passionately entwined once again.

Later, near noon on Sunday, he suggested that they get ready early for their flight back. He had a surprise for her.

It turned out to be a small store that specialized in Christmas items year 'round. She was delighted, buying up half the place, telling him which things would go best at the house in Connecticut and what would look great in the artist's cabin in the woods. He was glad.

When they returned to the city, Jillian checked with Henry about her grandfather's health. He'd been doing great all weekend; Amelia had stayed, and they'd decided not to go into the office that week but head straight out to Connecticut to stay until the Thanksgiving holiday. Douglas's doctor wanted him to take it easy, and in Connecticut he could get his rest and still stay in touch with the office easily, thanks to modern technology—and Amelia, who could have kept the office running from the North Pole.

They stayed at his apartment that night. And at two a.m., Jillian woke up screaming.

He held her, told her over and over again that there was no fire.

"I could feel it," she cried, sobbing. "I could feel it on my flesh."

"I won't let fire come anywhere near you," he vowed.

"You're a liar!" she suddenly accused him. "You promise me everything, but when the time comes, you won't be there."

"Jillian..."

But she jumped out of bed and ran into the bathroom, slamming the door against him.

Monday, at the office, Daniel Llewellyn walked in on Robert, tense, still angry. "Every bit of rat poison is out of here, Marston. Every bit."

"I'm glad to hear it."

Daniel suddenly slammed a fist down on the desk. "She's my family, damn it! I would never hurt her. None of us would." The passion in his voice seemed real.

"I hope not," Robert said. "I hope not."

Jillian entered Connie's cubicle. "What are your lunch plans?"

Connie looked up. "Plans? A sandwich, I guess."

"We're going to school."

"What?"

"I just talked to the bartender at Hennessey's. Madame Zena's real name is Shelley Millet. And guess what?"

"What?"

"She taught school with Milo."

"Really?" Connie said, surprised. "So," she said carefully, "we're going to go see Madame Zena—at school?"

Jillian nodded. "But don't say anything. To anyone."

"No, of course not."

Jillian got absolutely nothing done that morning. She was upset by what she had done to Robert, she was also determined to find out what was going on. And she was afraid that if he knew what she was up to, he would stop her. She knew that Connie thought she was crazy—Madame Zena had screamed at her, calling her a witch, upsetting her. But she needed to see her.

And she had to stop waking up screaming. She knew it upset Robert. She loved Robert with her whole heart. She didn't intend to lose him.

She was so nervous that someone in the office would try to stop her from leaving that she whisked Connie out of the building just after eleven-thirty. They shopped, had coffee, then went to the school early, waiting outside Shelley's classroom.

Shelley Millet, minus her costume, was tall, regal, and striking. Jillian expected her to be surprised and possibly also annoyed to see them.

She wasn't surprised, and if she was annoyed she didn't show it.

"Miss Millet, I'm really sorry to track you down this way," Jillian began, but Shelley Millet put up a hand to stop her.

"It's all right. I expected you before now, actually."

"Really?"

"Uh-huh."

"Can we take you for a drink, a snack, coffee—anything?"

"There's a place just down the street. Quiet, private."

A few minutes later they were sharing a booth at the small

luncheonette. It wasn't dark, there were no beads, and there was nothing spooky about the place whatsoever. Jillian haltingly explained about meeting Robert on Halloween, right after "Madame Zena" had called her a witch, and how she had passed out. Now she was having constant dreams of fire and waking up, screaming.

Shelley Millet stirred her coffee, nodding. "You are in grave danger."

"She is?" Connie said. "But how..."

"It was in the cards. And Milo told me."

Looking into the woman's copper eyes, Jillian shivered. "Milo?" she whispered. "My—Robert has mentioned talking to Milo, too. In his dreams."

"Yes, I know."

"You know?"

"Mr. Marston is on his way here now."

Jillian stiffened. "I came to you for help. Why would Robert come to you? He doesn't believe in anything out of the ordinary."

"How many people do?" Shelley Millet asked her, smiling. "Oh, when we're children, we believe in the Easter Bunny, Santa Claus...in fact, we're willing to believe in a lot when we're young. Then we grow up and we forget to have faith. Even in God. If we can't see it, it doesn't exist."

"Well..." Jillian moistened her lips, wishing for a moment that she hadn't brought Connie. "Madame Zena—Shelley, I love him. Robert, I mean. It was very quick, ridiculously quick. I'm sure there are people who could say that I can't really know how I feel, but I do. I love him. I want to be with him, I want to be happy, make him happy, but every once in a while, suddenly, out of the blue, I'm afraid. Terrified. And he thinks someone in my family is out to hurt me."

"No!" Connie gasped. "Why?"

"Because of Llewellyn Enterprises. Because of my grandfather."

"Jillian, I think that someone is out to hurt you, and so does Milo," Shelley said.

"Why doesn't Milo come to me?" she asked, feeling an aching in her heart, a strange poignancy.

"Let's cut to the chase here," Shelley said. "You and Milo were friends, right? Really good friends. You married him to give him access to the Llewellyn money, right?"

Jillian sucked in her breath. "Well...his HMO sucked! The cancer ward was like a zoo."

Shelley smiled. "That's understandable. But he was your *friend*. Never really your *lover*."

"I loved Milo. I loved him with my whole heart."

"That isn't exactly the same, is it?" Shelley said softly. "Your husband is coming," she added suddenly.

"Your husband?" Connie gasped. "You mean he's here now? Milo's ghost is with us? I don't feel cold or anything."

"Not Milo's ghost. Robert Marston is here."

"You married him?" Connie said incredulously, staring at Jillian as if she'd been stabbed in the back.

"Shush. We're not telling anyone yet."

"Yes, well, I can see you not telling *anyone*—but you didn't tell *me!*"

"Do you tell me everything that's going on with you?" Jillian demanded.

Connie stared at her, biting her lip. As Shelley had said, Robert was on his way in. He stared at her almost as accusingly as Connie had as he slid into the booth next to Madame Zena.

"Hi," Jillian murmured weakly.

He nodded curtly to her, then turned to Shelley. "Thank you for agreeing to see me."

"My pleasure. But there's something you all have to understand. I can only tell you what I see, what I believe, then you have to take it from there."

"So why am I dreaming about burning?" Jillian asked.

"It's from your past life," Shelley said.

"A past life?" Robert repeated.

"You said your mind was going to be open." Shelley hesitated. "You said that Milo Anderson was haunting your dreams."

"Yeah. But only at the house in Connecticut. Only in the room where he died. Except that—" He broke off, as if he didn't believe what he was saying himself. "I think he was in Florida."

"What?" Jillian and Connie cried in unison.

"A branch fell, nearly crushing Jillian. I ran to push her out of the way. I made it, but I still think...I don't know. It looked as if she was being pushed out of the way even before I reached her."

He looked away, shaking his head. He was saying these things, but he couldn't accept them.

Shelley Millet raised her hands, forming a circle with her long fingers. "Energy," she said softly. "All life is energy. Energy doesn't die. There is, in my mind, in my being, in my soul, no doubt that there is a supreme being. To us, he is God, to others he is Allah, to some he is the very spirit of the earth. The Vikings called him Odin; the ancient Romans named him Jupiter; the Greeks called him Zeus. Study mythology, the Old Testament, the battles of the angels, and it will shock you just how much of what we believe is similar to what we call legend, ancient stories, far too archaic for our modern sophistication. Christmas, Jillian. Think about it. A virgin birth, the son of God among men—nailed to a cross. But we believe, and our beliefs do not make us foolish, they make us rise above both the evil and the ordinary. The point is, I believe that the world is full of old souls. I think we get many chances. You knew one another before. You were in love with one another before. Something happened. Something horrible, to do with fire. Maybe someone back then was out to hurt you, Jillian, and perhaps Robert failed you."

"I will not fail her!"

Shelley smiled. "Maybe you had that same arrogance centuries ago, Mr. Marston. Maybe you're being given a second chance. Seize it. Don't throw it away. History may well be repeating itself."

"I don't understand," Connie said. "Just because someone hurt Jillian in another life—"

"I'm not a specialist on this particular subject," Shelley said. "But those who do study reincarnation believe that we come back most often with the same groups of souls around us. Perhaps they take on different relationships. Mrs. Murphy, perhaps you were a sister in another life, a mother, even a brother."

"I was a boy?" Connie said indignantly.

"Maybe," Shelley said with a shrug, then looked at Robert and Jillian in turn. "I do think you had a chance before, that your lives were cut short, and so you're getting a chance to try again. You may take that for what it's worth." She looked at Robert. "What does Milo tell you?"

Robert made an impatient sound. "Why is Milo in on all of this? I never met the man."

"Souls may pass at different times, like ships in the night. In another time, another place, he might have been your best friend."

"And I might have been a boy," Connie moaned.

"What does Milo say in your dreams?" Shelley persisted.

"That Jillian's in danger. That I..."

"What?"

"That I should read the book. And I *did* read the book. Well, some of it."

"And what was it?"

"An old volume on the English Civil War."

"May I suggest you finish it?"

Jillian stared at Robert. He looked haggard, and when his eyes touched hers, they still held reproach. But he loved her. Really loved her. She was certain that she saw that in his eyes, as well.

"I read part of the book, too," she said. "It was all about the secret affair between one of the king's soldiers and a lady."

"Did *you* finish it?"

"Well, no."

"Finish it. Maybe you'll find your answers," Shelley told them.

"I will finish it," Jillian said, staring at Robert. She leaned forward, her hands covering Shelley's. "Thank you. Really. Is there anything else you can tell us? Anything else you see?"

"Just one thing."

"Yes?" Jillian said anxiously.

"I see that Mr. Marston should pick up the check. Teachers don't make much money." She smiled. "I also see that you're both good people. And that either of you is welcome to call me at any time." She rose. "Finish that book."

"We're heading back to Connecticut for Thanksgiving."

Shelley's eyes suddenly seemed to haze over, taking on a greater glitter of copper. "That's good."

"Will Milo be there?" Robert asked. Jillian couldn't tell if he was being sarcastic or asking a sincere question.

"Maybe," Shelley said, smiling. "But he's on your side."

"Then, who is against me?" Jillian whispered.

"We don't get to see everything," Shelley replied.

"We're conveniently missing what's most important," Robert said.

"Maybe it's most important to put your faith to the test," Shelley told him. "But it's good that you're going to the house. Whatever is happening, you need to find out. You need to solve this. Before Christmas."

"Before Christmas?" Jillian murmured.

"You must."

"Why?" Robert demanded tensely. He reached out, taking her wrist.

Shelley shook her head. "Just believe, Mr. Marston. Believe in yourself. No matter what barrier lies before you, believe in yourself."

She freed herself from his grip, and hurried out of the luncheonette.

CHAPTER 14

"This is absolutely insane," Robert murmured.

They were back in the library in Connecticut. The household was even fuller than it had been last time, since Joe and Connie's children were there, along with Connie's mother. But for now Robert and Jillian were alone in the library, dinner eaten. Connie and Joe were tucking their children into bed. Eileen was wrapping gifts. Gracie was in the den, calling a distant cousin in Chicago. Since she had no immediate family of her own, she had been invited for the holiday, even though Thanksgiving was traditionally just for family and longtime friends. As Daniel's ever-faithful shadow, Gracie had been elated by the invitation. In fact, Jillian wasn't sure that there really was a cousin in Ohio, but she would never suggest that to anyone. Gracie seemed too alone in the world.

Most of the rest of the household was stuffed to the gills, entirely lazy, little more than a group of couch potatoes stretched out on every available piece of furniture and watching a movie.

With everyone else settled, Jillian and Robert had seized the first free time they'd been able to take to go to the library.

"Shelley said to finish the book," Jillian reminded him firmly.

He lifted his hands. "Shelley is a tarot card reader. I'm reading a book about events that occurred hundreds of years ago—because of a tarot card reader. This is absolutely insane."

"You made a point of seeing her," Jillian pointed out.

Robert shrugged, easing down into the overstuffed chair facing the desk. She was perched on the swivel chair behind it, the book in her hands.

"There are a number of letters in here, and diary entries—I read those the last time I was here," she said.

"Why?" he asked softly.

"Why what?"

"Why were you reading the book?"

"Because you had been reading it."

"Ah," he murmured, and smiled, settling more comfortably into his chair.

"The majority of the story was written by someone named Justin. He was the one who grouped the diary entries and the letters together."

"Yeah, I know. I was reading the parts Justin had written. Go toward the end. See if we can find out what actually happened. I think maybe she was executed—burned at the stake."

"Burned at the stake?" Jillian repeated, feeling a cold draft sweep over her.

Robert leaned forward. "Jillian, do you think that you might have read this book before? Maybe you started dreaming about burning because of the book, because what happened to this girl was so horrible."

She looked at him, shaking her head. "Robert, I never saw this book before you left it on the desk the last time we were here."

He didn't say anything, so she turned her attention to the book. "This part is written by Justin. It's near the end." She began to read.

It was nearing the Christmas season when last we came home, when last there was still what a man could call a home. We remained in the woods, hiding, for it was no longer safe to be among the King's men in Cromwell's England. Messages were sent to the house through Jane, our Lady's maid, and she came in the night, slipping away like a wraith to the forest. She laughed with the captain, walked among the trees with him, and stayed with him by the river until morning. The captain was concerned, telling her she must come away with us. But she told him that her father still lived. Sir Walter had taken all control; he ran the village as if he were king in his own right. Across England, there was talk again that devils walked. That in a lawless land, torn by war, Satan had taken hold. She swore herself strong and safe; she had but contempt for Sir Walter.

I heard them talking, down by the river, when dawn came. She had the ability to make light of the most serious situation; she was afraid for her captain, certain that it was time for him to fly to Scotland, where the King was still respected as the King. "Go, flee," she told him, and teasingly reminded him that Edward I had managed to murder most of the Welsh, while many a Scot had taken to the Highlands where no man could find them. They spun a tale that night between them, pretending that they both left the place they had once loved so much but that was now so torn by bloodshed. He said that there were beautiful green hills in Ireland, as well, and islands where even a man such as he might be-

*lieve in magic. But Lord Alfred, stricken, taken to his bed,
seldom even conscious of those around him, still breathed.
She would not leave, and she swore that she was safe.*

*But I knew Jane, knew her well, and she told me that Mor-
wenna lied, that her every day with Sir Walter was a fight
and a threat, and that one day Sir Walter would seize her. He
had threatened to take legal action against her many times.
She laughed at his accusations of heresy, saying surely anyone's pact with God could be construed as heresy these days,
that the Catholic Church had departed England and the In-
quisition was no longer in effect. He spoke to her of treason,
as well, and she asked how she could be guilty of treason
when she had honored her King but could do nothing to save
his life against the sham of a battle he now waged in court.*

*Old Jeremy, who had served Lord Alfred so loyally for
so many years, came with the dawn, warning that Sir Walter was searching for Morwenna. So she fled. But not before the captain held her in his arms, not before he vowed
that he would always be there for her in her time of need.*

*That night, we rode away, hearing that there would be
a meeting to the south, of those last cavaliers who had
sworn loyalty to the King. There was a plan being circu-
lated to rescue him from the grip of his persecutors. It was
night, we heard later, when Sir Walter went all but mad,
telling Morwenna that she would marry him, she must, he
was a Godly man and she had bewitched him, and it was
her one chance to save her soul. In anger, she told him that
she could not marry him, for she was already wed to another. And when he touched her, she showed him such re-
pulsion that he went into a tantrum, frothing at the mouth
like a rabid dog. He didn't call for the guards but took her
himself, by the hair, dragging her, hurling her deep down*

*into the dungeon, where the old women had been prodded
and poked, tortured into admitting their pacts with Satan.
She defied him still, telling him that Michael would come
for her. Then she was afraid, for he wanted Michael to
come, and she knew that he would kill Michael if he could.*

Jillian paused in her reading for a moment, looked up at
Robert. He was no longer slouched in the chair. He was sitting
straight, as if suddenly jolted into perfect posture.

"Robert?"

"What?" He looked at her, tearing his gaze from the corner of the desk.

"This is what she was telling us, right? Shelley Millet. That
we lived the events in this book. That our lives ended in tragedy
and somehow we have to keep it from happening again."

"I imagine so," he said, his attention still not all there. "She
said the same souls tend to come back together. So we need to
figure out who around us was Sir Walter, who was Justin, and
all the rest."

"I suppose."

Robert was dead silent for a moment. Then his eyes touched
hers. He cleared his throat. "Milo says that he was Justin."

"What?" A chill fell over her, colder than a blanket of ice.
"What?"

He lifted his hands, dropped them, cleared his throat again.
"Milo says that he was Justin."

"Milo?" she whispered.

He nodded.

"Milo is here?" she asked. There was nothing in the room.
Except the cold.

"I thought you *dreamed* about Milo?"

"I did." He looked at her for a moment. "I'm not sleeping, am I?"

"No. You swear that you—you who believe in nothing—see a ghost."

He swallowed, gritting his teeth, his gaze unmoving.

"Where?" she whispered.

He closed his eyes, then looked at her again. "Perched on the edge of the desk."

"You can see Milo? My deceased husband."

He nodded.

"Why can't I see him?" she whispered.

"He says that I need help far more than you, but other than that, he doesn't really know. He says he's been with you. You were taking a subway somewhere, and you were too close to the tracks. He shoved you back. And...he was in Miami the day the branch fell."

Jillian sat dead still for a moment, wondering if he was tormenting her, or trying to humor her through the situation.

"Why won't he let me see him?" she whispered.

"He isn't stopping you. It's just the way things are. I'm able to see him because I have to help you."

"How does he know I'm in so much danger?"

"Because the cat was poisoned."

"We're not going on about the cat again, are we?"

Robert looked at her. "I took the ashes from the furnace and had them analyzed, Jillian. There was rat poison in them."

"We've had rats in the office," she informed him defensively. "And Jeeves had been an alley cat. I'm sure instinct made him eat a rat."

"Jillian, he died on your desk. On the tray with your Halloween cookies and tea. The poison was probably on your tray."

"Robert, that is reaching."

"Is it?" He leaned forward. "Douglas has been seeing his lawyers in his office lately. He's also been arguing repeatedly with Daniel over something. Eileen watches you constantly with razors in her eyes, and Griff...well, God knows what Griff is really thinking. Then there's Theo, who's never really appreciated for being a good old grunt, an intelligent, middle-management kind of a guy."

"And what does Milo say?"

"Milo says you're in danger."

She sat back, folding her arms over her chest. "You bastard," she whispered. "You're using Milo to try to convince me that someone in my family is after me."

Robert rose with an impatient oath. "I don't believe any of this."

"You're the one who called the tarot card reader!"

"I called Shelley because I was trying to help you stop screaming in the middle of the night," he lashed out angrily. "And," he added more quietly, "I am not using Milo for anything. I don't want to see a ghost, especially the ghost of your last husband—sorry, Milo, nothing personal there," he told the corner of the desk.

She jumped away from the desk suddenly, totally freaked out. "And what does Milo say to that?"

"He said he didn't take it personally at all."

She clenched her fists by her sides. "I can't do this," she whispered. "I can't do this anymore."

She fled the room.

"Jillian!"

Robert ran after her. She ignored him, racing to join the others in front of the TV. Douglas was seated in one of the large wing chairs facing the television. Jillian curled up at her grandfather's feet, aware that Robert had followed her. She didn't look at him.

"Griff," she said, "want to go to the tree farm tomorrow? Chop down our own tree?"

"Only if it's not totally freezing," he replied.

She turned her attention to the movie, ignoring her husband. Later they had hot chocolate and cinnamon rolls. Everyone thanked Agatha for a terrific meal, then meandered upstairs.

Jillian went to her room, still angry, still unnerved—and still afraid. She hesitated. This was her grandfather's house, and he didn't know about her marriage. Out of respect, she and Robert had agreed that they would maintain their own rooms, especially since all they had to do to be together was move the wardrobe out of the way of the connecting doors. But the day had been so busy that they hadn't gotten that far yet, and now she was feeling uncertain. She was about to lock the hallway door and consider the situation when the door was shoved open even as her fingers were set to turn the lock. Robert.

"We're not going to play these games," he told her.

"Games? Do you know what you're doing to me, what—"

"Yeah, I was being honest with you. Making a fool of myself, a totally vulnerable fool. You may think I'm insane, but I love you. I married you because I love you, and I understand if you feel you need some distance in this house, but...don't lock me out, Jillian. Don't lock me out."

She stared into his eyes, then wound her arms around his neck, clinging to him.

A moment later she drew away uncomfortably. "Wait a minute. Is Milo here? Now?"

Robert smiled. "No."

"But..."

"He swore to me rather indignantly once that he never comes to this room, and never comes around when we're...together."

She leaned her head against his chest. "Does he know that I really loved him? That he was my dearest friend?" she asked softly.

He smoothed back her hair. "Jillian, he knows. Why else would he still be here? He loved you, too, with all his heart."

Amazingly, they both slept exceptionally well that night, wrapped in each other's arms.

On Friday morning Jillian insisted on getting the tree. Thanksgiving was over; it was officially, traditionally and totally time to set up Christmas.

For years she had gone with Griff to get a tree, but this year Robert refused to let them go alone. Since Joe and the kids were still sleeping, Connie decided to join them, as well. They sang carols in the car. Jillian told Griff it was his turn to play Santa for the kids that year. Griff said they were Joe's kids, so Joe should have to play Santa.

"That's the point—they'd recognize their father," Connie said, hitting him on the shoulder.

Snow still lay heavily on the ground when they reached the tree farm, but they were bundled in coats, gloves and sweaters, and the temperature wasn't brutal. Jillian led the way through row after row of pines to find just the right tree, with Connie laughing and Griff whining all the way.

They were alone in the wilderness, so it seemed. No other shoppers were out quite so early.

Griff took the hatchet and the first swing. It went wild, causing Jillian and Connie to laugh, taunt him and hop back. Robert didn't appear so amused. He took the hatchet and whacked down the tree with so few blows that Jillian found it almost frightening. Griff didn't seem to notice, though in the car, he teased her, saying, "Ditch the macho madman, Jillian. Marry me."

"We've discussed this before, Griff," she teased back. "We don't want to have two-headed children."

"We can avoid procreating—oh, no, I forgot. We have to procreate. Keep the Llewellyn dynasty going. Oh well, two-headed children it is. We can make *Ripley's Believe It or Not,* and become rich and famous in our own right."

Connie was giggling. "She can't marry you, Griff. She's already married."

Griff stared at Connie, as if amazed she could be so casually cruel. "Connie, Milo's dead," he reminded her softly.

"Yes, but—oh!" Connie gasped, seeing the way Jillian was staring at her. "Oh God, I forgot. What a mouth I've got on me. I'm so sorry."

Too late. Griff was staring at Jillian. "You've married him. *Already?*"

"Yes, she's married me, already," Robert said firmly, his eyes catching Griff's in the rearview mirror.

"Well..."

"Don't say anything yet, please, Griff. I haven't told Grandfather," she begged.

"Oh, like he won't be pleased," Griff muttered.

"I haven't told him. I hadn't told anyone," Jillian said.

"Connie knew," Griff said, sounding hurt.

"By accident. She overheard something, that's all. Griff..."

"So you stole her away and married her, just like that," he said to Robert. Then he shrugged. "Well, congratulations."

"Thanks, Griff. But, please..."

"Maybe we should just tell everyone," Robert suggested.

"Not yet," Jillian said.

"Right. Fine." Despite his words, he sounded angry. "You can tell people in your own good time."

Griff started to laugh. "I think you're crazy for not saying anything. Douglas is going to be thrilled. I mean, he's an old-fashioned guy. He's spent years trying to ignore the fact that Eileen and Gary slip from room to room when they're in this house. And not even Eileen has had the balls to tell him they practically live together. He ignores my lifestyle totally—just mentioning now and then that a promiscuous lifestyle is dangerous in this day and age. He's down on Daniel these days, though. I wonder what the old boy has done? If it's something nice and evil, he isn't sharing with me."

They reached the house then, where suddenly they had all kinds of help with the tree. Connie and Joe's girls were up, and they were thrilled with the prospect of decorating the tree. The entire household got involved. Eileen supervised from a sofa, while Gary and Daniel put up lights. Agatha and Henry worked together in the kitchen, making popcorn for strings to wrap around the tree. Joe helped Douglas sort through the boxes of ornaments, giving the unbreakable ones to Connie and Joe's girls, Tricia and Liza, one by one. Theo and Gracie lifted the girls when necessary to allow them to reach the higher branches. Griff called himself music management, sorting through the Christmas CDs to get them in the proper mood. Kelly Adair, Connie's mom, stood across the room and eyeballed the three, telling them where they needed more ornaments, while Connie and Jillian supervised from a closer range, rescuing ornaments when they fell from little hands.

The effort took most of the day. It was only when they stopped for a late lunch that Jillian realized she had not seen Robert for a long time.

She hesitated, deciding not to try to find him, since she meant to take the kids with her to the cottage that afternoon and start decorating there.

She tried to slip out with the least amount of fuss. Connie was coming with her. She took Crystal, her own horse, that day, while Connie rode Cream. Tricia rode in front of her, while baby Liza rode with her mother.

On the way, they sang Christmas carols. The girls were wonderful, fascinated by the deep snow, oblivious to the cold, enjoying the adventure.

They reached the cottage and began going through the many

boxes of Christmas items. Jillian managed to leave the others downstairs and walk up to Milo's studio for a few moments alone. She walked around the room.

"Can you hear me?" she whispered. "It's me, Jillian. Milo, what are you doing? What are you saying to Robert? What on earth is going on here?"

She stood still, closing her eyes, expecting to hear his voice.

"I thought I heard your voice once. On that subway platform," she said softly.

It seemed suddenly as if a breeze stirred in the room. She thought she could hear the soft rustling of curtains.

"Milo?" she whispered.

She closed her eyes. A whisper of air seemed to caress her cheek.

"Thanks for trying to help."

"Jillian, who on earth are you talking to?"

Her eyes flew open, and she spun around. Connie had come up the stairs. Jillian shook her head. "No one. I was just talking to myself."

"Hey, I saw Madame Zena with you, remember?"

"Yes, I remember. But I was just talking to myself."

"Have you read that book yet?" Connie asked her seriously.

"We've started."

"Started?" Connie said. "When we get back, you need to finish it."

They stayed another hour or so, making instant hot chocolate loaded with little marshmallows for the girls. Finally, they rode home. It was almost dark.

Jillian headed for the library as soon as she arrived.

As she had expected, Robert was behind the desk, already reading. He looked up when she came in. He was in a teal turtleneck, dark hair curling over the collar, eyes grave. He watched her for a minute before he spoke.

"You went to the cottage?"

"Yes, I would have asked you to come, but I wasn't sure where you were."

He set the book down. "Bull."

"What?"

"You went to the cottage without me to see if you could drum up Milo's ghost."

"What makes you say that?"

"Milo."

"He told you?"

Robert smiled suddenly. "No. But I knew that's what you were doing." He sobered. "Jillian, don't go off without me again, all right? Especially not here."

"I was with Connie and the kids."

"It doesn't matter."

She sighed, sitting across from him. "Did you finish the book?"

"Yes," he said softly.

"And?"

There was a soft tap at the door. It opened, and Connie stuck her head in. Jillian stood up quickly. "Connie..."

"Oh, come on, you two. I was there with Madame Zena!"

"Yes, and you also opened your big mouth in the car this morning," Robert said sternly.

"I'm sorry. Really."

"And," Jillian reminded her, "you're married to Joe. Daniel's right-hand man."

"Hey," Connie protested. "I don't tell Joe everything. I can keep a secret. Really. Besides...I've already read pieces of the book. And if I'm anyone, I'm Jane. Ye olde faithful maid."

"You read the book?" Jillian asked.

"Well, you two left it right on the desk. It wasn't like I had to prowl around to find it or anything. And I'm serious. You heard what Shelley Millet had to say. I'm your office assistant now—I was your maid back then. Not at all fair. I mean, I have friends who have done that whole regression thing. They were always princesses, or rich, brilliant women. I get to be office staff and domestic help."

"Connie, you have a great job."

"Yes, but I don't get to be the Princess Llewellyn."

"And you didn't get burned at the stake," Robert said sharply. He stared at Connie, then at Jillian, and began to read.

We were riding hard to the south when Garth reached us with the news; the Lady Morwenna was being held in the dungeon. Charges had been read against her; witnesses had been summoned. She was judged guilty of witchcraft and heresy against Almighty God Himself, and she was labeled a traitor against England and the English people. Come the 24th, Christmas Eve, she would be executed by the laws of her country and her God, burned at the stake until dead, her ashes scattered to the wind. Michael was outraged. He heard the news but could not believe it, could not accept it. Sir Walter would not dare commit such a deed. But looking at Garth, seeing the lines of trial and tension in his face, we knew it had to be true.

"We ride," Michael said.

"It's a trap, you know," Garth warned him. "He will set the lady upon the stake, then wait to seize you when you come."

"He will die when I come," Michael vowed. "We ride. Now. I swore that I would be there."

And so, with Garth struggling to keep up, we rode for home. Garth told us that Sir Walter's fury came mainly from her rejection of him, that even in the fierce cold of the dungeon, she refused to give in to his demands. She told him that before God she had a husband, and that her only act of treachery could be to betray him. Sir Walter swore that she would burn, here on earth, then do so again in eternal hell. She vowed that she would come back to seek revenge, but that his words were foolish anyway, because Michael would come for her. He had promised to come for her. With her whole heart, she believed that he would do so.

Garth fell back. He could not keep up with the fierce pace of our desperate run. Michael vowed again and again that he would arrive before the appointed hour. Yet I could see the fear in his face that he would not do so. We later heard that she stood for hours upon the pile of kindling and faggots, and even when the fire was lit, she swore that he would come.

Sir Walter did not have her strangled first, as would have been kind.

They say that her screams echoed through the day and into the night, though she could not have lived near so long upon her pyre, then rang across the hills forever after.

We came upon the scene too late by only moments, and yet what those moments had wrought. Michael had great talent with a sword, with firearms, with his fists. His greatest ability, however, was his aim with a bow and arrow. And so he saw where she stood, consumed in flame yet living still, and he strung his bow and let loose his arrow, and he killed her himself, striking her heart through distance and flame.

"Oh my God!" Connie gasped, leaping to her feet. "Jillian, when you met Robert, you passed out, grasping your heart. He shot you in the heart with an arrow—*he* killed you!"

"Connie, she was already half dead, being burned to cinders. He did her the only kindness he could," Robert interrupted patiently. "And this is a story, a book."

"It happened," Jillian said.

"You actually killed her," Connie accused him incredulously. He shook his head in aggravation, turning back to the book.

She was gone. Our lady was gone, but her screams never seemed to die away. Michael took up the chant with a thunder of rage, and we rode through the snow, so few of us, so many of them. But there had never been such a rage as seized us then. He had failed to believe that he could best the fire, but insanity came then, and he believed in his sword arm. We cut through the guards and the crowds. Most probably the common folk had no will to stop us, and once upon a time the guards had been Lord Alfred's men, so perhaps their own guilt caused their deaths. Blood stained the snow. He hacked through every man until he came to Sir Walter. Sir Walter he slashed to ribbons, until the head was all but severed, the torso a stump, the limbs strewn, and still it was not enough. Michael had his horse race over and over the body.

But Cromwell's forces were behind us. And so we rode north.

Robert looked up at Jillian, then at Connie. He placed the book on the desk and leaned back, lacing his fingers behind his head, stretching his legs out under the desk.

He smiled at Connie. "Milo said to tell you that you weren't necessarily the maid."

"What?" Connie gasped.

"Milo talks to him," Jillian murmured. "In dreams."

"He's here now," Robert said, still watching Connie.

"Oh, really? And how does Milo know?" she demanded.

Robert shrugged. "He says that he was Justin."

"Oh, sure. Milo was the loyal, trustworthy Justin, honest and brave. You were the great warrior, and Jillian was the lady. And now you're telling me that I didn't even get to be the maid?"

"Souls stay the same, so the belief goes. We're not all necessarily the same sex when we return. If you believe in that kind of thing," Robert told her intently.

"So who was I?" Connie demanded. "The wicked Sir Walter?"

Robert shook his head. "Connie, how on earth would I know? It's just a book. And I'm half crazy. I see ghosts, for Christ's sake."

Connie frowned, backing toward the door. "What did I ever do to you?" she whispered to Robert. "I encouraged her to love you," she said, looking as if she were about to burst into tears.

"Maybe you did," he told her, rising, following her. Jillian watched him with astonishment and dismay. "But you *are* up to something," he said to Connie softly.

Connie looked as if she were ready to flee. She bit her lower lip, backing away. "Well, she married you, right? The dynasty is created." She stared at Jillian. "Does this mean you're firing me now? Oh, and what about my husband? Is he out, too? After all, he works for Daniel, and there's bound to be a power struggle."

"Connie, stop it," Jillian protested. "Robert and I aren't taking over the company. Douglas is alive and well, and Daniel excels at his job. What is the matter with you?"

Connie suddenly burst into tears and fled.

Jillian glared at Robert, who didn't even seem to notice. He was just watching Connie's departure speculatively, eyes narrowed.

When it was time for bed that night, Jillian managed to get upstairs early, far ahead of Robert, and lock the door against him. She couldn't believe what he was doing.

Attacking her family.

And now her best friend.

She lay in her bed and whispered aloud softly, "Milo, help me. I'm the one who needs it."

But if Milo was there, he remained silent.

That night, she dreamed again about the burning. Fire all around her. A blaze, leaping up. Flames licking her flesh...

She screamed so loudly that she woke the whole house, and when Robert burst through her locked door to grab her and shake her, she was so terrified that she fell into his arms sobbing.

"Jillian needs a vacation," Theo whispered softly as they left her doorway.

Only Douglas remained, watching the two of them.

Robert straightened, holding her protectively to his chest, smoothing her hair. "It's all right, sir," he said stiffly. "We flew to Vegas. We're married."

"I should have suspected" was all Douglas said, then he turned and walked away.

It was late Saturday morning before Jillian was able to get to sleep again.

CHAPTER 15

Jillian was working, intent on the gold taking shape in her hands, and she was content.

Then Connie burst into her office.

"What is it?" Jillian asked.

"I *almost* had an affair with him."

"Who? What are you talking about?"

Connie swallowed, smoothing out a wrinkle that didn't exist in her skirt. Her wide blue eyes fell on Jillian again. "Daniel," she whispered.

"Joe *works* for Daniel."

Connie nodded, swallowing again. "I know, and I love my husband. He's fiercely loyal to Daniel, too. He was watchful when Robert first came. I think he hated Robert at first, because he thought he was here to oust Daniel."

"Connie," Jillian asked carefully, "what about the 'almost' affair?"

"We met for drinks a few times and discussed an affair."

"But you didn't..."

"I saw him a few times. We talked. We had drinks. We almost..."

"But you didn't?" Jillian repeated.

Connie shook her head.

"Does Joe know any of this?"

Connie shook her head vehemently. "I know you think I should tell him, but the point is, nothing happened. And if I tell him..."

"He'll accost Daniel, he'll want to quit, he'll want you to quit."

Connie nodded. "And it's over. Really over."

"Why are you telling me?" Jillian asked.

"You're my best friend," Connie said softly. "We're supposed to share."

"Ah," Jillian murmured a little skeptically.

"And because Robert is watching me. He's suspicious, and I don't see why he's so suspicious of me. The one you need to watch is Griff."

"Why Griff?"

"He's always talking about marrying you, which of course he can't do now, since you're already married. You see, Griff isn't Daniel. Griff would have to marry you to get the kind of power Daniel has." Connie sighed. "You won't tell him, will you?"

"Joe? I'd never tell your husband a thing like that, Connie. Anyway, I think you're right. Nothing happened, let's just leave it alone."

"Watch Griff," Connie warned her.

"I will," Jillian promised solemnly.

Connie left the office, Jillian staring after her. She could watch Griff. She could watch everyone. But as much as she watched, she didn't seem to be able to *see* anything.

She hadn't had the dream again since she left the house in Connecticut. Robert had moved half his things into Douglas's house, and he was with her every night. The new ad campaign was in full swing, and sales were skyrocketing. She was delighted, since the company was turning over a percentage to the charities of her choice.

The entire city was decked out for Christmas, and she could feel that she was really doing something for the children who needed help. Those with cancer, with AIDS, with other diseases, or with just bad luck in life. Orphans, children with debilitating injuries...

On top of that, she adored Robert more every day.

But she was still watching.

And worse, *he* was still watching.

Their days had been going smoothly. So smoothly—so busily— that Robert had almost begun to believe he had imagined the danger that had haunted them. Maybe the cat *had* eaten a rat. Maybe a branch *had* just fallen and a saddle girth had just worn through.

And maybe he had only imagined the ghost of Jillian's late husband.

Connie was still angry with him; he could tell every time he saw her. And he still didn't know what she was hiding.

He had to be vigilant still. There were undercurrents still humming through the offices. Douglas and Daniel continued to be at odds with one another. They kept their differences to Douglas's office, but Robert could sense the tension.

The office emptied out early that day. The executives of Llewellyn Enterprises were due on the ice at Rockefeller Center, where they were treating a group of underprivileged children to skating, dinner and a Broadway show. Jillian had gone over hours ago with Daniel.

Dealing with a major cable company had kept Robert at his desk later than he had intended. In the middle of his call, he realized he was missing one of the contracts he needed. Apologizing to the VP on the other end, he left his office, wishing he hadn't let his temp go for the day.

No one was around. Swearing, he hurried along the hall to Daniel's office, calling out to him. Daniel had apparently left, and Gracie was gone, as well.

Swearing some more, he looked through the papers on Gracie's desk. Nothing. He went into Daniel's office and opened his top drawer, hoping that the pertinent information would be in plain sight.

He froze where he stood.

A box of rat poison was shoved into the rear of the drawer, half hidden by a sheaf of papers.

Rockefeller Center was fabulous, Jillian thought. The night was beautiful, crisp and cold, and the famous tree was huge, and lit in all its usual glory. She, Eileen and Daniel were already on skates, greeting the kids as they arrived. They ranged in age from five to fifteen, and their excitement at the night out, their pure pleasure in putting on skates and sliding across the ice, was a humbling experience.

"Look at that little girl," Eileen whispered to Jillian. "Isn't she the cutest little thing you've ever seen?"

Surprised—Eileen didn't tend to be the warm and cuddly type—Jillian looked past her cousin to see the child to whom Eileen was referring. She was young, tiny, with golden ringlets and huge blue eyes. She looked a little lost, just standing on the ice, waiting.

"She's adorable," Jillian said.

"I'll bet she can't skate," Eileen told her.

"The big ones are usually around to help the little ones."

"Why don't you go help her?" Eileen suggested.

"I can, but if you think she's so cute..."

"I'm not good with children the way you are. You go help her. I'll watch."

Jillian stared at Eileen in exasperation. "You don't know if you're good with them or not, you hardly ever talk to them!" But there was a single tear forming on the little girl's cheek, as Jillian skated over to her. "Hi. Want to try taking my hand?"

The child looked up as Jillian stretched out a hand. The little girl took it, and they started around the ice. Jillian talked, pointing out the tree, the decorations, shop windows across the street. The girl was very small, so it was easy to catch her and help her along any time she started to slip. Still, though she smiled at Jillian, she never spoke.

Later Jillian passed the little girl to one of the older boys, who was steady on his skates. She helped some of the bigger children, especially one chubby little boy who was having problems in front of his friends. "Relax," she whispered. "Take both my hands and we'll cross over. We'll look great, I promise." She winked. He flushed, but he paid attention, following her every lead. After a while she heard the other boys calling out to him with a note of envy in their voices. Pleased, she left him with a little girl who had been trying to do the same easy glide.

She skated over to the edge, heading off the ice to take a seat beside Sister Catherine, one of the nuns in charge of the orphans. Sister Catherine was young, very pretty and popular with the children—and with adults, as well. Eileen had been sitting there, watching the action, chatting with the sister. Jillian gasped, smiling. "I can't believe it. I'm out of air."

"This is a wonderful thing you're doing," Sister Catherine told them. "Not to sound jaded or anything, but most corporations simply give money to charity. They get tax breaks for it and, often, more than the value of the donation in free publicity. Not that I mind that—I don't care what it takes to get help for the children. But you Llewellyns all come out here yourselves. Time is far more precious than money."

Eileen laughed softly. "Remember how I used to hate this

when we were kids? I always thought that the orphans would be dirty or something."

"Ah, but you were a big history buff, and you always got through it by pretending that we were the medieval nobility, washing the feet of the poor on holy days," Jillian reminded her, smiling.

"I was such a brat," Eileen admitted. She pointed out over the ice. "There's Theo. Showing off."

"And Daniel, looking like a pro."

"Gracie's on the ice—look!" Eileen said. "She's really good. I never saw her out there before. She can really skate."

"Maybe she's moving fast because it's so cold," Jillian mused, winking at Sister Catherine.

Sister Catherine laughed back. "The air *is* cold tonight, but the children never mind that. They enjoy this so much. The Christmas season is so special for children."

"And for Jillian. She never grew up," Eileen teased.

"Well, you've heard this before, but Christmas is for the child in all of us. And naturally it's one of the biggest events in the year to me," the nun said, smiling.

The little blond girl Eileen had commented on earlier, her smile almost as big as the Christmas tree, came skating toward them, wobbling only slightly. She gave Sister Catherine a beatific smile, beaming with pride.

"Jenny, you're doing so well. You're skating," Sister Catherine said and applauded.

Jenny nodded, then looked shyly from Sister Catherine to Jillian. She struggled for a minute, then said a soft, barely whispered "Thank you."

"Sweetheart, you're welcome."

As Jenny skated off, Jillian realized that Sister Catherine was staring at her. "What?" she said, touching her face. "Did my nose grow?"

"No. No, there's nothing wrong with you at all. It's just

that...I've never heard Jenny talk before. Her parents died traumatically just a year ago, and she was left screaming for help, which came too late. I believe that's the first time she's spoken since then. It's a miracle."

"It's great, but I don't think it qualifies as a miracle," Jillian said.

"Isn't a miracle when the unbelievable happens—not when a little girl with nothing really wrong with her decides to talk again?" Eileen asked skeptically.

"I believe in miracles big and small," Sister Catherine said, grinning. "I accept them in all sizes, and I just say, 'Thank you, Lord.' This was a little miracle. And do you know why I get lots of little miracles?"

"Why?"

"Because I'm willing to let them happen."

"Jilly needs a miracle," Eileen said casually.

"Eileen..." Jillian murmured.

"Why? Maybe I can help," Sister Catherine said, looking at Jillian curiously.

"She keeps dreaming about fires and burning up," Eileen said. "And then she screams."

"I haven't had the dream in a while," Jillian murmured.

"Were you ever in a fire?"

"No," she said, then thought about the book and Morwenna's horrible death. "Not in this lifetime," she added lightly.

"Well, they say dreams mean something," Sister Catherine said.

"Maybe she sees her family as tendrils of flame, lapping at her soul and sanity," Eileen intoned dramatically.

Sister Catherine grinned. "Dreams are usually a nighttime reflection of the daytime world. Remember being a child and telling Santa what you wanted for Christmas?"

"Sure," Jillian said.

"Now," Sister Catherine told her, "since we're a bit too big for Santa, what you do is this—you just look up, find the brightest star and say, 'Merry Christmas, Jesus. Happy Birthday. This year, please, for Christmas, I'd very much like to stop dreaming about fire.'"

"I like it," Eileen said. "And you can add, 'Please, protect me from the bogeyman.'"

"I've got it," Jillian said out loud. "Dear Father, please, for Christmas, no more nightmares, and protect me from all evil." She added silently. *And please, please, please, don't let the bogeyman be someone in my own family.*

"You know," Sister Catherine said, turning her gaze upward, "*He* can give better than any department store Santa."

"I'll remember that," Jillian said. Then she jumped up. "Look at the time. It will be a miracle if we make the play."

"Trust me, we'll be there on time," Sister Catherine said calmly.

"And how do you know that?" Eileen asked.

"I told you, I get all my little miracles. I just believe that they'll happen."

Robert didn't make the skating party, but he was there for the play, and when they took the kids out to eat after, he was great. Jillian felt a surge of pleasure watching him. Though he seemed a bit preoccupied, he laughed, cut meat, pushed in chairs, distributed napkins, rescued a few drinks, and never once made a child feel awkward.

But he seemed to be avoiding her family, she realized. Douglas had gone home early, right after the theater, Amelia at his side. But Daniel, Theo, Griff and even Gary had joined them for the evening, and every one of them spent time with the children.

When the evening was over, the kids thanked everyone. Jenny spoke to Jillian again, saying thank you again and nothing more, but Jillian was still delighted. And the little girl gave Robert a big hug, which seemed to surprise him.

"She's a pretty little thing," he told Jillian, one arm around her as they stood on the street, shivering a little as they watched the children get back on the bus. Daniel and Griff were inside, settling the bill. Eileen, Gary and Theo had gone on home. "I bet you looked like that when you were little."

"Maybe. I don't remember."

"Well, I'd like a dozen like her."

"A dozen girls? No sons?"

He looked at her, angling his head, smiling. "How about a dozen of each?"

"Wow, we'll be busy."

"But it sounds like fun, huh?"

"It does. But I think two dozen children may be a few too many."

"Maybe. I'll let you work on the number. As long as it's more than one."

"Four."

"I like it."

She smiled, putting her arms around him. "You know, I love you more and more every day."

"I love you, too," he told her, but there was an odd tension about him. She could feel it in the heat of his body, in the tautness of his muscles.

"Just think, only a few more days and then we're off to Connecticut again for Christmas. Time together, the scent of pine, packages all wrapped up in string."

"I was thinking of not going to Connecticut for Christmas," he told her.

"What?" she asked incredulously.

"It's our first Christmas together. We could go somewhere alone."

She hesitated, drawing back, watching. "Robert, I love my family."

"I didn't say that you shouldn't."

"But you don't want to be with them for Christmas."

He stared down at her. It was growing colder by the second. "I'm sorry. Too many things have happened. It's hard to trust them."

"Robert, I don't know how many Christmases Douglas has left."

"I don't know how many *you're* going to have left!"

She searched his eyes, deeply blue, almost black in the shadowy light. "I can't leave my grandfather on Christmas, Robert. I can't. And I won't."

"Morwenna died on Christmas Eve."

"Sometimes you believe in the book, and sometimes you don't," she charged him. "Whatever's convenient for you. If history is somehow repeating itself, if we *are* old souls trying to make things right in a new life, running away isn't going to solve anything."

"And what if you have a homicidal cousin?"

"None of my cousins would ever kill me—especially at Christmas," she said vehemently.

To her dismay, Griff was coming up to them. She prayed that he hadn't heard her. If he had, he made no comment, just asked Robert, "Did you drive over? Daniel said to check with you. If not, I can give you a ride."

"Thanks, Griff. I drove today."

"Cool. Good night."

Griff started off; then he turned back, a curious expression his face. "Hey, cuz, I'd never kill you at Easter, either. And certainly not on St. Patrick's Day."

"Great," Jillian moaned, watching him walk away. "Now his feathers are all ruffled."

"Maybe they should be."

"Just what is your problem?" she demanded angrily.

"Daniel had rat poison in his desk."

"Maybe he was killing rats."

"Maybe he killed the cat."

"He wouldn't. He likes cats."

"Yeah, well, the cat wasn't supposed to die. You were the intended victim, Jillian."

She shook her head, backing away from him. "You're wrong. And I'm not staying away from my family on Christmas, Robert. I'm not."

He sighed. "Jillian..."

"I'm going to take a cab."

"The hell you are."

"No, you know what? I'll get a ride with Daniel."

"Jillian!" When she started to walk away, he went after her, catching her arm, spinning her back around. "Okay, have it your way. We'll be with your family for Christmas, Jillian. Let's go home now, can we?"

Neither of them was happy, but she gave in. They drove the distance in silence. Robert, usually fairly calm behind the wheel, swore at the drivers around them the whole way.

At the house, Jillian hurried upstairs to shower, then rushed into bed. He didn't come up until later. She heard him as he shed his clothing, but he didn't come right over. He had picked up the snow globe Milo had given her and was examining it.

Riders in the snow.

After a while he came to bed. It was the time to make up. One of them should have rolled toward the other. They should have talked, touched, laughed, made love.

But they kept their distance.

That night, she didn't dream about fire.

She dreamed instead of a massive dragon with Eileen's face. *Jillian, precious Jillian. Perfect Jillian, Douglas's beloved. You'll need a miracle, a miracle, a miracle....*

Then Robert was there, a perfect fairy tale prince, riding

through the snow, ready to fight the dragon. His sword was drawn, his arm was ready.

But Eileen was laughing at him. *He was the one who strung the arrow. He was the one to shoot Morwenna straight through the heart....*

She jerked awake. He was at her side, instantly alert. Immediately, his arms were around her, his eyes anxious, even in the shadows. "The burning...?"

She looked at him and laughed. "No, no, I'm sorry I woke you."

"What, then?"

"Eileen. She was a dragon. But it's okay—you were fighting her off." She was smiling, but he frowned. "Really. She was a big, fat, black dragon. It was actually very funny."

He eased back, watching her. "You're really all right?"

"Absolutely. Why are you looking at me like that?"

"Because I'm wide awake now."

"Meaning...?"

"I wouldn't want to take advantage of you or anything, but if we're even remotely thinking about two dozen children, it would never be too soon to start."

She laughed, and then, still laughing, she threw herself into his arms. "It seems I'm wide awake myself," she whispered.

Three days later, they all gathered once again at the house in Connecticut. They spent the first few days shopping like crazy, then insanely wrapping, throwing themselves entirely into the Christmas spirit. Eileen and Gary were behaving a bit strangely, whispering all the time, with Eileen far more quiet than catty, which was definitely different for her.

The relationship between Connie and Joe was still strained, and Jillian wondered if it wouldn't be better after all if Connie told her husband the truth.

Connie's mom, the kids, Amelia and Gracie, who seemed to

have become one of the crowd, seemed to be the most cheerful among them—unaware, perhaps, of the underlying currents of unease. Admittedly, though, despite the tension she sometimes felt, Jillian had a wonderful time at the parties they held during the week. One was for the sales staff and buyers, another for the charities with which they were associated, and the last for the children of St. Mary's Orphanage, a follow-up to the skating party. Jenny came back for that one and played with Tricia and Liza, who didn't mind that she didn't speak. When she left, she once again said, "Thank you" to Jillian.

Griff went missing at one point during the party. Douglas needed him for something, and Jillian went searching for him.

She found him in the library. Reading the book. She grabbed it from him, not sure why she felt red-faced.

"Hey," he protested. "What's the matter?"

"Nothing."

"Is that your personal property?"

"No."

"Then, may I finish reading it?"

"Not now. Grandfather is looking for you."

"Fine."

"Now."

"I'm coming," he told her.

She turned around and left him. Later, when she went back for the book, it was gone. The fact that Griff had it disturbed her greatly, and she wasn't sure why, unless it had something to do with Connie's warning.

She didn't want to let Robert know. He was already growing more and more tense as the holiday approached.

On the morning of Christmas Eve, at the breakfast table, Douglas tapped his spoon against his glass. "I have an announcement," he told them.

"Oh my God!" Griff cried out dramatically. "He's changed the will. In memory of Jeeves and in honor of our new black cat, the entire Llewellyn fortune is to be left to a home for wayward alley cats."

"Not a bad idea, Griff," Douglas said. "But no. I wanted to let you know that after a tremendous amount of persuasion, Amelia has agreed to be my wife."

Jillian gasped with pleasure, jumping up. "Amelia! Oh, merry Christmas."

Amelia smiled back. "He bought me the most beautiful ring."

"There you go," Griff said, throwing up his hands. "The patriarch has had it with all of us. He's marrying a sweet young thing, and they're going to produce all new, far better behaved, offspring."

"That's it, Griff, dear," Amelia said. "I always wanted my first child before my seventieth birthday."

Eileen stood up suddenly, looking very pale. "Joke, Griff, just go on—joke!" she exclaimed. Then she suddenly burst into tears and went running upstairs.

"Wow," Griff said, looking totally lost and confused. "I didn't think she wanted the money that badly."

Gary stood, stared at Griff, threw his napkin down and went after Eileen.

"It isn't the money," Connie said softly.

They all stared at her. Then, suddenly, Jillian thought she understood. "Is Eileen pregnant?" she gasped.

"No, it's more than that," Gracie murmured.

"I think you're right," Robert said very softly. "I think she's lost a baby."

Douglas stood. "Well, I didn't mean to make such a happy occasion for me such a sadness for my granddaughter. Excuse me." He was going up to see Eileen, Jillian knew. But he paused, looking back. "Jillian, Robert, though I believe most of the family has guessed, I think it's time you shared your news, as well."

"Jillian," Griff declared, "*you're* pregnant."

"No, I'm not pregnant. That I know of," she added as a quick afterthought.

"But we are married," Robert said.

No one moved.

"That's all?" Daniel said after a moment.

"I can even tell you when you went off and did the deed," Theo said, laughing.

"We all knew," Griff told them. "Well, if you'll all excuse me, I still have some Christmas presents to wrap."

"I'm going up to see Eileen," Jillian murmured. She glanced at Robert, then left the table, anxious to talk with her cousin.

Upstairs, she found that Douglas had been and gone, and Gary was nowhere in sight, either. Eileen wasn't especially welcoming when she told Jillian to come in, but she at least allowed her to enter.

Jillian sat by the bed. "Why didn't you tell me?" she asked softly.

"There wasn't that much to tell," Eileen said with a shrug, looking away. "I was stunned when I found out, and I admit all I thought at first was wow, how great, I've beaten Jillian to something at last. Then...then I realized I wanted the baby. It was this wonderful life, a person. Gary and I had created a person. And then I lost it."

"Oh, Eileen, I'm so sorry. I didn't know."

"How could you?" Eileen asked bitterly. "You're off in your own little world with Robert. The perfect mate for the perfect grandchild. Maybe Grandfather really did hire him so you two could create your own dynasty. Which you will now, of course. You're perfect. *You'll* never have a miscarriage."

"Eileen, anyone can miscarry. You'll have another baby. And

Gary will probably be thrilled, because you'll finally break down and marry him."

Eileen turned away from her. "Jillian, I'm being nasty to you. Don't you dare go being nice to me."

Jillian sighed softly. "Eileen, I'm so sorry. But things will get better."

"I even thought of adopting the little girl. But she liked you better."

"You mean Jenny? Eileen, you made me go skate with her."

"Jillian, please, just leave me alone. Just—just for now."

"Sure. But you're wrong about that little girl, Eileen. She just wants love. Love her, and she'll love you back."

Jillian started out of the room.

"Jilly?"

"Yes?"

"You're not going to believe this, what with the way I've just treated you, but..."

"But?"

"I do love you."

"I love you, too," Jillian said, and left her.

She walked back downstairs and was surprised to hear her grandfather's voice coming from the library—and it was rising. She heard a male voice reply to him—an angry male voice. At first she thought her grandfather and Daniel were at it again.

Then she realized it was Robert talking.

She shouldn't eavesdrop. Not even on those two.

But she walked closer and just stood there, her hand on the knob.

"Now you want me to stop. Now, when I have something! You told me to watch out for her. You even hired me because of my past. And I *have* watched out for her, I've done everything in my power to be with her every minute—"

He broke off, as she pushed open the door and stepped in. She felt as if she were burning from head to toe.

She stared at her grandfather first. "You hired him to watch out for me? As a well-educated bodyguard?"

"Jillian," Douglas protested. "It wasn't like that."

"And you!" She spun on Robert. "You've done everything in your power to be with me every minute. You sure have. You slept with me. You even married me."

"Jillian..." He stood, speaking through clenched teeth. "You're acting like a fool."

"A fool? I must be stark raving mad! I listened to you. I listened to you pretend that Milo was in the room, and I fell for everything you said. Grandfather, how dare you? Well, do you both want to know something? I don't want your protection. I'd rather cast my lot with the rest of them."

She spun around and strode down the hallway. But she could hear them behind her.

"Jillian, wait!" Robert shouted.

"Robert, you've got to wait, give her a minute to think."

Her grandfather might slow him down, but Robert was coming after her. She hurried down the corridor, grabbed a jacket from the hall closet and ran outside. She wasted no time but headed straight for the stables.

She didn't talk to Jimmy; she didn't go for a saddle. She just threw a bridle on Crystal, leapt up bareback and went racing out into the snow.

She rode for hours, thoughts tumbling through her mind. He had married her because he'd been hired to. She'd been so much in love—and he had been on guard duty! In a way, he'd shot her through the heart in this lifetime, too.

It was Christmas Eve. The light was already beginning to fade. And she needed to get back to the house; she wanted to spend the holiday with people she loved.

Including Robert.

It was, after all, Christmas, and she had to give him a chance.

She rode back to the house, heading toward the stables. As she got close, she saw the house door open. Gracie came running out. "Jillian?" she said, shivering as she reached the horse's side.

"Yes, Gracie?"

Gracie, hugging her arms across her chest, shivered, smiling. "You're wrong about Robert. He loves you so much."

Jillian flushed, wondering just how much the whole household knew.

"Thanks, Gracie."

"He's been out searching for you. I think he was heading for the cottage. Jillian, if he loved me that way, I'd be at that cottage, giving him a chance."

Jillian hesitated, still hurt. But she couldn't believe that everything had been a lie. He had been with her through too much. Maybe even through a second lifetime, a second chance. And she'd been in his arms, made love with him; surely that emotion hadn't been a lie.

"Thanks, Gracie," she said. "Thanks so much."

She turned Crystal around, patting his neck, and started for the cottage at a lope that quickly became a gallop. She reined in when she reached the cottage. There were hoofprints in the snow. Someone had been there. Was he still there now? If he was, she didn't see his horse, but she had to go in and check. She had to *hope.*

She leapt from her horse and raced inside. Someone had been there. A fire was burning in the hearth, water was boiling on the stove.

"Robert?" she called as she pulled off her gloves, walking around the ground floor. "Robert?" He didn't answer. Maybe he was upstairs in the studio. She walked up, then sighed, blinking back tears. The room was empty. It was her own fault. She had run away. She hadn't given him a chance. But this was Christmas Eve. He would give her another chance when she finally found him, she was certain.

She walked over to the easel where Milo had worked. "I miss you, too, you know, Milo. So much. I wish you had appeared to me."

"Jillian."

She heard her name, weakly at first. Then more strongly. Coming from the stairs.

She turned. Blinked.

Milo.

Not really. Not Milo in the flesh. Milo, barely there, a reflection on the air, nothing more.

"Milo," she whispered.

"Jillian, get out. Run!" he told her. It seemed difficult for him to talk to her, to form words.

She shook her head. "Milo, I'm not afraid of you."

"It's not me, Jillian. Just...run."

"Why?" she demanded.

He tried to speak, but his image blurred, faded.

Like a wisp of smoke.

Smoke!

Then she knew. She heard the crackle of flame, and the wisp of smoke was suddenly a billowing. Fire!

Jillian started to race back down the stairs, but the flames were bursting upward, blocking her escape.

It was her dream come to life, tongues of fire, hungry, rabid, reaching upward. Reaching for *her.*

She opened her mouth and began to scream.

And scream...

C H A P T E R 1 6

Robert had ridden for hours. He'd gone to the cottage, but finding no sign of Jillian there, he had returned to the house, hoping against hope that she would be back. When he didn't find her, he was ready to head out again, but he decided to accost Douglas and Daniel first, in case they could help in any way.

"She's out there somewhere, and I don't know where."

"She's an excellent rider, and she knows this terrain. She's going to be all right," Douglas said firmly, but Robert could tell he wasn't sure himself.

Theo walked in from the kitchen. "I'll go with you, Robert," he said. "Maybe I can think of a few places to look that might not occur to you."

"Great, thanks."

"Griff's coming, too. He's gone down to the barn to get our horses," Theo said, pulling on a pair of gloves.

He left, and Robert stared from Daniel to Douglas. "Douglas, you were afraid of something happening to Jillian, afraid someone in this family was behind it. You don't want that to be true, and neither do I. But you *are* worth a small fortune, and that can bring out the worst in people. You and Daniel have been fighting for weeks. What's going on?"

They were going to answer him, by God. In the past hour, the fear he had been feeling had doubled, tripled. He hadn't wanted to come here, to this house. At first it had been just gut instinct, but then he'd thought about the book. Morwenna had refused to leave her home because of her father. Jillian had insisted on coming here because of her grandfather. It was frighteningly similar.

As he'd ridden in search of her, he had hoped the ghost of Milo Anderson would appear to lead him in the right direction, which he knew was totally insane.

But all he had now was that insanity. He had to use it.

"The argument has nothing to do with Jillian," Daniel said heatedly.

"What *was* it about?" Robert persisted.

"My sex life. Are you happy?"

Robert stared at Daniel, frowning.

"I'm not pleased with his choices," Douglas said.

"And I'm not pleased that he thinks he has a right to pass judgment on my choices," Daniel said flatly.

"There was rat poison in your desk," Robert charged him.

Daniel's frown seemed sincere. "In my desk? I got rid of all of it when you told me about the cat."

"It was there."

Before Daniel could respond, Griff burst into the room. "There's a fire."

"Where?" Douglas exploded.

Robert could barely breathe. "Where?" he repeated, terror filling him. Fire. She had dreamed of fire, had awakened screaming with terror. Fire...

"Where?" he thundered.

"I think it's the cottage. If we—"

He was out of the house before Griff could finish speaking. He'd taken Igloo that day; he leapt back on him now. Griff reached his side, along with Theo, who was shouting that his horse was gone. "Go, go both of you! I'll catch up. Who the hell has Cream?" he muttered. "Go!"

Robert needed no encouragement.

He had never ridden so hard in his life. Desperate as he was, he became aware of each slight sound, each nuance of scent. The day was cold, crisp. The sky was blue. His horse's hooves made thunder, striking upon the ground. Distant thunder, muffled by the thick blanket of snow. The cold seeped into him, though he was sweating with fear.

His horse's hooves seemed to beat out words. We will not make it. We will not make it.

He knew, suddenly, that history *could* repeat itself.

He knew that he had ridden through the snow before and failed. Now he had a second chance to save her. And if he failed again...? His heart was sick, and he was afraid.

"Robert, you'll kill yourself, and we'll never get to her!" Griff called to him.

"We're almost there! The cottage is just ahead."

"Oh Lord!" Griff shouted. "The flames..."

Robert gritted his teeth. He had to believe. But in what? Miracles? That he could ride into the fire and save her? He would. By God, he would.

With the fire racing up the stairs, she'd had no choice but to retreat—once she'd realized that she would die if she didn't stop panicking. At first she had felt rooted to the spot, but now she hurried to the rear of the studio, then rushed into the bathroom to soak a towel to put over her face to filter out the smoke. Then she'd looked out into the night. It would be a long fall, but she would land in the snow. She wouldn't let herself think about the rocks below the snow, cold and hard. Anything had to be better than the flames.

She could feel the flames, though they were not touching her. She knew the feel of fire.

She refused to know it again.

She opened the window, then realized with a moan that the storm window was up. As she searched desperately for something with which to break it, she could feel the floor growing hotter beneath her feet. She was suddenly terrified that it would collapse, dropping her into the fire.

He would come. He would not fail her again. She had to believe in the power of this second chance.

"Jillian!"

The voice was coming from outside. She rushed back to the window.

Robert was there, with Griff racing up behind him.

Robert was gesturing for her to get away from the window. She saw him dismount and pick up a dark object, large enough that it had not yet been fully covered by the snow. He drew his arm back, and she moved quickly away from the window.

The glass shattered inward. She leapt back as shards smashed around her. The object he had thrown rolled toward her, but she paid no attention. Robert was here!

Fire suddenly roared, breaking up through the floor. She rushed to the window.

Below her, the porch was being consumed in flames. Robert had remounted and sat on his horse just beyond the flames, staring at her. She realized that what he had thrown had been an old cannon ball. Milo had found several on the property and had kept them stacked outside. A cannonball that could still explode.

"Go." The word was a whisper. And then she felt herself being shoved past the flames to the window.

Milo!

Below her, Robert was urging his terrified horse up to the edge of the burning porch. "Miracles!" he shouted. "You jump!"

Robert and the horse were almost directly below her; flames shooting everywhere around them. Around her.

Licking at her heels.

Nearly touching her flesh.

"Jump!" he yelled to her.

And she jumped....

She seemed to fall forever. In slow motion, she fell through time, the flames below her, but beyond them, so close, Robert. The man she loved. Loved in this life—and the last.

She landed in his arms, an inferno raging around them; cutting off all escape. Was that how it would end this time? The two of them burning together? But Robert looked into her eyes, features grim and dark with soot.

"Close your eyes," he commanded. "Hold your breath."

He slammed his heels into Igloo's flanks. The horse shrieked, balked, reared.

And then Igloo leapt forward into the fire. Through the fire. He ran past the heat and into the cold, a world of snow and ice. Cold air wrapped around them, and her flesh was not burned. She seemed to hear nothing as they ran, no hooves upon the ground; they simply raced upon air, through the silence of a white world of snow, through time eternal....

Then sound returned, and she heard Igloo's hooves hit the ground. Robert reined him in, and they turned, heading back to where Griff still waited.

They watched the house explode, the fire seeming to reach the sky.

It didn't matter.

It wasn't touching them.

Daniel and Theo had nearly reached the cottage, riding double on old Blossom, when they started back. Douglas was frantic, Daniel said. Then he looked closely at her and insisted that they had to get back to the house and call a doctor. She was probably suffering from smoke inhalation, he said when he heard her cough.

Sitting on Igloo, held close in Robert's arms, she assured Daniel that she was fine, but she could tell that he didn't believe her.

Back at the house, Douglas was standing at the door. His knees crumpled when he saw her; she ran to hold him up. Amelia hugged her, Henry cried, and Agatha rushed around with warm blankets and pots of tea.

It was some time before Griff said, "Just how the hell did the fire get started?"

"I don't know, but we'll find out," Douglas said with rough determination. "But for now, clean up and get some warm clothes on before I lose one of you to pneumonia."

Soot, the cold, none of it mattered. In her bedroom, Jillian did nothing but hold Robert for what seemed like hours. Then they showered, and finally they made love. They said little, too afraid to speak.

"Was that a miracle?" he asked her at last.

"Your lovemaking?" she teased. "Well, you were very good. Exceptional, actually. But a miracle...?"

"Jillian..."

"It's a miracle. It's *all* a miracle," she whispered.

After their lovemaking, Robert dressed and went down to join the others, while Jillian opted for a bubble bath.

Eileen and Gary were in the living room with Douglas, Daniel, Theo, Griff and Robert. Jasper McClean, the sheriff, had come and gone, telling them they would have to wait for the ashes to cool before the investigators could even begin to find out what had caused the blaze.

"You folks were mighty lucky," he had told them. "A cottage

like that, with no fire escape... Well, it's gone now. But Douglas, don't you worry. We'll get to the bottom of it."

Now, when it was just family, they knew it was time to get to the truth.

"Did someone start it on purpose?" Eileen asked incredulously.

"I think so," Robert said. "I think someone rode out there and purposely set the place on fire—knowing that Jillian was inside."

"Not me—I don't even like to ride," Eileen said.

"I was here arguing with you," Daniel reminded him curtly.

"You were at the stables, Griff."

Griff stood defensively, hands on his hips. "Yeah, right. I can see where you're going. Because of that book. Reliving history, that's what you two think."

"What are you talking about?" Douglas asked .

Robert shook his head, staring at Griff.

"I'm the bad guy, right—because I'm related, and I'm always joking with Jillian about marriage? So that makes me Sir Walter?"

"You tell me," Robert said.

"Hell, no!"

"Don't look at *me*," Theo charged.

"Well, who was out today?" Robert demanded.

Daniel exhaled. "Oh my God. Where is Jillian now?"

"Taking a bath," Robert said.

"Get up there with her," Daniel insisted. "Until we know what really happened, you can't leave her alone."

She was relaxing, eyes closed, in the bubbles, when she heard the noise. She looked up, thinking Robert had come back.

It wasn't Robert.

"What are you doing here?" she asked, more confused than angry.

"Daniel deserves that business. He's the oldest male, and he's worked for it. He's put his life into it."

"The business will go to all of us. Not that that has anything to do with you." She sank lower in the tub, hiding beneath her camouflage of bubbles. "Look, I appreciate what you do for Daniel, I know he values your help. You—"

She broke off, frowning, as she stared at Gracie.

"You told me to go to the cottage!"

"But you got out," Gracie shot back. "Daniel would never do anything to discredit you. Everyone adores you. You're even in the commercials. You outshine him every day, in every way you can. He loves you too much to see what you're doing to him. But he loves me, too. I know it. He needs me. So I went to him. I have my talents, you know. Talents outside the office. Daniel doesn't even realize yet just how talented I am. You just haven't been watching, paying attention. You could have found out so much, but you were only worried that your assistant, your friend, might have been having an affair with Daniel. I was worried, too. But all Connie was doing that night in Connecticut was telling him that she loved her husband, and that she hoped she and Daniel would always be the best of friends. I know, because I was listening. And now you have to notice me."

"Gracie, get out," she said wearily. Then her breath caught when she saw Gracie produce a gun. She stiffened in the midst of her bubbles, so much suddenly so clear.

"Gracie!"

The door burst open. Robert was there.

"She's got a gun!" Jillian shouted.

Robert made a flying leap.

Gracie fired.

"A miracle," Sister Catherine told Jillian on Christmas Day, shaking her head in disbelief.

"A miracle," Jillian echoed. "Can you imagine what a clever woman she was? She killed the cat, then hid the poison in

Daniel's desk, knowing I would never seriously suspect him of anything, even if the poison were found and somehow connected to Jeeves's death. She figured I would go riding, and even that I would insist on Robert taking Crystal again, so she rigged the saddle. She knew where the shoot was going to be in Florida, so she hired a couple of local college kids to weaken the branch. They thought it was for a movie stunt. The sledding accident was more like grasping at straws, but she planned that, as well. It was a long shot that might have worked. Anyone is welcome to use any of the cars in the garage, so Gracie drove down the road and ran into the fence herself. When we were all fooling around, she managed to see to it that I was the one heading toward the break in the fence. She couldn't be sure that a car would speed by, but I might have been seriously hurt or killed anyway. And then there was the fire," Jillian finished softly.

"Which Robert saved you from...but what about the bullet?"

"Robert hit Gracie's arm, ruining her aim. The bullet hit the tub, ricocheted, then hit Gracie. They say she'll be fine, though, so she can stand trial."

Connie came running out of the dining room then, smiling. "The bird is on the table. Time for Christmas dinner."

"Sister," Jillian said, "we'd all love it if you would say grace. I have to warn you, though. We usually all put in a few words, a thank-you from each family member for what the year has brought. It's a tradition. But it would be wonderful if you would begin for us."

A few minutes later, Sister Catherine did just that. "Thank you, Lord, for the food that we are about to eat. Thank you for gathering us together here today. Thank you for second chances—"

"Thank you for this Christmas," Jillian said, interrupting first, and far earlier than she had intended.

"Thank you for our daughter," Eileen said softly, smiling down at the little hand wrapped in hers. Sister Catherine had brought Jenny, who had taken to Eileen and Gary immediately. The adoption would not take long.

"Thank you, God, for my family," Douglas said. "And," he added with a wink, "my new almost-blushing bride."

"Thanks for watching out for my cousin," Griff said gruffly.

"Thanks for protecting us all from harm," Daniel said, feeling guilty for not realizing the depth—and danger—of Gracie's obsession with him.

"Thanks for the really great girl I know you're going to find for me this year," Theo said. He smiled at Sister Catherine. "You sure you're wedded to the Church?"

"I'm afraid so. However, if I weren't..." She gave him a teasing grin.

Jillian spoke again. "Thank you," she said, looking heavenward. "And thank you, Milo, wherever you are. I don't think you'll be coming back now. And, God, thank you so much for Robert. For my life. For *our* lives. Thank you very, very much—"

"For miracles," Robert said.

And then he kissed her.